International Praise for Miss Read

"Miss Read reminds us of what is really important. And if we can't live in her world, it's certainly a comforting place to visit." —*USA Today*

"If you don't know Fairacre, you are twenty novels behind."
—*New York Times*

"[Miss Read] has achieved a sort of universality."
—*Chicago Sunday Tribune*

"Miss Read has three great gifts—an unerring intuition about human frailty, a healthy irony, and, surprisingly, an almost beery sense of humor. As a result, her villages, the rush of the sun and snow through venerable elms, and the children themselves all miraculously manage to blend into a charming and lasting whole." —*The New Yorker*

"Humor guides her pen but charity steadies it . . . Delightful."
—*Times Literary Supplement*

"We need more books like this . . . quiet, homey stories about down-to-earth people." —*Anniston Star*

"Miss Read has created an orderly universe in which people are kind and conscientious and cherish virtues and manners now considered antiquated elsewhere . . . An occasional visit to Fairacre offers a restful change from the frenetic pace of the contemporary world."
—*Publishers Weekly*

"Testimony to the gallantry of ordinary folk . . . I like Fairacre."
—*Omaha World-Herald*

"Miss Read has created a world of innocent integrity in almost perfect prose consisting of wit, humor and wisdom in equal measure."
—*Cleveland Plain Dealer*

"Someone has said she writes for ordinary people extraordinarily; when I read her I keep thinking of the acute perception and wit of Jane Austen. [Miss Read] is unique, and oh, so pleasant to read."
—*Chattanooga Times*

"Miss Read [possesses] a tranquil eye in the midst of our loud and windy times." —*Patriot Ledger*

Books by Miss Read

CHANGES AT FAIRACRE

Miss Read

Illustrated by J. S. Goodall

HOUGHTON MIFFLIN COMPANY
Boston   New York

To Mary and Eric
with love

First Houghton Mifflin paperback edition 2001

For information about permission to reproduce selections from
this book, write to Permissions, Houghton Mifflin Company,
215 Park Avenue South, New York, New York 10003.

Visit our Web site: www.houghtonmifflinbooks.com.

Library of Congress Cataloging-in-Publication Data
Read, Miss.
Changes at Fairacre / Miss Read;
illustrations by John S. Goodall.
p.   cm.
ISBN 0-618-15457-4 (pbk)
I. Title.
PR 6069.A42C48   1992
823'.914   CIP

Printed in the United States of America

EB 10 9 8 7 6 5

PART ONE
FAIRACRE

1   A Visit To Dolly Clare

SPRING came early to Fairacre that year. Half-term was at the end of February and I had seen the school children off the premises, at four o'clock on the Friday, to run home between hedges already beginning to thicken with plump buds.

A few celandine already starred the banks, and in the cottage gardens, and in mine at the school house, the daffodils were beginning to follow the fading snowdrops and early crocuses.

In all my years as head teacher at Fairacre School, I had never before seen such welcome signs of spring at half-term. I could remember the lane deep in snow in earlier Februaries, awash with puddles or glittering with ice. There might perhaps have been a flutter of yellow catkins or a few hardy sticky buds showing on the horse chestnut trees, but this balmy weather was rare and wonderful.

Bob Willet, our school caretaker, church sexton and general factotum in the village, was not quite as euphoric as I was.

'You wants to look further afield,' he told me as the last of the children vanished round the bend of the lane. 'There's blackthorn out already, I see, and you know what that means: a proper sharp spell comin' along. We'll get a frost afore the week's out.'

'Well, I'm going to enjoy this while I can,' I told him. 'Why I might even cut the grass.'

'More fool you then,' said my old friend roundly. 'You

be asking for trouble. Getting above yourself just because the sun's out.'

'I'm going to see Miss Clare during the weekend,' I told him, partly to change the subject.

He brightened up at once. 'Now you give Dolly Clare my love. Amazing old girl, ain't she?'

I agreed that she was, and we parted company amicably.

Dolly Clare, who lived at the next village of Beech Green, knew more about Fairacre School than anyone in the neighbourhood. She had attended it herself as a pupil, and later as a teacher. When I arrived to take up my headship, she was nearing retirement and in charge of the infants' class.

She was a dignified figure, tall, straight-backed, white-haired and extremely gentle. I never heard her raise her voice in anger, and the small children adored her. Her teaching methods were old-fashioned. The children were expected to sit at their desks and to work at them too. There was mighty little roaming aimlessly about the classroom, and if a child had a job to do it was expected to finish it tidily, and with pride in its accomplishment.

By modern-day standards the infants' room was unnaturally quiet, but there was happiness there and complete accord between teacher and pupils. The children trusted Miss Clare. She was fair, she was kind, she looked after them with steadfast affection. They were content to submit to her rule and, in truth, a great many of them were happier here, in the warmth and peace of the schoolroom than in their own homes, so often over-crowded and noisy with upraised and angry voices.

In such a rural community, farming was the major industry. The horse then ruled, and there were carters, farriers, wheelwrights and horse doctors in attendance upon the noble beast, who drew the plough, pulled the carts, provided the family transport and generally governed the ways of the agricultural community.

Families were large and it was nothing unusual to find parents with eight or ten children. In the early days of Miss Clare's teaching the school had almost one hundred pupils. The school leaving age was fourteen, but many left earlier if a job cropped up. It was no wonder that Fairacre School was such a busy and crowded place. Long desks held children in a row, and there was little chance of fidgeting going unnoticed.

By the time I arrived the school took children up to the age of eleven, and after that they went on to the neighbouring village school at Beech Green, where George Annett was the headmaster. Here they stayed until they were fifteen, unless they had qualified for a place at the local grammar school in Caxley, and had departed thither after their eleven-plus examination, knowing that they could stay until eighteen, if need be, possibly going on from there to a university, or perhaps higher education of a technical kind.

From the first, I felt the greatest respect and affection for my colleague, Miss Clare. She was a mine of information about Fairacre and its inhabitants, for she had taught most of them and knew their foibles. She had started life in the local market town of Caxley where she and her older sister Ada began their schooling.

Her father, Francis Clare, had been a thatcher and there was plenty of work to be done. Not only were there a great many thatched cottages and barns in the neighbourhood, but at harvest time the newly-built ricks were thatched, and Francis was in great demand.

At the age of six Dolly and her family moved from Caxley to a small cottage at Beech Green, and there she grew up and still lived. The one love of her life had been killed in the 1914–18 war, and perhaps this accounted, in part, for the warm devotion which generations of young children had enjoyed under her care at Fairacre School. They gave her the comfort and affection which a family of her own would have supplied in happier circumstances, and both Dolly and her charges benefited.

She had shown me soon after we met the contents of an oval gold locket on a gold chain which she wore constantly round her neck. On one side was the photograph of a handsome young man, and facing it a lock of his auburn hair.

Dolly Clare and I worked in perfect accord until her retirement. Since then I had visited her at least once a week in the Beech Green cottage which had been thatched by her father and, more recently, by a man to whom she had given her father's tools when he had died. Frequently she came to stay with me at the school house, and was a welcome visitor to the school itself.

The fact that she out-lived her own generation and knew very little about her sister Ada's children and their progeny, meant that her friends were doubly precious to her. I was honoured to be among them.

A few years earlier she had told me that her cottage and its contents had been left to me on her death, and that I was to be one of the two executors. Such overwhelming generosity stunned me, and made my future secure for I had no real possibility of buying property, and of course the school house went with the post of head teacher. Dolly Clare's wonderful gesture had given me an enormous feeling of gratitude and relief. I knew that I could never repay or thank her adequately.

Later that Friday evening, when I was still relishing the thought of half-term stretching before me, there was a knock at the back door. There stood Bob Willet, holding a

shallow box which contained an assortment of vegetables.

'If you're going to see Dolly Clare could you give her these?'

'Of course. Come in for a minute. The wind's turned, hasn't it?'

'Ah! Gone round east a bit.'

He put the box on the kitchen table, and dusted his hands down his corduroy trousers.

'All from your garden?' I inquired, admiring the bronze onions, the freshly-scrubbed carrots, a snowy caulifower and some outsize potatoes.

'All except the marmalade,' he grinned. 'I never grew that, but Alice had made a bat n and thought Dolly'd relish a pot.'

'I'm sure she will. Have a cup of coffee?'

'Don't mind if I do.'

He sat down and looked about him. 'You got a new kettle?'

'The old one sprang a leak.'

'Hand it over, and I'll solder it for you.'

'As a matter of fact, I took it to Caxley.'

Mr Willet clicked his tongue disapprovingly. 'What you want to do that for? Wasting good money.'

'Well, I didn't want to bother you. You do enough for me as it is.'

'Rubbish! I don't do nothin' more'n I do for most folks around here. And they could do most of the jobs themselves, but they're too idle. With you it's different.'

'How?'

'Well, you're a woman, see, and not over-bright about doin' things with your hands.'

'Thanks!'

'No offence meant, Miss Read. I mean, you can do things I can't. Understand forms and that. Write a good letter. Cook a fair dinner – not as good as my wife Alice's, I must allow, but not at all bad. You has your points, but kettle-mending ain't one of 'em.'

He accepted his mug of coffee, and I joined him at the table with my own.

I did not take umbrage at Bob Willet's assessment of my abilities. As he often says: 'Speak the truth and shame the devil!' I faced his strictures with fortitude.

'And how was Dolly when you last saw her?' he inquired, stirring busily.

'As serene as ever, but she is so frail these days. I don't know that she should live alone.'

'She wouldn't want to live any other way. The only person she'd have settled with was her Emily Davis.'

Emily had been a contemporary of Dolly's from the earliest days at Beech Green. Their friendship, begun at that village's school, had survived until Emily's death some years before. The two old friends had planned to live in Dolly's cottage, but their time together was short, for Emily had died, leaving Dolly alone again.

Luckily Dolly had good neighbours who kept an eye on her, and George and Isobel Annett, the teacher at Beech Green school and his wife, lived close by and were as attentive to the old lady as if she were a near relation. Our vicar, the local doctor, and many Fairacre friends called regularly, and she was fortunate enough to have a stalwart and cheerful cleaner who came twice a week to perform her duties, and often simply to visit her friend.

She was a spry young Welsh woman called Mrs John, and had helped me out once in the school house when Mrs Pringle, our dour school cleaner, had let me down. She had two young children, always immaculately turned out, and her house was a model of good housekeeping. She and Miss Clare were fond of each other, and a great deal of Dolly's knitting ended up on the John children's backs.

'Still keeps herself busy, I suppose?' queried Bob Willet, putting aside his empty mug. 'Tell her I'll do a bit of gardenin' for her any time she wants.'

'I will,' I promised.

'Best be getting back. Got the watering to do in the greenhouse, and Mr Mawne's got summat up with one of his window catches. He's another like you. Supposed to be schooled proper but can't do nothin' much in the house.'

'Then it's a good thing we've got you to look after us,' I told him, and watched him stump away down the path.

It was cold and grey the next morning, and Tibby, my elderly cat, was as loth to get up as I was. However, the thought of the freedom from school was cheering enough to get me going, and by the time I was ready to set off to Miss Clare's, the sun was attempting to dispel the heavy clouds.

I had been invited to lunch, and after some protestation on Dolly's part I had agreed if I could do the cooking.

Consequently, I carried in my basket, six eggs and some minced ham ready for the omelette I proposed to make. I had also made an orange jelly and an egg custard – very suitable fare, I considered, for two old ladies – and only hoped that my modest endeavours would have met with Bob Willet's assessment of 'a fair dinner'. I also took some fresh fruit.

With his box of vegetables on the back seat with my basket, I set off for Beech Green. The roads were wet from an overnight shower, and the grass verges were besmeared with dirt thrown there throughout the past winter months by passing traffic.

About a mile along the road I overtook a small figure trudging along with a plastic carrier bag flapping in the breeze. It was one of my pupils, young Joseph Coggs.

I pulled up beside him. 'Where are you off to?'

'Brown's, miss.'

'Want a lift?'

A dazzling smile was the answer, as he clambered into the passenger seat.

Brown's was Beech Green's general store, and I wondered why Joe had been dispatched on a journey of two miles. After all, we had a very good shop in Fairacre.

'And what are you buying from Brown's?'

'Soap powder, miss.'

'Can't you get that at our shop?'

'Not till us have paid the bill.'

'I see.'

We drove along in silence. A pigeon flew dangerously close to the windscreen, and Joe drew in a deep breath.

'Reckon that frightened him,' he said.

'It frightened me too,' I told him. 'Might have smashed the windscreen.'

Joe pondered on this. 'Could you pay for it?'

'The insurance would cover it.'

'How?' asked Joe, mystified.

To my relief, Brown's shop front hove in sight, and I was spared the intricacies of explaining the principles and practice of car insurance to my passenger.

I drew up, and Joe began to open the door. I reached to the back seat and handed him over a banana from my collection of fruit.

'Eat it on the way home,' I said, 'and don't forget to put the skin in the litter bin over there.'

Ever the teacher, I thought, even on holiday!

'Thank you, miss. And for the ride. Me shoe was hurting.'

Poor old Joe, I thought, as I drove away. Shoes that hurt had been his lot for most of his young life, and he would get little sympathy from the rest of the hard-pressed Coggs family.

Dolly Clare was sitting by a bright fire when I arrived, but rose with remarkable agility for such an old lady.

'I've been counting the minutes,' she told me. 'It's so sweet of you to give up your half-term. Company means a lot when you can't get out.'

I looked about the snug sitting-room. As always, it was cheerful with shining furniture and even a few early poly-anthus flowers in a glass vase.

'Emily and I planted them years ago,' she said as I admired them. 'These are the progeny. They do well here, and so do cowslips. I suppose because they are derived from downland flowers. Emily and I picked so many prim-roses when we were children here at Beech Green, but there aren't as many now as there were in the coppices.'

She followed me into the kitchen where I set out my culinary arrangements, and handed over Bob Willet's present.

'The dear thing!' she exclaimed. 'And all so useful. And

homegrown too. I shall write him a note without delay.

Back in the sitting-room I inquired after her health.

'Nothing wrong with me but old age. I have lots of friends who pop in, and Mrs John is vigilant. I only hope I slip away one night like Emily, and don't cause a lot of bother with a long illness.'

It seemed to me that she was even smaller and more frail than when I had last visited her, but she seemed content and happy to talk about times past, and particularly her memories of her friend Emily.

'It's strange, but I think of her more than anyone else. Even my dear Arnold, who would have been a very old man by now, is not as clear in my memory as Emily. I suppose it is because I met her when we were children and one's impressions are so fresh. I have the queerest feeling sometimes that she is actually in the house with me.'

I made a sound of protest. Was she getting fanciful, I thought, getting hallucinations, becoming fearful?

As if she read my mind, she began to laugh.

'It's nothing frightening, I assure you. In fact, just the opposite. I feel Emily's warmth and sympathy, and find it wonderfully comforting. With Arnold, alas, I seem to have lost contact. I remember how dearly we loved each other, but I can't recall his face. For that I have to look here.'

She withdrew the gold oval locket on a long chain and opened it. I knew the portrait well, but studied it afresh before she returned it to be hidden under her blouse.

'And yet, you see, Emily's face is clear as ever to me. What odd tricks the mind plays! I can remember how this cottage looked when I first saw it at the age of six, far more clearly than I can recall places which I've known in the last ten years or so.'

'The brain gets cluttered up,' I said, 'as the years go by. The early impressions are bound to be the sharpest.'

'One of the joys of living in this house for most of my life,' went on Dolly, 'are the pictures I remember of my parents' life here. Times were hard. In those days if you didn't work you didn't eat. It was as simple as that. No cushioning by the state against hardship, and we had a very thin time of it if work was short.'

'How did you manage?'

'We always kept a few chickens, and a pig, of course, as most cottagers did in those days. My mother was a wonderful manager, and could make a shilling go as far as three. We went gleaning too after the harvest, and always had a sack of flour. And neighbours always helped each other in time of sickness and accident.'

'What about parish relief? Wasn't there something called that?'

'Oh, one dreaded "going on the parish"! Mind you, the people in the big houses were usually very generous and sent soup or puddings and such like to needy folk. Somehow we made do until more work came along. In a way, my father was lucky. He was known as a first-class thatcher, and he was in work most of the time. But I can still see my poor mother standing at the kitchen table with a morsel of cold rabbit and onion from the garden wondering whether to make a pie, with far more crust than filling, or to chop it up with hard boiled-eggs and some home-grown lettuce. I think I was about eight at the time, and I remember I persuaded her to make the pie! I didn't like lettuce.'

'She sounds a wonderful woman.'

'We all had to be, and it stood us in good stead in wartime and throughout our lives.'

She began to laugh. 'All this talk of rabbit pie has made me quite hungry. What about us going into the kitchen to see about that delicious omelette?'

So we went.

2   Falling Numbers

DURING half-term I enjoyed the company of another old friend. Amy and I had met at college, taught at neighbouring schools for a while, and kept in touch after her marriage. She lived in a village a few miles south of Caxley, our local market town. She was all that I was not – well-dressed, sociable, much-travelled, lively-minded and, of course, married.

Her husband, James, was a high-powered business man who had an office in the city, and had to spend a good deal of his time visiting European centres of finance, and some in America and Japan. He was energetic, good-tempered and, even in middle-age, devastatingly good-looking. It was not surprising that women were attracted to him and, although he and Amy made a devoted couple, one could not quite accept that *all* his trips were business ones, whatever he said.

I saw Amy frequently, partly because she was alone very often, and also, I flattered myself, because our friendship meant more as the years passed.

She was sitting in her car when I returned from our village shop with some groceries, an unwieldy French loaf swathed in tissue paper and a packet of soap powder which reminded me of Joseph Coggs's errand.

As always, she was elegantly clad. Her tweed suit was of misty blue, and the cloth had been woven in Otterburn, I knew. The matching jumper was of cashmere, and James's sapphire engagement ring added the final touch to Amy's ensemble.

'You should have rung,' I said, opening the door, 'and then I would have changed from this rough old skirt.'

'I don't mind your rough old skirt,' said Amy kindly. 'It's an old friend by now. Incidentally, how long have you had it?'

I stood in the middle of the kitchen and pondered.

Amy removed the loaf, took off the paper and put the bread in the bin.

'Must be getting on for eight years,' I said at last. 'I bought the stuff at Filkins when we toured the Cotswolds one Easter. Remember?'

'Well, it wears very well,' replied Amy. I began to feel pleased. Amy is rather censorious about my appearance.

'It needs cleaning, of course,' she added. 'And hems are up this season.'

'I'll ask Alice Willet to shorten it,' I said meekly, and put the kettle on.

'Well, what news?' I asked over the tea cups.

'Not much. James is as busy as ever, and is doing a Good Deed.'

'Well done James!'

'I hope so, but I can see it is all going to be rather fraught. He came across an old school friend who is down on his luck. Been made redundant, and James is searching for a job in one of his companies that would suit the fellow. But the thing is he's rather a problem.'

'How? Just out of prison? Suffering from something?'

'Not exactly.'

Amy blew a perfect smoke ring, an accomplishment of hers which she knows impresses me inordinately, although I deplore the habit of smoking, as she is well aware.

'He's been terribly depressed because of losing his job, and his wife has left him. Luckily the children are off their hands, but he's one of those chaps who can't do a hand's turn in the house, so he's half-starved and lonely with it.'

I gave an involuntary snort.

'Oh, I know you aren't sympathetic, but not everyone can cope as you do. Even though it is a muddle,' she added unnecessarily, eyeing an untidy pile of washing awaiting the attention of the iron. 'James has invited him to stay for a few days, and I wondered if you would come to dinner next weekend, and cheer him up.'

'Of course I will. You know I always enjoy your meals.'

'It's not just my *meal* I'm inviting you to,' said Amy. 'It's your *support* I need on this particular occasion.'

I promised to do my duty; Amy relaxed, and I did too.

One good thing, this unhappy man was married. He might not be a contented husband at the moment, but at least Amy would not have designs on him as a future husband for me.

Over the years I have been the victim of Amy's machinations. In vain I tell her that I *like* being single. She refuses to believe it, and a procession of males, whom Amy considers suitable partners for an ageing spinster, have been introduced to me. Some I have liked and have remained friends with, some have been harmless and quickly forgotten, and some have been frankly appalling, but I don't hold it against dear old Amy. She was born a match-maker, and will continue her endeavours until death claims her, and I have had ample experience now in evading the state of matrimony. We both play the game like old hands, but I must confess that I find it rather trying at times. This new acquaintance should not give me any trouble.

'What's his name?' I asked.

'James calls him "Basher".'

'Well,' I expostulated, 'I can't call him *that*!'

'I suppose not. It may be Michael or Malcolm. Something beginning with 'M'. I'll find out before you come.'

(As it happened, he turned out to be 'Brian'.)

'By the way,' said Amy, 'I came across Lucy Colgate the other day.'

Lucy had been at college with us, and I had always detested her. Amy was more tolerant.

'I thought she had married,' I said.

'She has, but I can never remember her married name. She was buying fish in Sevenoaks.'

'And what were you doing in Sevenoaks?'

'James had a board meeting, and I went along for the ride. I was doing some shopping when I bumped into Lucy. We had coffee together.'

'And how was she?'

'As tiresome as ever. Intent on impressing one with her worldliness and high spirits.'

'Well, that sounds like Lucy! Do you remember how she used to boast about climbing over the cycle sheds to get in after hours at college? She always wanted to be the Madcap of the Fourth. What is it these days?'

'Oh, sex changes and abortions and various diseases which used to be happily unmentionable, but now people like Lucy feel obliged to parade even when having morning coffee. I think she imagines that she is shocking people like us. "Opening Our Eyes to Life As It Is," you know.'

'It's time she grew up,' I agreed, 'but she never will. Poor old Lucy! I suppose she still feels a dare-devil under all those wrinkles.'

'No need to be catty. It doesn't suit you,' said Amy primly. She put down her cigarette and then surveyed me closely. 'Nevertheless, we have certainly weathered the years better than Lucy Colgate,' she announced with great satisfaction.

And we both dissolved into laughter.

* * *

Half-term ended with a night of heavy rain. It drummed on the school house roof, and splashed and gurgled into the two rainwater butts.

I sloshed through puddles in the playground and met Mrs Pringle in the lobby. As usual she was taking the wet weather as a personal affront.

'Love's labour lost trying to keep these floors clean in this weather,' she grumbled. 'There's a puddle the size of a football pitch outside the Post Office, and half our lot are playing "Splashem" in it.'

'Splashem' is a simple Fairacre game which involves waiting by a sizeable puddle until some innocent victim appears. The far-from-innocent instigators of the game then jump heavily into the water sending up a shower which drenches their victim. At the same time, the triumphant shout of 'Splashem' is raised. Everyone involved gets wet feet and the unlucky innocent gets soaking clothing as well. It is a game which only a few enjoy, and I have been as ferocious as the outraged parents in trying to stop it. On the whole, the playground is free from it, but on the journey to and from school the malefactors still indulge.

'I'll give them all a wigging,' I promised Mrs Pringle.

'What they wants,' said she, 'is a good hiding. It's a great pity you teachers have got so soft with 'em all. As bad as the Caxley magistrates. I see as Arthur Coggs got something called a *conditional discharge* for fighting in the market place. Nothing but a *let off*, when he deserved a *flogging*.'

'Well, we can't go back to flogging and the stocks and hanging,' I said. 'We've got to put up with justice as it is.'

'More's the pity,' replied Mrs Pringle, bending down to pick a leaf from the floor. She was puce in the face when she straightened up, and her corsets creaked under the strain.

'I'm not the woman I was,' she said with some satisfaction. She must have noticed my expression of alarm. 'First thing in the morning my bronchials are a torment. Nearly coughs my heart up, I does. Fred says I should give up this job, and I reckon he's right.'

I have heard this tale so often from Mrs Pringle's lips, as well as second-hand comments from Fred, her husband, that I have grown quite callous.

'No one,' I told her, 'wants you to work when you aren't fit. If you really find the job too much then you must give in your notice.'

'And leave my stoves to be polished – or *half* polished more like – by some other woman as don't know blacklead from furniture polish? No! I'll struggle on as best I can, till I drop.'

At that, she preceded me into the classroom for a final flick round with the duster.

As I expected, she was limping heavily. Mrs Pringle's bad leg, which 'flares up' regularly, is a good indicator of that lady's disposition.

Today, after my trenchant comments, the leg was even more combustible than usual.

Ernest rushed into the lobby, leaving wet footprints, but luckily Mrs Pringle was busy taking umbrage out of sight.

'Can I ring the bell, miss?'

'Carry on, Ernest,' I said.

School had started again.

At mid-morning a neighbour of Bob Willet's appeared, bringing bad news.

She was the mother of three of my pupils as well as an older child at Beech Green school. The family, the Thompsons, were comparative newcomers to the village, and generally approved.

The father was employed by the local electricity board and went daily to Caxley. Mrs Thompson helped in the village shop in the mornings while the children were at school, but she gave this up during the school holidays.

'She's a good little mother,' Alice Willet had told me, and this was high praise indeed.

The children were well cared for, not overbright, but well-mannered and happy. I was very fond of them and they had settled cheerfully among the others.

I had heard rumours and, as I had feared, Mrs Thompson had come to tell me that her husband had been posted elsewhere, and that they were obliged to leave Fairacre.

'And we don't want to go. Not one of us,' she asserted, 'but it means more money, and if he turns this down he might not get another chance in the future. I'm real sorry about it, Miss Read, and the children don't want to leave any more than we do.'

'Have you got to find a house?' I asked, secretly hoping that this would mean keeping my pupils a little longer.

'No. There's a house with the job, so we can go in at Easter. It all looks fine on paper, but that doesn't change our feelings.'

'Well, at least I shall have them for the rest of the term,' I said. 'But we shall all miss them. They've been model pupils.'

I accompanied her to the outer door. The rain was pelting down again, but a large umbrella stood in the corner of the lobby and Mrs Thompson assured me she would be adequately sheltered on her return to her duties at the shop. I thanked her for letting me know about her plans, and watched her departure across the playground.

I returned to the classroom with a heavy heart.

At playtime, after the dire threats about 'Splashem' to my flock, I broke the sad news to my assistant Mrs Richards, formerly Miss Briggs. She was as upset as I was.

'But this will bring our numbers down to well under thirty,' she cried.

'Nearer twenty,' I told her. 'Mind you, we've been almost as low before, and always managed to evade closure.'

It is one of the shadows which hangs over many villages these days: none wants to lose its village school, and local newspapers, the length and breadth of the country, carry sad stories of battles to keep village schools thriving.

I thought of my recent conversation with Miss Clare, and the large numbers which once thronged Fairacre School. So much had changed over a life time. At eleven years of age, my pupils moved on, instead of staying until fourteen as in Dolly Clare's day. Families were much smaller. With the advent of the car, parents could deliver their children farther afield to a school of their choice. Salaries had increased, and many parents could now afford the fees at local private schools which, for one reason or another, they preferred for their children.

I had faced this problem of dwindling numbers through-out my years at Fairacre. So far we had been spared, but for how long? Many small schools had managed to combine with others for activities such as games, or had shared facilities for common ventures such as film shows, peripatetic lecturers, demonstrators and so forth. This was fine when the schools were fairly close.

Fairacre unfortunately was isolated, except for the neighbouring school at Beech Green. If we had to close, it was most likely that the Fairacre children would be taken by bus the two or three miles to the larger school, where George Annett was head teacher and had an excellent staff. I had no doubt that my little flock would settle there happily, in more modern surroundings and with the added attraction and stimulation of larger numbers which would allow team games such as cricket and football which my youngsters sorely missed.

But what would happen to this venerable old building with its leaky skylight and lobby walls flaking paint everywhere? And what about my beloved school house across the playground, where I lived so contentedly?

Even more alarming, what would happen to me?

All conjectures about the future were brought to a sudden return to the present, by the appearance of a tearful infant dripping water everywhere, who had become the latest victim of 'Splashem'.

I strode out of the classroom into action.

Mr Willet, of course, had heard the news of the Thompsons' departure long before I had, and he seemed to find great satisfaction in telling me so.

'I thought about that old saying,' he said, when I remonstrated with him, 'that one about ignorance being bliss. Seemed to me a pity to shake you out of your fool's paradise.'

I felt somewhat nettled by this remark.

'I'm shaken all right,' I told him crossly. 'This is one step nearer closure, you know, and we shall both be out of a job.'

'Won't worry me,' he said sturdily. 'I can turn my hand to anything. Gardenin', carpenterin', decoratin', grave-diggin', there's allus summat to do. Now with you it's different. What can you do except teach school?'

'I can cook –' I began.

'Not good enough to get a proper job.'

'Well, I could work in a shop.'

'You ain't that quick with money.'

'Or learn to type, and go into an office.'

'The young 'uns would run rings round you. They has *computers* anyway.'

'Perhaps I could do market research. You know, walk about Caxley High Street with a clip-board, and annoy everyone with my questions when they were hurrying home to cook the lunch.'

'You wouldn't be bossy enough.'

I began to feel somewhat mollified by this remark.

'I mean,' he continued, 'you're bossy enough in school with the kids, but you'd never stand up to anyone your own size.'

'Thanks!' I said, back where we had started. 'So what do you suggest, other than the Caxley Workhouse?'

'That closed years ago,' he reminded me. He looked me over speculatively.

'I s'pose you might get married.' He sounded doubtful.

'A desperate measure,' I laughed. 'And not one I'm going to consider.'

'Maybe you're right,' he conceded and began to move towards the door. Then he stopped and turned.

'The first of those new houses is up for sale. Might get some children there, with any luck.'

Mr Roberts, our local farmer, had sold a strip of land a

year or so earlier, and three good-sized houses had been put up by a local builder. They were fairly innocuous in appearance and had decent gardens, but their prices were steep by village standards.

The sale of the land had provided plenty of gossip at the time. Bob Willet told me that his grandfather had always gone to work at Springbourne by a footpath which had once crossed that piece of land.

'Used to save the old boy a good mile,' he told me. 'But after the war that path was never claimed. Roberts's old dad was a cunning one, and it served his purpose to let the path be covered by his crops. There was plenty around here did that, and we lost no end of old footpaths then.'

However, despite local protests, planning permission was granted, and Fairacre now had three new 'executive' houses, whatever that meant.

'It would be marvellous,' I said, 'if we had three families with lots of children coming to live there.'

'Make a nice change,' agreed Bob. 'Mighty few young 'uns in Fairacre coming along as it is.'

'Has anyone heard if the houses have attracted any buyers yet?'

'Two or three of them yuppy types. Real tinkers.'

'Tinkers?' My mind flew to a collection of shabby caravans, washing spread on hedges, swarthy men busy with clapped-out cars, and litter everywhere.

'Two-Incomes-No-Kids. T.I.N.K. or tinkers,' explained Mr Willet. 'If that sort comes, it'll be years before you get any of theirs into the school.'

'Well, I shall live in hope,' I told him. 'After all, Fairacre School is still alive and kicking.'

'Just,' agreed Bob Willet, departing.

3   At Amy's

THE following Sunday I prepared myself for Amy's dinner party.

I hoped that it would not be a large one, and was comforted by the thought that Amy had muttered something about six, which would save putting in the leaf of the table. However, knowing Amy, she might well have fallen victim to her own generous instincts and I might find myself among twice the number first envisaged.

In my modest wardrobe I have had, for more years than I can recall, a black velvet skirt and waistcoat to match. What is more, the waistcoat has pockets large enough for handkerchief, purse and spectacle case. They can also accommodate an indigestion tablet, although I knew that this would be quite unnecessary after a meal at Amy's.

The thing was, Amy had seen this ensemble many times over the years, worn with a white silk blouse, a white lace blouse, a black and white spotted blouse, and a fine white woollen blouse for draughty houses.

While I was worrying about the alternatives, a navy-blue foulard which was too tight in the waist, or a pink-flowered silk which I thought made me look like mutton dressed as lamb, I remembered that my only pair of black patent shoes was at the mender's, so that ruled out the black velvet duo.

Now I had only to choose between the navy-blue and the pink. I spent most of the afternoon vacillating between the two, as I marked history test papers in the garden.

The sun was warm, and out of the wind it was possible

to enjoy this early warmth. The rain had done some good, and already the early daffodils were showing their buds. My red pencil slipped to the ground, and I closed my eyes against the sunshine.

Did other women fuss so about their clothes, I wondered? Heaven alone knows, I am the most undressy person alive, as Amy frequently tells me, and my wardrobe is scanty. What did women do who had twenty outfits to choose from? Went quite mad, I supposed, worrying about shoes and jewels and so on to go with the right clothes. Thank heaven I only owned Aunt Clara's seed pearls for my evening adornment, and one or two pieces of costume jewellery.

How did royal ladies cope? Did they choose their own emeralds and rubies or was that decision left to the Mistress of the Wardrobe, or whoever it was? And think of the horror of having to choose something from hundreds of ensembles! I supposed I was lucky with just the choice of my too-tight navy blue or the too-juvenile pink, and fell into a light doze.

When I awoke the sun had vanished behind a cloud, and my arms were covered in goose pimples.

I went into the kitchen and put the kettle on. It should be the pink. My new cream handbag and matching shoes would be quite suitable, and Aunt Clara's seed pearls would tone beautifully.

I proposed to be the belle of the ball. It would make a nice change.

'Well, you *do* look pretty!' cried Amy when I arrived. 'You should wear pink more often. It's so *youthful*. It makes you look like a bridesmaid.'

This was exactly what I had feared, but I did not enlarge on the theme.

Amy herself was in a filmy grey frock patterned with leaves and looked, as always, exactly right.

I was the first to arrive, so we had time to discuss the other guests before they joined us.

'Only Horace and Eve Umbleditch,' said Amy, 'to make a nice comfortable six. And if poor Brian is depressed we can always count on Horace to keep the ball rolling.'

I agreed. Horace, a fellow-teacher, was always an asset in company, as I had known for years.

'And is this Brian likely to be depressed? Where is he, by the way?' I asked.

'Getting dressed, I hope. He was late coming back from Caxley and had a quick shower. He's not a very tidy shower-taker, I'm afraid.'

'I think you are noble to have him at all,' I said truthfully. I imagined a gaunt sad figure drifting about the place, hollow-eyed and monosyllabic, mourning his lost wife and job. My heart bled for him just a little, but even more profusely for my gallant old friend.

'Oh, it won't be for long,' said Amy. 'James is looking out for something suitable for him. Ah! Here are Horace and Eve.'

She made her way to the front door, and I heard welcoming greetings from James and Amy, and Horace's well-known hearty voice.

I have always been fond of Horace, and he had been among the many local bachelors and widowers whom Amy had presented to me, over the years, as suitable husbands. Neither Horace nor I had had the slightest desire to satisfy Amy's ambitions, but we had always enjoyed each other's company. He taught at a local prep school and had recently married the school secretary. I imagine that Horace's loud voice was the result of years spent in making himself heard above hordes of little boys.

We sat with our glasses, exchanging news. I always feel
that the inhabitants of the country south of Caxley are
much more sophisticated than we are north of the town,
and this evening the talk was of opera, a local bridge
tournament, and the disgraceful condition of the nearby
golf course. Eve and I launched out on a discussion of
Caxley shops and their superiority over Oxford, Reading,
Winchester and other large conurbations, until we both
confessed we had not visited any of the latter for years and
so then enjoyed a refreshing fit of the giggles.

Amy appeared somewhat distracted and was obviously
listening for the arrival of Brian from upstairs. It would
not have surprised me to see her go in quest of him, but
she was spared that.

The door opened and Amy's visitor was revealed. Far
from being gaunt, hollow-eyed and the picture of melan-
choly which I had envisaged, Brian turned out to be pink
and bouncy, gleaming with soap and good health, and only
a few inches over five feet. He apologized for being late.

Amy introduced him to us all as: 'Brian Horner, who
was at school with James, and is staying here for a while.'
He had a nice smile, a low voice, and a firm handshake. He

did not seem to be at all cast down by his circumstances, and I wondered if he were really as unhappy as Amy and James seemed to think.

He was put next to me at the table and although I knew that this time Amy was not thinking of matrimony, I remembered her request 'to cheer up Brain' and set about doing my duty to support my hostess.

As it happened, I had very little work to do. Apart from fixing a bright smile on my face, and laughing politely at Brian's jokes, all that was required was a listening ear.

Brian turned out to be one of those people who can eat and talk at the same time. He did both with great speed, and kept us all regaled with tales of recent holidays – the cottage in Wales which was so damp that fungi grew on the inside wall, the hotel in Greece where the hot tap in the bathroom refused to turn off creating a private sauna *en suite*, and the skiing holiday with no snow.

He told his tales well, and although I had the feeling that he was rather monopolizing the conversation, I put it down to nervousness which so often makes people garrulous. At any rate, it made my duties much lighter, and I was able to enjoy Amy's lovely meal.

Afterwards we sat round the fire with our coffee, and I had time to talk to Horace and his wife who were thinking of moving into a house of their own, a mile or two from the school.

'If we don't do it now,' he said, 'we never shall. It's just too easy to stay on in the school premises until I retire, but then where should we live?'

I told him that those were my feelings about my own school house, and later I was invited to visit them in their present tied home.

The party broke up about eleven. Brian, who had taken only a small part in the conversation about the new home, sighed rather heavily as he said goodbye to Eve and Horace.

'You don't know how lucky you are to be making domestic plans. That's something I miss so dreadfully.'

It was one of those remarks upon which it is impossible to comment, but the pair looked somewhat startled, simply making their adieux and expressing pleasure at making his acquaintance. Perhaps, I thought, watching his sad face, he really is as unhappy as Amy says.

I rang her at playtime next morning to thank her for a splendid evening.

'And did you like Brian?' she said.

'Yes, indeed.'

'Oh, good. He was most complimentary about you.'

I am quite accustomed to this sort of remark from Amy after meeting males at her parties, but could afford to ignore any implications of future romance as Brian was already married, although a grass widower at the moment.

'James thinks the world of him,' went on Amy. 'He is a few years older than James, and was captain of cricket when James was in the fourth form. Quite a hero, according to James, was our Brian. They keep harking back to cricket matches they remember, and going to see Bradman at the Oval when they were boys. The air is thick with Trent Bridge and Lords, and I must say, I find it a trifle over-powering.'

'Any sign of a job for him?'

'There's a possibility of something in Bristol. Another Old Boy, equally cricket-crazy, I gather, has a business there, and James said he would be ringing him today.'

'Good. Must go. I can see a fight developing in the playground. Between *girls* this time!'

I put down the telephone hastily, and went to the rescue.

Hostilities having been quelled, we all returned to the classroom where peace reigned as soon as the children got to work on their pictorial maps of the village of Fairacre.

It grew comparatively quiet, broken only by the stutter of coloured pencils, the drone of a bee, newly-emerged from hibernation, bumbling up and down the Gothic window, and the distant bleating of sheep in a field belonging to Mr Roberts. Soon it would be lambing time and the shepherd would be keeping his vigil. It was good to look forward to may blossom in the hawthorn hedges, tulips in cottage gardens, cowslips on the downs, and lighter evenings to relish such joys.

Meanwhile, I let my thoughts stray to my conversation with Amy. I sincerely hoped that she would soon be free of Brian, and that James's admiration for his school-fellow would result in a steady job, safely in Bristol.

I had noticed before this peculiarly male trait of hero-worship which seems to persist, to a certain extent, throughout a man's life. Usually the object of veneration is a sportsman, as in this case. Many times have I watched a man picking up the newspaper, turning immediately to the sports pages, and brightening or despairing at what was to be read there. The leaders of the nation, the heroes of war, those most eminent in the arts are as nothing compared with the man who scored a century or kicked the winning goal.

Women, I mused, seemed to get over the hero-worshipping stage with commendable speed. The 'school-girl's crush' faded by the time the sixth form was reached, and she herself became briefly the object of adoration. Strange that the male should take so long to get over it. Stranger still that it should persist, in so many cases, for the rest of a man's life.

Well, perhaps Brian would benefit from James's feelings.

I remembered that the Bristol business man was also a devotee. Between the two of them, Brian should find a haven.

At that moment, the door opened and Patrick appeared, his gap-toothed grin well in evidence.

'And where have you been?' I demanded.

'Out the back,' he replied. This is the vernacular in Fairacre for the lavatory. 'You never took no notice when I asked. And I *had* to go. So I went.'

I apologized. This did not seem the right moment to explain, yet again, the problems of the double negative. No doubt there would be plenty more occasions.

I put Brian Horner's affairs away, and returned to my own.

Before afternoon school, Mrs Pringle, our dour cleaner, arrived to perform her usual task of washing up the dinner things.

'You'll have to do without me this time next Wednesday,' she told me. 'Just had word from the Cottage that they wants to see my leg.'

The Cottage is our local Caxley Cottage Hospital. Sometimes it is known as 'The Caxley', but this is somewhat confusing as our local bus and our local newspaper are both known as 'The Caxley'.

One catches, or meets people, on 'The Caxley' (bus). To appear in print in *The Caxley* (newspaper) can be a matter of pride or shame according to which page one is given prominence. Naturally, to be mentioned under the heading Court Proceedings can be embarrassing. The Wedding page or Local Charity Events can be a pleasure, and if a personal photograph is included (even if it does look like 'An Explosion in a Pickle Factory', to quote P. G. Wodehouse), it is an added bonus to one's self-esteem.

'So I shan't be able to do the washing-up, or put your place to rights.'

'Well, never mind,' I said. 'I can do it with the children, and it doesn't matter about my house.'

'*Doesn't matter?*' boomed Mrs Pringle, turning puce. 'I was all set to do that brass of yours, and not a minute before time, I may say. I thought of getting Minnie to step in for the day.'

At this my blood ran cold. Minnie Pringle is a niece, with as much sense as a demented hen. I have suffered from her ministrations in the past, and the thought of her at large in the school lobby with the dinner crockery was bad enough. Left to her own devices in my house was not to be borne.

'Definitely not!' I exclaimed. 'We can managed for one day without bothering Minnie.'

Mrs Pringle drew in an outraged breath. Her puce cheeks took on a purplish hue.

'I was only trying to help,' she said at last. 'Small thanks I gets for *that*, I can see. I'll say no more. Just to let you know I'll be catching the one o'clock Caxley to The Caxley next week.'

She limped heavily from the classroom, leaving me to wonder if she would possibly be reading *The Caxley* on The Caxley when she went for her appointment at The Caxley.

As usual it was Mr Willet who came to the rescue later.

'My Alice heard as our Madam Sunshine is off to hospital on Wednesday. You want her to wash up? She says she's willing. And she'll do whatever's needed at the school house.'

'I'd be glad of her help here,' I told him, 'but my house won't hurt. According to Mrs Pringle there's so much wants doing there that another week's neglect won't do much harm.'

'Right. I'll tell her. Mr Lamb mentioned it.'

Mr Lamb is our Fairacre post-master, and much respected, though I had often had the unworthy suspicion that he perused much that passed through his hands.

Bob Willet must have read my thoughts on this occasion.

'There was a postcard from the hospital,' said he. 'I don't say Mr Lamb exactly *reads* things like that, but he sort of *imbibes* them, as he's sorting out the mail.'

It seemed best not to comment.

On the next Saturday morning I had occasion to visit the Post Office myself. Mr Lamb was busy hanging up a multitude of various coloured forms around the glass enclosure which, we all hoped, would protect him in the event of robbers breaking in.

There was a young woman there and, to my delight, she had a boy of about four or five with her. A new pupil, I wondered, with my hard-pressed school in mind?

'Do you know Mrs Winter?' said Mr Lamb. 'She's come to live in one of the new houses.'

I introduced myself and expressed hope that she would enjoy living in Fairacre.

'I'm going back to make coffee,' I added. 'Would you like to join me?'

She smiled and accepted.

'Have you got a dog?' asked the boy.

'No, but I've got a cat.'

He looked pleased. They seemed a cheerful pair, and I looked forward to learning more about them.

We bought our stamps and bade farewell to Mr Lamb.

'What a nice man he is,' enthused Mrs Winter as we

went back to the school house. 'He's introduced me to quite half a dozen people.'

'He did the same for me years ago,' I told her. 'And in those days one still had the older generation calling on the newcomers. It's a pity that nice habit has died out. Really, I suppose, I should have called on you, instead of leaving it to Mr Lamb.'

Over coffee, it transpired that she knew more about me than I had realized.

'You see, I worked with Miriam Quinn for several years and I believe she is a friend of yours.'

'Indeed she is,' I exclaimed, 'although I don't see quite as much of her now that she is married to Gerard Baker and lives in Caxley. How is she?'

She gave me all the news, and it turned out that she herself had succeeded to Miriam's post as personal secretary to the great Sir Barnabas Hatch, the financier.

'It's partly through Miriam that we decided to buy this house in Fairacre. She had always said how happy she had been in the village, and I visited her at Holly Lodge once or twice.'

'And will you continue with your job?'

'I shall indeed. Not only do I enjoy it, but we certainly need two incomes to pay our mortgage.'

'Does Jeremy go to school yet?' I ventured, watching the young boy engrossed in a picture book on the sitting-room floor.

'Play school twice a week,' said his mother, 'but he starts at the prep school in Caxley in September. It has a first-class Kindergarten group, and both my sister's children go there. We can drop him off each morning as we go into the office. My husband works for the same firm, but in another department.'

My hopes for a new pupil were dashed, but I did my best to hide my disappointment.

I showed her round the house and garden, accepted an invitation to tea one Sunday, and we parted company at the gate.

'A very nice addition to the Fairacre community,' I told Tibby on my return to the kitchen.

My encounter with Jane Winter and her little boy gave me much food for thought over that weekend. How things had changed at Fairacre School even in my own time there, let alone in Dolly Clare's! For one thing, there had been almost double the number of children on roll when I took over. The ancient log book showed almost a hundred pupils at the beginning of the century, but of course they could stay at school then until the age of fourteen. Nowadays they left at eleven.

But that was only one reason for the fall in numbers. Smaller families was another. The drift from the land another one. The two or three local farmers who employed a dozen to two dozen men as ploughmen, carters, hedgers-and-ditchers, harvesters, thatchers and piece-workers of all skills, now coped with the two or three employees and barns full of expensive agricultural machinery, supplemented by contractors called in for seasonal work.

There had also been a natural desire by parents to see their offspring better catered for than they had been themselves. A great many in Fairacre remembered the hard times of the thirties, and intended that their children should never be as deprived as they were in their youth. After the war, many of the farm labourers changed jobs and moved into the towns where wages were higher and the hours of work shorter. Consequently, children attending the school were few and far between.

And then there came the pleasures and convenience of owning a family car. Their parents' world had been limited to the miles they could walk, or ride on horseback or in a carriage. For many of that generation and earlier, Caxley was as far as they had ever ventured. Very few had seen the sea, some seventy miles away, and fewer still had been to London, less than seventy miles to travel. Now, it seemed, they could spend their leisure anywhere in the British Isles, or even farther afield.

Even more pertinent, from my point of view, the car could take children out of the village to nearby schools of their parents' choice. The preparatory school at Caxley, to which young Jeremy Winter was bound in September, was a case in point. It had been a thoroughly reliable and thriving school for many years, and was deservedly respected in the community. Many local people had passed through its hands, and in the old days had usually gone from there to the ancient local grammar school. One could see why the Winters would have no difficulty in taking the child in by car, and it was absolutely right that they should have the school of their choice. But it did not help my numbers, alas!

The proliferation of cars in the village certainly contributed, in some measure, to the plight of my own school and many others in the same quandary. But what could be done about it?

When I first came to Fairacre public transport was adequate. There were several buses a day to Caxley and back, and from there one could proceed to larger towns such as Oxford, Reading, Andover, and even Salisbury with a little planning. Now we had several days in the week with no buses at all.

There had been a branch line on the railway to Caxley, much used by school children and other daily passengers. When it closed, in company with hundreds of other lines after the war, there was a definite loss to the community.

To have a car in Fairacre is now a necessity rather than a luxury, and what was once an added pleasure to life is now a vital means of getting to one's living.

Well, there was mighty little I could do to halt the dwindling of my flock. Perhaps the other two new houses would provide some future pupils for Fairacre School.

But somehow I doubted it.

4   Newcomers

MRS Pringle returned to her duties after her visit to hospital. Her mood was more militant than usual.

'That new doctor I saw this time said I was to lose two stone and take *more exercise*. "*More exercise, young man,*" I says to him, "if you saw how much exercise I have to take, day in day out, at my work – which is Real Work, I'll have you know, not just looking at legs and writing out bits of paper for the chemist – you would get a real shock." He didn't say nothing after that.'

It was my private opinion that Mrs Pringle had not delivered the tirade quoted but wished she had, and I was being the recipient of her wishful thinking.

'A mere boy he was too,' she went on, puffing about the classroom with her duster. 'Could've been my grandson except I'd have learnt him better manners if he'd been one of mine, I can tell you.'

'Has he prescribed any medicine or ointment?' I enquired, really in order to stem this vituperative flow.

Mrs Pringle sat down heavily on the front desk, chest heaving under her flowered overall. I confronted her glaring eyes as bravely as I could.

'Much too posh for that, this one was. Going to get in touch with our own doctor, I gather, and says he'll see me when I've lost the first two stone. *The first two stone!* He'll have to wait a bit, and that's flat.'

She heaved herself to her feet and made for the floor. It was no surprise to see that her limp was much in evidence.

* * *

March was almost over and before long we should be breaking up for the Easter holidays.

Our vicar, the Reverend Gerald Partridge, paid his usual weekly visit and gave a talk to the children about the coming Holy Week followed by the Festival of Easter.

I always enjoy his visits, and so do the children, but much of his discourse is far above their heads. He had been a brilliant student, I had heard, at his theological college, and this I could well believe. But his beliefs were couched in such obscure and learned language that I found as much difficulty in understanding him as did my class.

However, he has a lovely voice, and kindness oozes from him like honey and this we all appreciate. The children are quite content to listen in peaceful bemusement as the words flow round them, and we all feel rested and happy.

On this particular afternoon, after the children had gone out to play, the vicar broached the subject of our falling numbers.

'I know,' I said. 'It is worrying, but what's to be done?'

'We've faced this before. It was the worrying part for you that my wife and I were concerned about. You can be sure that if the worst happens, which pray to God it won't, we shall all see that you can stay on in the school house.'

'I have no doubt that the education committee would be humane enough to allow that,' I agreed. I wondered if this were the moment to tell him about Miss Clare's wonderful bequest to me. So far, I had kept silent about it, although I had a strong suspicion that the news had been common knowledge for some time in the neighbourhood. I decided to take the plunge.

'As it happens,' I began, 'I don't think I should be entirely homeless –'

'Ah yes! Dear Dolly Clare's house. I had heard of her plans that you should have it.'

How *did* the news get about, I wondered for the hundredth time? I had said nothing, Dolly had said nothing, that I knew. Her solicitors presumably were like the proverbial clams. I suppose things are air-borne in rural parts. There seems to be no other explanation.

'It's true,' I said. 'I am an extremely lucky woman, and Dolly says I can stay at her house whenever I like.'

'Well, that's a great weight off our minds,' sighed the vicar. 'You are going to have a roof over your head one way or another.'

I went with him to the door. A few spots of rain were falling, and I called the children inside, waving goodbye to our chairman of governors at the same time.

Within two minutes the heavens opened and the windows were streaming with rain. At least I had collected my little flock before the chance of playing 'Splashem' had been a temptation.

The rain continued through the night and I lay in bed listening to it gurgling into the water butts. I heard the thump of the cat flap on the kitchen door, and a second thump very soon afterwards. Obviously Tibby had not spent long out in the garden, and had returned to warmth and a dry bed with the minimum of delay. I too enjoyed my bed, and thought how extra snug it seemed with the rain splashing outside.

In the morning it had cleared, and a bright sun was already sparking the raindrops on the edge. A spring morning in this downland country is a joy, and my garden was looking at its most hopeful. The ancient plum tree, brittle with age, was a mass of white blossom, and the grass was 'pranked with daisies', as Robert Bridges put it. I decided then and there that the children should learn his poem *Spring Goeth All in White* that very afternoon, in readiness for all the pleasures of the spring now, and those about to come.

The clematis was showing buds and, in the two tubs by my door, scarlet early tulips made a splash of colour against the faded brickwork of the house. Farther off in the border the daffodils made a brave show behind the mixed colours of velvety polyanthus. I savoured the freshness of it all before going in for my breakfast. Everything was so clean, so new, so hopeful. Before long the weeds would come, and the greenfly. The birds would peck at the polyanthus and primrose, and scatter the earth everywhere as they scratched for insects. The grass would need mowing, the paths would need weeding, the flowers would need deheading.

Never mind! That was in the future. It was bliss enough to relish this early morning vista of young life and fresh beauty, and I proposed to look no further.

On the following Sunday I went to tea at Jane Winter's new house.

I had looked forward to this for some time, for I have the usual curiosity about how others live, and we have had so few really new houses in the village that this was going to be an extra excitement.

Since my arrival in Fairacre, a number of cottages had been sold and renovated. With the decrease in the number of farm workers, many of their homes had gone on the market. Some, but not many in Fairacre, had become weekend cottages for Londoners, but more had been taken by couples working in Caxley, or retired people from the neighbourhood.

This, of course, was traditional. The young couples wanted a garden, and a pleasant place to bring up a family. The retired couples often wanted to leave their town homes which had sometimes been their business premises as well, and were looking for something peaceful and pretty, and easy to run.

The Hales were typical of such people. He had been a history master at Caxley Grammar School for most of his career, and they both enjoyed retirement now in Tyler's Row, a row of small and once shabby cottages which they had converted into one house. The Hales had proved to be a great asset to Fairacre, supporting the church and school, and well to the fore in helping with all our village activities. No doubt the Winters too would join in, although their business commitments would mean that their time was limited.

The front garden of the Winter's house was still rather raw, but the border had been planted with dwarf conifers of varying shapes and hues, and would look pleasant before long. It was obviously planted with an eye to saving labour in the future, which I thought wise. The Mr Willets of this world get scarcer weekly, more's the pity, and what one cannot do has of necessity to be left.

'Come and see the back garden,' said Jane, leading me round the house. There was a newly planted lawn, young grass already sprouting, and the whole area covered with lines of black cotton supported by a forest of sticks.

'The birds are such a pest,' said Jane, 'but I think we're winning. We're planning to have a rockery in the corner, and a long border with perennials at that side. And we're going to get a shrubbery going next autumn.'

'No vegetables?'

'Simply not worth it,' she said. 'We are surrounded with first-class market gardeners, and I can always pop into Tesco's or Sainsbury's from the office. Besides, when would we find the time to tend a vegetable garden? I know my father spends all his days planting peas and training raspberries, but then he's retired.'

It all made good sense, but again brought home to me the change in Fairacre ways. The older people in the village

still maintain their vegetable plot in the back garden, and
when I came here first a great many grew vegetables in their
front gardens as well. The idea of spending money, and
energy, in bringing stuff unnecessarily from Caxley on the
bus was unthinkable. Only foreign produce such as oranges
or bananas needed to be transported, the bulk of fruit and
vegetables came from one's own patch and was eaten in
season. All the peelings, the outer leaves of cabbages and
lettuces and so on, went to the pig, for almost all cottagers
had a sty, and even in my own days, most gardens had a
family pig in the corner.

Needless to say, there was no pig in this garden. It was
very well planned, and given a few years it was going to
look lovely, as I told my hostess.

We went indoors to be greeted by Jane's husband Tom,
a large and cheerful man who was engaged in bandaging
young Jeremy's knee.

'Nothing serious,' he assured me. 'It isn't a hospital job,
is it Jeremy?'

The child nodded agreement. There were still signs of
tears, but he seemed to be over the shock.

'Our paving stones are still wobbly,' explained Tom, 'and we shall have to get them laid properly, I can see.'

The drawing-room was large and light, and the furniture new and comfortable. Jeremy was prompted into handing round sandwiches and cake, which he did nobly despite the limp, but his father was given the job of delivering teacups.

It was all very jolly, and I enjoyed meeting new people and admiring their splendid possessions. It was stimulating to see the latest bathroom equipment, the modern double-glazing, the fitted cupboards and up-to-date gadgets in the kitchen and the adjoining utility room. The washing machine and tumble drier, as well as some large objects which I could not recognize, were housed here, while the kitchen itself was reserved for the cooking arrangements and also had a large table where meals could be taken. This, I could see, was already the heart of the house, as it is in all real homes.

After tea and the inspection of the house, we returned to the sitting-room and helped Jeremy with a large jigsaw puzzle of Mrs Tiggywinkle.

'He loves Beatrix Potter,' commented Jane.

'What a right-minded child,' I said.

'But I still wish we'd chosen "Benjamin Bunny",' said his father, studying a mottled piece of jigsaw. 'These prickly bits are the devil to sort out.'

I returned home with a pot of home-made jam, a picture drawn by Jeremy, and the comfortable feeling of having made new friends.

Later that evening, as I soaked in my very ordinary white bath, I dwelt on the beauty of the Winter's new home, and particularly on the luxury of their bathroom. The walls were painted a pale green, and the bath, wash-basin, bidet

and lavatory echoed the colour. Even the soap was green
and the towels too. It was a most beautiful sight.

And yet, not all that long ago, as I well remembered,
almost all the water in our village was that which fell from
the skies, and ended up in water butts and tanks. It is true
that there were several deep wells, and my school house
possessed one in which the water was pure and ice-cold.
But bathrooms were few and far between, and in my early
years at Fairacre I took my bath in front of the kitchen fire
enjoying silky rain water in a galvanized iron tub.

Very few houses now were without a bathroom. My
own had been adapted from a tiny box room between the
two bedrooms, and very well it suited me.

I remember how excited I was when main water was laid
through the village, and I turned on my new bath taps.
Here indeed was luxury!

There was no doubt about it, I thought as I towelled
myself dry, Fairacre folk were a great deal better off these
days. Gone were the buckets of hot and cold water to be
carried into the house. Better still, gone were the earth
privies at the end of the garden which, no matter how well
embowered in lilac and elder bushes, were not a pleasure
to visit at any time, and at their very worst on a dark wet
night.

I would not wish to go back to those days, and yet I
wondered if my delight in hearing rain splashing against
my windows and gurgling into my water butts did not
stem from that long ago time when rain water was welcome
and held so dear.

Amy called in one evening, soon after the Sunday tea
party, and I told her all about the new house.

'I wish you had somewhere like that to live,' she said
somewhat wistfully.

I looked at her in surprise. 'But I've got this – and I love it! You know that.'

'Yes, of course I know it,' said Amy, sounding more like her brisk self, 'but what about the future? What happens if the school closes? *When* it closes, one might say, from all I hear.'

Again, I had to make a decision. Should I keep my secret, as I had done for some years now? Or was it a secret after all? The vicar seemed to know all about Dolly Clare's generosity, and I had no doubt that most of Fairacre knew too.

I resolved to tell Amy that after one or two bequests, I would inherit Dolly's house and its contents. And having told her it was gratifying to see that she really had had no idea of my good fortune, and she was greatly stirred. Amy has a warm and quite emotional nature hidden under the sophisticated veneer, and she rose to give me a hug.

'Gosh, what a relief! I am so *very* pleased for you. Dear old Dolly, she is as far-sighted as she is generous. It is the perfect answer to your problems, isn't it?'

I told her how I felt about it.

'It solves our problems too,' she went on. 'James and I have often thought about what might happen to you when you retired, and he had plans for some kind of trust fund.'

'Good heavens!' I exclaimed. 'It's uncommonly kind of you both, but I shall have a pension, you know, and probably find digs somewhere, or a flat to rent.'

'Well, that doesn't arise now, does it?' said Amy.

'You are a good pair,' I replied. 'Always helping lame dogs over stiles – though I can't ever remember seeing a lame dog being helped over a stile, come to think of it. No doubt it would resent the attention, and bite the helping hand ungratefully. Anyway, how's your latest? Brian, I mean?'

'Still with us, although his daughter took him off our hands for three days last week.'

'So the Bristol job didn't materialize?'

'We don't know yet. The fellow who was at school with James and Brian is in Australia on some high-powered business lark, and then he will want to consult the other directors, so it looks as though we shall have our Brian for some time.'

'Well, I reckon you are both noble. I often think of that somewhat outspoken Spanish saying: "After three days fish, and visitors, stink!"'

Amy laughed. 'Well, at least Brian doesn't do that! He's the most frequently-bathed man I've come across.'

She rose to look out at the garden. 'I can see why you're so fond of this place. It is a little gem.'

'I know.'

'Does it run to a cup of coffee, by the way?'

I burst into apologies.

'Anything will do, my dear, as long as it isn't "This-week's-offer" from the village shop.'

'You shall have the very best,' I assured her, hastening to the kitchen.

5 Easter Holidays

WITH the end of the Spring term in sight, I began to busy myself with innumerable forms and returns which had to go to the local education authority.

More pleasurably, I began to plan some modest entertaining at the school house. During term time my evenings and weekends seem to be filled with such domestic activities as washing and ironing, answering personal letters, attacking anything particularly urgent in the home such as a leaking tap, a spent light bulb, or some feline disorder of Tibby's.

There are also school duties which have to be done in the peace of my sitting-room, such as the ever-present marking, planning of lessons and occasionally the highly necessary job of sorting out a large cardboard carton known euphoniously as 'The Bits Box'.

This useful aid to education contains such objects as cotton reels, buttons, kitchen paper towels, plastic boxes which once held margarine, Gentleman's Relish and other choice comestibles, lengths of elastic, string, raffia, lace, mysterious pieces of metal from old corsets, broken clocks, kitchen gadgets, and heaven knows what beside.

This jumble of rubbish is a constant source of delight to my children whose powers of invention are sparked off by blissful trawling in this rich sea. From the detritus they fabricate windmills, ships, cars, furniture for their dolls' houses or a host of ingenious objects. The Bits Box is much prized, but needs attention now and again. An insufficiently cleaned cereal carton, for instance, soon gets the attention of the school mice who bustle out at night when all is quiet. Sometimes the box itself, redolent of its varied cargo, has to be replaced with a fresh one.

This holiday, however, I intended to invite the Winters and Miriam and Gerard Baker to lunch with me. I should like to have invited Amy and James too, for they are generous in their hospitality to me, but they were going to be away and, in any case, seven people in my small dining-room was rather a squash. They would come on another occasion.

The invitations were accepted to lunch on a Saturday, and I began to ponder on the meal. I enjoy cooking, but it is not much fun providing for one person. It was going to be much more exciting planning an elegant spring luncheon for five.

It seemed a good idea to browse through several glossy magazines for ideas, and these were so absorbing that I found myself studying articles on child behaviour, breast-feeding, bird migration and the pollution of our beaches, before realizing that I had spent an hour in these pursuits and was no farther ahead with my culinary plans.

I turned to the pictures. That rum and chocolate and coconut cake looked really impressive, but the recipe had over a dozen listed ingredients. Also one needed several bowls in use, including one lodged over hot water whilst engaged in melting butter and chocolate together.

I like something simpler. Ten to one the milkman would call at a crucial moment of butter-and-chocolate merging, and all would be lost. Then think of the washing up of all those messy saucepans, bowls and spoons. Besides, a lot of people did not care for rum, or coconut, for that matter.

I turned to another magazine. Did I want a loan in order to buy a house? Was I adequately insured against accidents in the home, hospital treatment, and car crashes? Was my marriage unsatisfactory? (Well, no. I was not bothered about that, priase be.) Had I ever considered becoming a counsellor, or a warden at a residential home?

This was getting me nowhere. I turned firmly to the cookery pages. This was better. 'Spring On The Table'. A rather ambiguous title, surely? However, the pictures were splendid, and the salmon soufflé looked just the thing. But, come to think of it, one really wants the guests absolutely ready and waiting at the table in order to present them with the perfectly-risen dish. Suppose the Winters were late, or the Bakers, for that matter? Too risky, I decided. Far better to be less ambitious and have something I could prepare the day before, such as cold gammon and chicken.

But I am a messy carver, and it might be one of those cold cheerless spring days when one would relish a Lancashire hot-pot or steak-and-kidney pudding, and forget such elegant dishes as cold soup sprinkled with caviare.

I had a look at *Mrs Beeton*. Under April she gives a comprehensive dinner menu for ten people, for eight and for six, and I studied the last eagerly. Would my four guests enjoy six courses starting with tapioca soup, and going on to sweetbreads, oyster patties, haunch of mutton, capon and tongue? Would they have room, after that lot, for rice soufflé, lemon cream, Charlotte à la Parisienne, or even rhubarb tart? I doubted it, and doubted too my ability to provide it.

In the end I settled for a round of gammon, a tongue, both cooked beforehand and carved in the privacy of my kitchen before the guests arrived. In this way, the more shapely and presentable slices could be neatly arranged with some hardboiled eggs on a lordly dish for handing round, whilst the fragments could be hidden in the fridge for home consumption another day. This, with a cheese and tomato quiche, new potatoes and a salad could follow a warming bowl of mushroom soup; and I proposed to make apple meringue and a treacle tart which no doubt the men would like.

All this mental effort had quite tired me, and I went to bed early. I had forgotten to bring up my library book, but *The Diary of a Country Parson* is always by my bed.

I opened it at Wednesday, March 12, 1794, and read with delight the dinner that Parson Woodford provided for five guests that day.

> We had for Dinner some Skaite, Ham and Fowls, a whole Rump of Beef boiled etc., a fine Hen Turkey rosted, Nancy's Pudding and Currant Jelly, Lobsters, Bullace and Apple Tarts, Cheese with Radishes and Cresses.

My own menu looked decidedly parsimonious beside that. But how much more digestible, I thought smugly, as I turned off the light.

The day after we broke up I went to visit Dolly Clare, carrying some magazines and a bunch of daffodils. It was a blustery day with a hint of rain in the air which misted the windscreen and dampened the roads.

I found Dolly sitting by the fire looking as serene as ever but, to my eyes, thinner than usual.

'I don't really want much in the way of food,' she confessed when I enquired after her health. 'I suppose I don't need it these days. I get so little exercise. Mrs John brings me a delicious lunch each day, but it's really too much. Very often half is left, and it seems such a terrible waste.'

'Have you told her?'

'Yes, indeed, but the dear soul continues to bring it. I haven't the heart to say more.'

I told her about Parson Woodforde's dinner party and my own plans. As always, she showed the liveliest interest.

'Tongue!' she cried. 'Now I always liked tongue, but haven't had it for years.'

'Come and join us,' I said. 'I could fetch you in the morning, and bring you back after tea. Will you come?'

She shook her head and laughed. 'My dear, I'm really not up to visiting anyone these days, but it's lovely to be invited. I shall just think of you enjoying that tongue.'

'I shall bring you some on the Sunday,' I promised. 'Better still, I'll bring you enough for two and perhaps you'll let me have it with you.'

She readily agreed, and when I made my way home I felt glad that I could do something, even if it only rose to putting aside some helpings of ham and tongue, to tempt my old friend's appetite.

I had a week before my little party, but before that occurred I was going to be at the mercy of the decorators.

Luckily they would be working upstairs, painting mainly, but also doing some much-needed tiling round the bath and wash basin.

It was one of the reasons for staying at home this Easter holiday. I wanted to keep my eye on the progress of the work, to catch up with such things as taking curtains and bedspreads to the cleaners, having the sweep, getting two decrepit teeth seen to, and shopping for some summer clothes.

Also, I needed to watch my expenditure, and even the most modest guest house would strain my resources at the moment. The painters, the cleaners and the dentist would deplete my bank account seriously enough, without my gadding about in foreign, or even local, parts.

And there was another reason for staying at home. I was worried about Dolly Clare, and did not want to leave her. I called as often as I could, and I knew that Mrs John was in and out several times a day. The doctor too was kind and attentive, dropping in to see her at least once a week, but I wished that I could do more.

I had suggested that she should come to stay with me for as long as she liked, but she was adamant about staying in her own home, which I well understood. I wanted to be at hand if she needed me, though, and this was probably the strongest reason for being glad that I was not going far during this particular holiday.

On Monday morning the two decorators arrived. I had not seen them before, but they had been recommended to me by Mrs Richards's husband Wayne, who was a builder. They seemed a cheerful pair and arrived in a battered van which rattled with pails and paint pots inside, and had an aluminium ladder along the top.

'I'm Perce,' said the fat one.

'I'm Bert,' said the thin one, and I led them upstairs to survey their task.

'Oh dear, oh dear!' sighed Perce.

'Looks a bit rough,' agreed Bert, lugubriously.

I refused to be alarmed. I have come across this sort of approach before. It means another twenty pounds on the bill, if taken seriously, but as I already had their estimate carefully tucked away in my writing desk, I did not worry.

'Bert's going to rub down in the bathroom,' Perce told me, 'while I tackle this 'ere bedroom.'

This was the spare room. Once done, I proposed to sleep in there while they did their worst in my own bedroom.

'D'you mind if we has the tranny on?' asked Bert, patting his portable radio lovingly.

'As long as you keep the volume down,' I said in my most schoolmistressy voice. 'I've some letters to write, and some phoning to do.'

I left them to their work and descended to my room.

Ten minutes later there was a tap on the door. Bert smiled at me. 'You wouldn't have such a thing as an old dustsheet for the floor? The one we've got's a bit skimpy.'

I mounted the stairs and produced a dust sheet from the bottom of the airing cupboard. From the bathroom came the sound of someone screeching and gulping out what I supposed was a song. Fortunately it was somewhat muffled by the closed door, but the heavy drumming made the house throb.

I returned to my letters, only to be disturbed by Perce slamming the front door, and I watched him ambling across to the van. He clambered in and drove off.

He had still not returned when I climbed the stairs again with a mug of coffee for Bert at ten-thirty.

'Where's Perce?'

'He had to go back to pick up some thinners. He won't be long.'

Morning prayers appeared to be emanating from the radio, and I added my own to them. The bathroom was so thick with dust from the rubbing-down operation that it was difficult to breathe, but Bert seemed unperturbed.

I went downstairs to my own coffee. Before I had taken a sip, Bert appeared. 'Could you spare a minute, miss? There's a nasty crack across the top of the door. It may need some time spent on it if it's to be a proper job.'

I climbed the stairs again, and surveyed the crack. It looked pretty superficial to me.

'You must do what is best,' I said. 'If it needs filling, or whatever, then do it. But I should get Perce's opinion when he gets back.'

'Right. I'll do that.'

I went back downstairs to my tepid coffee. Why, I wondered, do men seem to need so much assistance, not to mention praise and commendation, for their tasks? I did not consult anyone about my teaching affairs – just got on with them, and faced the consequences.

At twelve o'clock Perce returned, and joined Bert upstairs. A quarter of an hour later, they both went to the van, and sat inside with their lunch boxes on their knees, and the radio on full blast.

Tibby wandered in, mewing protestingly.

'I know, Tib,' I said. 'I know.'

To give them their due, Perce and Bert were almost finished by Thursday of that week, and I felt that I could begin my preparations for the Saturday lunch without too many requests for pieces of old rag, a dustpan and brush, a kettle of boiling water, old newspapers, a cold chisel, (are there *hot* chisels, I wondered?) and even *'the right time'*, now and again. (Who, in any case, is going to give an enquirer the *wrong* time?)

I started on the quiche first, and enjoyed rolling out the pastry to bake it blind. It was going to be filled with cheese, tomatoes and eggs for I had an idea that Miriam Baker, née Quinn, had become a vegetarian. Of course, I thought, rolling busily, if she was one of the really strict ones, vegan or something, the eggs would be turned down, and in that case she would simply have to graze on the salad.

There is something very soothing about cooking if one has the kitchen to oneself and nothing too demanding to cook. With the work almost completed upstairs. I pursued my own plans happily. The tongue and the gammon were waiting to be boiled. I had most of the shopping done. Last minute jobs such as mixing the mustard and taking the egg stains from the forks before general cleaning of the silver, and making sure that there were enough matching napkins – not easy in a household of one – now loomed, but I was beginning to feel that I had the whole campaign well in hand.

I might have known that Fate would pull the rug from under my feet.

Perce and Bert told me at five o'clock that the bathroom tiles would need to be changed over the wash-basin as they were 'too big in a funny sort of way'. (*How* funny? Strange? Comic? Sinister?) They would have to get a smaller size in the morning – that is, Bert said, shaking his head, if they made that particular size in that colour. Should they bring a few samples out to show me? If they couldn't get the same thing, would I like a different one – say, in a *toning* shade? They could get plain white, of course. It was up to me. After all, it was my bathroom, they said fairly, and looked relieved at the thought.

'Does this mean,' I demanded, 'that you won't finish to-morrow?'

They looked aghast at such a direct question.

'Not our fault, miss. Just a bit of a slip-up over the sizing. If we can get the right ones first thing, we ought to get everything done tomorrow. What's the rush anyway?'

'The rush, as you call it, is that I shall have people here on Saturday, and no doubt they will use the bathroom. I want it to be finished.'

Now they both looked hurt.

'Well,' said Bert sadly, 'if that's how you feel, I think we'd better settle for white tiles behind the basin.'

'There's just a chance we might be able to order the same as the others, of course,' added Perce, 'but them tile firms take their time sending down.'

'The same if you can get them, white if not,' I said, in the tone I use to infant malefactors. 'But the job's to be finished by tomorrow. Understand?'

'Very well, miss,' sighed Bert, more in sorrow than anger, in the face of such feminine unreasonableness. 'We'll call in at the stores on our way home.'

I watched them clamber into the van. They were busy talking to each other. It was fortunate, I suspected, that I could not actually hear their comments.

That same evening, while the ham and tongue simmered comfortably on the stove, Mrs Pringle arrived.

'I had to go over the school,' she said, 'so I thought I'd pop in.'

'Do sit down. Coffee?'

'No thanks. It gives me heartburn. But I thought I'd give your brass a rub up with these visitors of yours coming.'

I was torn between gratitude for the kind offer and

irritation at being disturbed in the midst of my preparations.

'Well,' I began, 'I don't think there's any real need, but
if you like to come for an hour tomorrow afternoon, I
should be grateful.'

'Better make it two,' said she. 'Besides the brass, I expect
that bathroom will want doing, and I see them men have
made plenty of dust everywhere. You don't want your
visitors drawing their fingers along the top of the doors
now, do you?'

'My guests,' I retorted, 'would do no such thing, and if they
were so ill-mannered they would deserve to get dirty fingers.'

Mrs Pringle snorted derisively, which made me seethe
even more.

'Why,' I continued, 'you might just as well suggest that
my visitors would scrabble about in the *chimney* while they
are at it!'

'And that,' said Mrs Pringle, puffing to her feet, 'can do
with the sweep, and that I do know.'

She limped to the door.

'See you tomorrow,' she said.

As always, she had enjoyed the last word.

Bert and Perce appeared the next morning bearing two boxes.
One held plain white tiles, the other some beetroot-coloured
ones with a green sprig of some unknown shrub in the centre.

'All we could get in that size, miss,' they said. 'That's a
very tricky bit of wall there, over that basin. Too close to
the door like, and that mirror on the wall takes up a deal of
room. I said to Bert at the time we was measuring: "Here's
trouble," I said, didn't I, Bert?'

'You did, Perce, you did.'

'You didn't measure it correctly,' I said bluntly, and
they looked wounded.

'So which d'you like?' said Perce at last.

'I don't like either,' I told them, 'but it will have to be the white, I can see that, so you'd better get on with it.'

They went aloft bearing the tiles. The box of beetroot ones remained on the table, and I studied the sprig carefully. Could it be yew? Or rosemary? Come to think of it, it looked remarkably like a piece of butcher's broom which examiners like to present to botanical students for identification. There was a catch in it, if I could only recall what it was after some forty years. What looked like a leaf was a stem, or else what looked like a stem was a leaf. Unless it was something called an adventitious root, of course.

I decided not to waste any more time on the matter, and put the box of tiles in the front porch for Perce and Bert to return to the van. Those sprigs, let alone the colour, would have driven me mad in a fortnight.

I was now quite reconciled to living with the white ones.

6 A Change of Address

SATURDAY morning was all that an April morning should be. The small birds sang as they went about their nest-building, the daffodils waved their trumpets and the blue sky was dappled with high slow-moving clouds.

My four guests were due at twelve-thirty, and as most of the preparations were done, I even had time to peruse the fashion pages of my daily newspaper.

It appeared that ethnic colours – whatever they might be – were the only possible choice for our summer outfits. Such bourgeois *ensembles* as navy-blue and white, beige and cream were evidently anathema to the fashion writer. Wide belts of leather studded with bronze, or simply thick chains with dangling medallions would encircle the waists of those who had such attributes.

Hats were out too — vivid kerchieves of scarlet or yellow would bind our heads to make us look like Russian peasants. Cardigans, it seemed, were also forbidden. This necessary adjunct to an English summer had been thrown overboard for vivid shawls and ponchos. What you did with your arms whilst attempting to carry a tray and keep your wrap round your shoulders, was anybody's guess, as buttons were taboo. What a blessing I had so little money that last year's despised garments would form the bulk of my summer wear!

'Lucky old Tibby,' I said to the cat, as I threw aside the

paper to go about my duties. 'Only one rigout for winter
and summer! And it always fits.'

The Bakers and the Winters arrived within five minutes of
the half hour, much to my relief.

We all know the friends that are bidden for, say, 'twelve
to half-past', and cotton on to the half-past bit and arrive
at five to one when the potatoes have turned to mush, and
the Yorkshire pudding is black round the edges.

Frankly, I far prefer people to arrive too early, even if I
am struggling into my clean blouse, and the white sauce
has still to be made. At least they are *there*, and you have
them under your thumb, so to speak, and are spared the
anxiety of wondering if they have:

a) forgotten

b) had a crash on the way, in which case who should one
ring first to apprise them of the accident and give the
address of the hospital?

c) been told the wrong day, and may turn up tomorrow
when the food is ruined.

My good friends were welcomed most warmly. The
women knew each other, of course, and there was immediate chatter about their old employer Sir Barnabas
Hatch, but Gerard and Tom had not met. However, within
minutes, over their sherry, they were discussing the merits
of Manchester United and Tottenham Hotspur, and I was
able to slip away to put out the food.

It all seemed to be much appreciated. Appetites were
hearty, and the ham and tongue was consumed by Miriam
with as much enjoyment as the others. Nevertheless, the
carefully prepared vegetarian quiche seemed equally popular
with all. I felt positively smug at the compliments and was glad
that I did not live in earlier, more formal times when young
ladies were adjured never to comment on the food offered,

and to eschew all talk of money, religion and politics; not that the latter two subjects cropped up very frequently, but money, or rather the lack of it, was a more common theme these days.

It was the reason, Jane Winter surmised, for the lack of buyers for the remaining two new houses.

'The price has been reduced by several thousand,' she told us. 'Perhaps we should have waited.'

'Nonsense!' said Tom cheerfully. 'We bought when we wanted to, and got a decent packet for the last place. It's simply that there's not the money about now.'

'There are several "For Sale" boards in our road in Caxley,' said Gerard. 'You can understand people's reluctance to lower the price, but it will have to come.'

'Have you seen any possible buyers at the new houses?' I asked Jane, hoping she would tell me of couples with large families of school age, all bent on living in Fairacre and attending my school.

'One or two elderly couples,' she replied, dashing my hopes. 'Retired people, I think. I spoke to one very pleasant woman. She'd be an ideal neighbour, I'm sure, but they thought the price excessive.'

'He'd had a bakery in Caxley High Street,' said Tom. 'I think it was 'Millers''.'

'Oh, that's a marvellous shop,' I exclaimed. 'It's been there for generations. One of the founders was a brother of an old boy who farmed round here for years. The brother – the baker – used to live over the shop. I had tea there once with one of his daughters. You could see all the life of Caxley from their sitting-room windows.'

'These people moved from there long ago, I gather,' said Jane. 'Now they want to be even further out.'

I found this understandable, but sad. Of course, it had always been thus. The High Street traders, as they grew prosperous, moved to the higher and hillier suburbs of the town, probably only a mile away in Victorian times. Their descendants built their homes a little farther out, on the fields which ringed the town. With the coming of the car, the present generation could live ten or twenty miles away from their business. Many, of course, had sold long ago, which accounted for the national, rather than local, names over the shops in the High Street.

Times change, we know, but I gave a wistful thought to that long-ago tea party overlooking a busy, but not, as now, traffic-clogged Caxley High Street.

My thoughts were interrupted by a question from Miriam about Miss Clare.

'I shall be seeing her tomorrow,' I told her.

'I don't know her as well as you do,' said Miriam, 'but she always struck me as one of the most well-balanced people one could wish to meet.'

I heartily agreed, and gave a brief account of Dolly's early days at Beech Green and Fairacre.

Gerard became vastly interested and wondered if he

could have a television interview with her. Always the professional, I thought!

'Would she come to Lime Grove?' he asked, eyes shining.

'I doubt it. She's very old and very delicate now. It's as much as she can do to get upstairs to bed.'

'We could do it at her house,' continued Gerard. 'Shall I call on her on our way home?'

'Good heavens, Gerard! Have a heart! I should think the very idea would make her collapse.'

The conversation turned to other things, and then the Winters said that they must go and collect Jeremy from his friend's house where he had been invited for lunch, and so the party began to break up.

'I can't tell you how I envy Jane,' said Miriam, as we waved goodbye to the Winters.

I wondered whether she was considering her own childless state, but other matters were on her mind.

'I do so miss the office,' she told me, in a low voice, so that Gerard, who was inspecting the garden, could not hear. 'Barny could be a sore problem at times, but he was always stimulating, and I miss the hurly-burly of all the arrangements to be made, and the comings and goings of interesting people.'

'Can't you apply for another job? I should think anyone with half an eye would snap you up.'

She looked pensive.

'I'm beginning to think about it. Barney has said that when Jane has her holidays he would like to have me as stand-in. But I wonder if that would work. Even if it would be enough.'

'Something will turn up,' I told her, wondering just what.

'When you women have stopped chattering,' said

Gerard, approaching, 'we'll offer our sincere thanks for a lovely time, and let you have a rest.'

They departed, leaving me with much to ponder.

The next day I set off to see Dolly Clare, taking the promised picnic with me. It so happened that I met Mrs John on her way home from calling at Miss Clare's.

'She's looking forward to seeing you,' she told me. 'I've just had to break the news that I shall be away for a week or two. My father is very ill in Cardiff. They seem to think that he is near his end, and I must go to help my mother. Mrs Annett knows, and she has promised to keep an eye on things, but I didn't like telling Miss Clare, I'd be away.'

'It can't be helped, and in any case your family must come first. I'll see what I can do, and give you a ring before you go.'

'Thank you. Actually, I shall set off on Tuesday morning.'

'I'll remember,' I said. 'You've been absolutely marvellous to her, and I know she has always appreciated it.'

I drove on, my mind full of plans.

Dolly was pottering about in her garden. She used a stick for support these days, and moved very slowly, but she was still upright and greeted me with a smile.

We wandered about the garden together. The fruit trees were in small leaf, and the hawthorn hedges beginning to show buds. After a while we went indoors, and I wondered if she would say anything about Mrs John's departure to Wales. It would be typical of Dolly, I thought, to say nothing, independent spirit that she was.

We enjoyed our cold collation, and I was glad to see that she ate a good helping of tongue. The remains I insisted on leaving in her cool tiled larder for another meal, and was about to help her upstairs for her usual rest.

'Rest?' she protested. 'I don't have such a thing when I have visitors. I can have a rest any time. Visitors are rarer and more precious.'

So we sat and talked, but still nothing was said about Mrs John. At length, I broached the subject.

'I met Mrs John on my way here. She tells me that she is obliged to go to Wales. I just wondered if you would like to come and stay with me?'

I had been thinking of this, and other plans, ever since meeting Mrs John. It was true that the workmen were due to tackle my bedroom, but that could be postponed, or I could sleep downstairs for that matter. In any case, the spare bedroom was now in pristine condition should Dolly agree to use it.

But, as I guessed, she would not consider it.

'I shall be perfectly happy on my own. Isobel Annett will pop in, I know, and I have the telephone if I should need help. It's very kind of you, but you have enough to do.'

'Then I have an alternative to offer,' I told her. 'Let me come here to live while Mrs John's away. I can easily drive to school from here, and you would not be alone at night.'

'There's absolutely no need –' began Dolly, but I cut in with a very cunning argument.

'I shall be terribly anxious about you. You shouldn't be alone for hours at a stretch, and I've worried for months now about your sleeping here on your own. Suppose you fell? Or someone broke in?'

She was silent for a moment, and then began to laugh.

'Very well, you artful girl, you win! And thank you very much, my dear.'

So it was settled, and I made up her spare bed then and there ready for my sojourn. My routine could easily be altered. I should leave Dolly about eight-fifteen each morning, having given her breakfast, and go to Fairacre to let in the workmen, to pick up the post, feed Tibby, and go over to the school. At the end of the school day I could spend half an hour or so in my house, feed Tib again, see all was well, and return to my temporary home with Dolly.

To say that I had been anxious about her was perfectly true, and I felt considerable relief at these new arrangements. I only hoped that Dolly would not find my presence too irksome. As a single woman myself, I knew how precious one's privacy was, and I was determined to bear that in mind.

The following day was the last of the Easter holidays.

Bert and Pearce arrive to tackle my bedroom, and set to work with unwonted briskness. I commented on their progress when I took up their coffee.

'Well, you wants us gone, I expect,' said Bert. 'We likes to oblige.'

'Besides,' said Pearce, 'we've got another job waiting over at Bent. They're getting a bit shirty.'

Bert gave Perce what is known as 'an old-fashioned look', and I guessed that he would be rebuked for his moment of truth when I had left the scene.

But mention of Bent reminded me to ring Amy and to tell her of my temporary change of address.

'Good idea,' said Amy. 'I wonder you didn't think of it before.'

'I certainly did,' I protested, 'but you don't know Dolly Clare. She "won't impose", as she says, or I should have been there months ago. Tell me, how are things with you? Brian still with you?'

'Not for much longer. There's been a general reshuffle at the Bristol place as they've opened a new office in Scotland. Brian starts as treasurer in the Bristol office as

soon as things have settled down there. To give the chap
his due, he's willing to push off into digs in the Bristol
area, so maybe he'll do that. James seems to think it
would be unkind to encourage him to go. Still thinking of
those heroic cricket matches of long ago, I surmise.'

'Men are trying,' I replied, and was about to tell her of
my troubles with Bert and Perce in residence, but fearing
that I might be overheard, I forbore to relieve my feelings.

'I was going to invite you to come with me to a charity
concert next week, but I suppose you don't feel able to go
out in the evenings if you are with Dolly.'

'It's nice of you, but I'm going to stay put while I'm at
Beech Green.'

'Fair enough. There'll be other things later on, I'm sure,
but it looks as though I shan't see you for some time. I'm
going with James to see a new factory in Wales. He's a
director of the firm, and I shall be staying on down there
with my aunt. She's ninety-two, and will no doubt walk
me off my feet.'

'Any more jaunts?'

'I may go up to Scotland later. James is also on the
board of this firm Brian's joining, so we may go up to see
how the new office is settling down. But that won't be
until June. I'll see you before then, I hope.'

'As soon as Mrs John gets back,' I promised, 'we'll get
together for a meal somewhere.'

At that moment, Bert appeared. 'Sorry to bother you,
miss, but have you got such a thing as an old kitchen
knife?'

'I heard that,' said the voice on the telephone. It sounded
highly amused.

'See you sometime,' I replied, putting down the receiver.

'Now, Bert,' I said, 'do you really want an old kitchen
knife or "*such a thing* as an old kitchen knife"?'

'We wants an old kitchen knife,' explained Bert, looking puzzled.

'Then say so,' I retorted. 'Though to tell the truth, all my kitchen knives are the same age, so you will have to take care of it. What's it wanted for, anyway?'

'There's a bit of something stuck under the skirting board. An old kitchen knife –' He caught my eye. 'I mean, a kitchen knife'd shift it easily.'

He followed me into the kitchen and I found him the desired object in a drawer.

'And bring it back,' I said.

'Yes, miss,' replied Bert meekly.

For a moment he looked exactly like Joseph Coggs, and my conscience smote me.

But not for long.

That evening I telephoned Mrs John and told her my plans, and hoped that she would have better news of her father when she reached Cardiff.

After that, I walked down to see Bob and Alice Willet to ask for their help at Fairacre while I was away at Beech Green.

As always, they were able and willing.

'We'll look after things, don't you fret,' said Bob sturdily. 'And that cat of yourn will be fed regular. If I can't do it, then Alice will, and Tibby'll get double rations if she's on the job.'

'Well, I think animals miss their owners more than we reckon,' contributed Alice. 'I'll see Tib has any little tit-bits like our chicken liver or meat scraps. Cats like fresh stuff.'

Bob cast his eyes heavenwards. 'That cat's got fatty heart as it is,' he told me. 'Wouldn't hurt it to go on a few days' fasting.'

But I knew it would not with the Willets to look after it,

and handed over the keys, and explained about the where-abouts of the tinned cat food and the milk arrangements.

'We'll all feel better knowing you're with the old lady,' said Bob, accompanying me to the gate. 'I suppose ideally she should have someone living there all the time, but I can't see Dolly Clare standing for that.'

The sun was going down as I passed through the village on my way home. The scent of narcissi and early stocks drifted in the warm air. Soon there would be lilac blossom and mock orange adding their perfume, and then the roses, which do so well in Fairacre, contributing their share too.

Above me, the rooks were winging homeward, black wings fluttering against a golden sky. They were building high this year, I had noticed, a sure sign of a good summer. Dolly Clare had told me that soon after I had come to live in Fairacre. Dolly Clare had told me so many things, just as she had told all those lucky children who had passed through her hands.

There were a great many of us who owed a debt to Dolly Clare. I looked forward to trying to repay her, in a small way, over the next few months.

7   'Love To Fairacre'

THE summer term began with a spell of hot dry weather. Even the wind was warm, and the distant downs shimmered in a haze of heat.

My move from the school house to Miss Clare's had caused the minimum of fuss. Each morning I drove the few miles from Beech Green to Fairacre, having given my old friend her breakfast in bed, and seen to her needs.

Isobel Annett, the wife of the headmaster at Beech Green School and once one of my assistants before her marriage, had arranged to call on Dolly at regular intervals during the day, and other friends also gave a hand while Mrs John was in Wales. I was back around five o'clock having seen to my school and home duties, and we spent the evenings together, before retiring to sleep in adjoining rooms under the thatched roof.

It all worked out very easily, and if Dolly sometimes found so many visitors irksome, she was too well-mannered and sensible to show her feelings. Secretly, I think she was relieved to have support, and was now accepting that she could do less and less on her own. After a life time of independence this must have been a difficult problem to face, but she did so with her habitual grace and good temper.

Sometimes, on these light evenings of early summer we went for a drive, usually threading our way through narrow lanes, fresh with young foliage, up to the cool heights of the downs above Beech Green.

On our way, Dolly would point out various landmarks:

'That cottage,' she would say, 'was where Mrs Cotter lived when I was young. She had ten children, and they all streamed out of that tiny place with polished boots and brushed hair, and the girls in starched white pinafores when those things were in fashion. Heaven knows how she did it on a carter's wage – but she did.'

As we approached a little spinney she would tell me that the very best hazel nuts grew there, and down in a fold of the downs she and Ada, her sister, used to go on September mornings to find mushrooms, in the dewy grass.

And once, as we drove along the lane which eventually led to Caxley, she pointed out an ancient sycamore tree, with limbs as grey and lined as an elephant's, which over-shadowed the road.

'I said goodbye to my dear Arnold here,' she said quietly. 'I never saw him again.'

Her hand stole to the locket about her neck, and we drove in silence for a time, our minds troubled by 'old unhappy far-off things, and battles long ago'.

At school, the fine weather was especially welcome. The children relished their playtime outside, I relished their ab-sence from the classroom for a precious quarter of an hour, and Mrs Pringle relished the comparative cleanliness of the school floors. An added bonus for her was the fact that her beloved stoves were not sullied with the inflow of fuel and the outflow of ashes.

She became almost pleasant in her manner, and expressed her approval of my move to Miss Clare's.

'Not that it couldn't have been made months ago,' she added. 'She could have done with help long since.'

I pointed out as mildly as I could that Dolly Clare wanted her independence, and that I had in fact offered my services on several occasions.

'Well, better late than never, I suppose,' she admitted grudgingly. 'And I will say that house of yours is a far sight easier to clean with only Tib in it.'

She bent, corsets creaking, to pick up a drawing pin from the floor.

'That could cause a mort of trouble,' she puffed, putting it on my desk. 'Minnie's Basil had a nasty septic foot after stepping on a tack. Minnie had to take him to The Caxley. Hollered something terrible, she said.'

Knowing Basil as I did, I was not surprised.

'Minnie's going to take all the kids to that new pleasure place they've built the other side of Caxley. Sounds lovely. Switchbacks and a giant dipper, and one of them swimming pools with great tubes you can dive down. The kids'll love it. She wanted me to go too, but I told her my switchback days are over, and I'm not flaunting my figure in a bathing suit even if my leg allowed it.'

It seemed wise to me, but I had to be careful not to agree too enthusiastically in case my old sparring partner took umbrage.

'I'd better bring the children in,' I said, making for the door. Diplomacy or cowardice, I wondered? In any case, the thought of Minnie's children at large on all that machinery made my blood run cold. Which would come off worst, I wondered, the children or the equipment?

'Miss,' shouted Patrick, red in the face with indignation, 'John swored at me. He swored twice. He said –'

'I don't want to hear about it,' I said dismissively. 'Go indoors, all of you.'

'But it was about *you* he swored,' protested Patrick. 'He called you a bad name. He said you was –'

'Never mind,' I said firmly. 'Go back to your desk.'

We had hardly settled down before the vicar arrived bearing a large envelope.

'This really should have come to you,' he said apologetically, after greeting the children. 'I can't think why it was sent to me.'

'Well, you are Chairman of the Governors,' I pointed out.

The envelope contained a sheaf of papers from our local naturalists' society and pictures of a dozen endangered species, as well as innumerable forms for donations, competitions, free tickets for this and that. They all managed to flutter to the floor, much to the delight of the milling crowd who rushed from their desks to rescue them. Such diversions are always welcome to children, and it took some time to restore order.

The vicar smiled benignly upon the scene, and when comparative peace reigned again he asked about Miss Clare.

'I thought I might visit her on my way to Caxley this afternoon,' he said. 'Would it be convenient?'

The Reverend Gerald Partridge, in common with most clergymen these days, was in charge of several parishes, and Beech Green was one of them.

He had been calling regularly on Dolly, but usually in the morning when Mrs John was around. I told him that Dolly would be glad to see him at any time, I knew.

'And you are happy together?'

'Perfectly. At least, I am, and I think Dolly is relieved to have someone in the house.'

'Good.' He surveyed my class. 'And how many on roll now?'

'Twenty-one, including the infants.'

The vicar sighed.

'Of course, there are those two new houses,' he said brightening.

'Have you heard anything?' I asked hopefully. 'The boards are still up.'

'Well, no. But we must live in hope. They are both very

well suited to families. Four bedrooms, I gather. Very hopeful. Very hopeful.'

He gave me his usual sweet smile and departed, oblivious, for once, of the children.

'He never said nothing to us,' said John-the-swearer reproachfully.

'If the vicar never said nothing, he must have said something,' I pointed out, embarking yet again upon the use of the double negative. A fruitless quest, as I should know after all these years, but as the vicar had just remarked, we must live in hope.

Mrs John returned a week or so later, bringing her mother with her for a little break after the sad days following her husband's death.

She was very like her daughter, small and nimble, with the same large dark eyes. She had been a nurse in her young days at one of the foremost Welsh hospitals, and she still had the lilt of the Welsh tongue. It was plain that mother and daughter got on very well together.

Dolly Clare was as pleased as I was to have Mrs John back again. Her presence eased my anxiety, and I suspect that Dolly found her assistance in dressing and other daily activities much more deft than my own efforts.

But I was greatly moved when my old friend asked me to stay on at the cottage.

'It is such a comfort to have you here,' she said, 'particularly when I wake in the night. If it's not an imposition, I should love you to continue here.'

There was nothing I wanted more and Mrs John was pleased too, so that my new routine continued, living in two homes at the same time whilst teaching went on undisturbed.

* * *

On the first Friday of June, I took Dolly's tray upstairs as usual, just before eight o'clock. There was not much to carry for she only had two slices of brown bread and butter, some marmalade, and a cup of weak tea.

She seemed to be asleep, and I put down the tray quietly. She opened her eyes, and smiled at me.

'Thank you, may dear. Just off?'

'Yes. Just off.'

'Goodbye then.'

She sat up slowly, and added as she always did: 'Love to Fairacre,' as I turned to go.

It was my turn to do playground duty at mid-morning, and above the din of exuberant children I heard my telephone ringing.

Hastening into the school house I lifted the receiver. It was Mrs John on the line, and she sounded distraught.

'It's sad news, I fear. She's gone. I found her in her bed when I got here ten minutes ago.'

'I'll come over at once.' I said, and went to arrange matters with my assistant, Mrs Richards.

* * *

I had always imagined that the death of my dear old friend would leave me shattered, probably in tears, and certainly trembling and shocked. But to my amazement, although I felt desolate, my mind was clear and I felt capable of dealing with all the practical problems which I should have to face.

There was a kind of numbness of body and mind which, I had no doubt, would soon desert me, but for which I was grateful when I entered the cottage and found Mrs John. She had obviously been crying, and she was shaky, but she was in control of her feelings.

'She must have gone soon after you left,' she told me. 'I thought she had fallen asleep again, as the breakfast wasn't touched.'

'We'd better go up,' I said.

She led the way up the familiar stairs.

'Mother came with me this morning,' she said, 'And she's done all that was needed. She's better at these things than I am, her being a nurse.'

I could not reply. This was my first encounter with death, and I wondered how I should react.

But there was nothing at all to fear. Dolly lay in her bed as I had seen her so many times. A light breeze lifted the curtain at the open window, and ruffled Dolly's fine white hair. She was in a fresh cotton nightgown, and the gold locket was still around her neck.

'I didn't quite know what to do with that,' said Mrs John, following my gaze.

'Leave it there,' I replied. I could not have removed it. As far as I was concerned, I felt it should accompany Dolly to her grave.

Mrs John carried the tray downstairs, and a little later I followed her.

'I rang the doctor,' she said. 'He's out on his rounds,

but they said they could get him on the car phone, and he'd call as soon as possible.'

'And I'll ring the undertaker,' I said.

I was still in the dream-like state which cushions one from immediate shock, and I found I could do these routine jobs without undue emotion.

'It was good of your mother to cope with things,' I said. 'It's something I've never had to face, but I think I could have done it for Dolly.'

'I was glad too,' said Mrs John. 'As soon as she'd done, she went home to get the children's dinner ready.'

How life jostles death, I thought. But rightly so, for life must go on.

There was a knock on the door and the young doctor, who had succeeded dear old Doctor Martin, came in.

'This doesn't surprise me,' he said, after the first condolences. 'She was very weak when I came two days ago. She was a grand old girl – never complained. I shall miss her.'

I took him upstairs, and waited while he examined Dolly.

'If you'd pick up the death certificate at the surgery,' he said, standing up, 'I'll do it as soon as I get back. It's a simple case of heart failure. Everything has just worn out.'

Gently he drew the sheet over Dolly's face, and I began to have my first tremors.

A few minutes after his departure, a van drew up. Two kindly men from the Caxley undertaker's went aloft with a stretcher, and very soon they descended slowly bearing Dolly, still shrouded in her white sheet.

'She'll go straight to our Chapel of Rest,' said the older man, 'should you want to visit her.'

He dropped something on a side table as he resumed his task, and I watched Dolly go through the cottage door and down the garden path for the last time.

When the van had gone I saw that Dolly's locket lay on the side table. Somehow it seemed cruel to have parted her from it.

I drove back to school, still numbed, told Mrs Richards the news, read one of the Greek legends to the children, heard them recite one of Walter de la Mare's poems and saw them off home. Then I went back to the school house, fed Tibby, made a cup of tea and rang the vicar.

He was greatly concerned, more, it seemed, on my account than Dolly's, but I assured him that I was perfectly calm and that I intended to go to the cottage the next day to write to any relatives I could find, and to tidy up Dolly's things. He suggested that either he or Mrs Partridge would accompany me, but I refused as politely as I could.

I sat down in my quiet sitting-room and drank my tea. It was only then that I remembered that I had had nothing to eat since my breakfast at Dolly's, some eight or nine hours earlier.

It reminded me of that untouched breakfast tray.

I must have been the last person to whom Dolly spoke, and I recalled those last three words:

'*Love to Fairacre.*'

It was now that grief engulfed me. My whole body shook as I returned the cup, clattering, to its saucer, and the tears began.

I seemed to spend all the evening crying, powerless to control my emotions. I did not cry for Dolly, now freed from pain and the indignities of old age. I cried for myself. I should never see or talk to Dolly again, and that, truthfully, was the cause of my tears and my desolation.

For now I knew. I was bereft.

8　Making Plans

NEWS of Dolly Clare's death was common knowledge within twenty-four hours and there were tributes to her from everyone. During her long life she had touched so many other lives as teacher and friend, that it was plain that her influence would linger for many years in Fairacre, Beech Green, and many places farther afield where old pupils had settled.

The funeral had been arranged for a date some ten days distant at Beech Green church, and she was to be buried in the churchyard there, beside her parents Francis and Mary.

In the meantime, I was doing my best to track down any living relatives. I put an obituary notice in *The Caxley Chronicle* and hoped that I might hear of some descendants of her sister Ada.

The son, John Francis, had gone overseas after his mother's death, but somewhere there must be descendants of Mary, the daughter. No one seemed to know what had happened to her.

Dolly Clare had lived so long that almost all her contemporaries had gone, but one elderly lady living in a retirement home in Caxley, wrote to the vicar telling him a little about Dolly and the family, and from this it appeared that Mary had married twice, but no names could be discovered.

I very much doubted if we would hear any more about Dolly's family.

* * *

The funeral took place on a beautiful June morning.

The vicar took the service, a simple one with three of Dolly's favourite hymns. The church was full of roses and sunshine, a fitting setting for the small plain coffin at the chancel steps, whose occupant had always loved flowers and the joys of summer.

There was a large congregation, but most of the people slipped away as just a few of her closest friends accompanied the vicar to the graveside. It was a peaceful spot, shaded by a lime tree already showing flowers. Francis and Mary's gravestone was patterned with moss and lichen, but I saw that there was room below the inscription for Dolly's name and dates, and this I proposed to have done as soon as possible.

Some friends took advantage of the general invitation to come to the cottage for refreshments after the service, and

when they had gone, I locked up the house, and drove back to my duties at Fairacre in time to serve out school dinners.

I thought of Mrs John's remark as I cut toad-in-the-hole into squares: 'Mother went back to get dinner for the children.'

So had it always been. My bedtime reading at the moment was Virginia Woolf's essay about my favourite clergyman, eighteenth century Parson Woodforde. I had come across her remarks on the entry: 'Found the old gentleman at his last gasp. Totally senseless with rattlings in the Throat. Dinner today boiled beef and Rabbit rosted.'

'All is as it should be; life is like that,' she comments.

Everyday life for me was certainly bearing this out.

After my night of weeping, some peace had returned. Although, from now until the end of my own days, I knew that there would always be this poignant sense of loss, yet there was no need for prolonged grief. A long and lovely life had ended, but Dolly would be remembered by many, for years to come. There had been no children of her own as immediate heirs, but all those who had passed through her hands had come under her wise and gentle influence, and this must shape their views and outlook for the rest of their lives.

It was with gratitude, not grief that Dolly would be remembered.

Amy came over to see me one evening soon after the funeral and said that I was looking distinctly peaky.

'Well, if you must know,' I responded, 'it's exactly how I feel.'

She had been in touch by telephone during my stay with Dolly Clare, but this was the first occasion that we had seen each other face to face for some considerable time.

She looked deeply concerned, and I began to feel guilty.

'No, I'm really all right. There was quite a bit to do tidying up Dolly's affairs as executor, and of course I was horribly shocked when it actually happened, but I am over that now.'

'Well, you don't look it. I think you want a tonic, plenty of good food and sleep, and a few days' holiday. Come and stay with us next weekend as a start.'

'I'd love to, but I can't. Perhaps towards the end of the month. We're getting a week off then.'

'Half-term?'

'Sort of. The powers that be are feeling their way towards a four-term year sometime in the future, and this is part of the preliminary trial. Actually, I hope it comes off, though I can't see it happening before I retire.'

'A week at the end of June,' said Amy thoughtfully, and I knew from her expression that she was planning something for me.

To distract her I asked after James and the semi-permanent lodger Brian.

'He's decided to look for digs near Bristol, so we haven't seen so much of him recently. James seemed to think that I was instrumental in pushing him out, but I can assure you I'm quite innocent. I think the idea of ejecting a hero who had once scored a century against Eton or Harrow, or possibly both, was more than James could face. Anyway, I told him that my conscience was as pure as driven snow, and that it was Brian's idea entirely, which it was.'

She began to smile.

'Mind you, when he broached the subject, I didn't cling to his arm with tears in my eyes to dissuade him. And it is lovely to have the bathroom to myself again, I must admit.'

'What about a turn around the garden, like Jane Austen's young ladies?' I suggested.

It was a perfect June evening. Mr Roberts had a field of beans somewhere nearby and there was a wonderful scent of flowers. The wistaria was in bloom, and the Mrs Sinkin pinks, which do so well on our chalky soil, added their scent to the evening air. The ancient Beauty of Bath apple tree had grey-green velvety marble-sized fruit on it and, judging by the plum blossom, we were going to be well off for fruit this year.

After our stroll, which we took with our arms round each other's waists like true Jane Austen characters, we sat on the garden seat to resume our conversation.

'Are you proposing to live at Dolly's now?' asked Amy.

'Not immediately. There's quite a bit to do there, and I don't want to make a long-term decision just yet.'

'Very sensible.'

'Besides, I've everything I need here, and it's so much closer to the school. I certainly do intend to go to Dolly's cottage eventually, as she wanted, but I'm staying here until the end of the summer term, and then I'll see how things go.'

A blackbird came out of the flower border followed by one of its young which was rather larger than its parent. It squawked incessantly as it badgered its harassed father for food, and we watched the two running back and forth across the lawn in their searchings.

Amy slapped her leg and the birds flew off.

'Mosquito!' she exclaimed. 'Just as we were enjoying Paradise.'

'We'd better go in,' I said getting up. 'Every Eden has its serpent.'

'I must go anyway,' said Amy, and I walked with her to the car.

'Tell me the dates of your holidays,' she said.

I told her, and she nodded looking rather mysterious.

'Ah! I have some thinking to do,' she said, and drove off.

Now what is she up to, I wondered?

Soon after Amy's visit Mrs Pringle apprised me of the fact that her niece Minnie had been obliged to go to hospital for a few days.

'So there am I,' she said dourly, 'stuck with those little 'uns of hers. If you could see your way clear to having Basil in school for a day or two, it would a be a real help.'

I felt sorry for my old cleaner and said we could manage Basil in school hours. She seemed relieved, which was more than I was.

Ideally, he should go into Mrs Richards's class. He was not yet five, but lethargic in the extreme. I knew from experience that it took him some time before he could let us know that he needed the lavatory – and then too late.

I decided that I would keep him with my own class. He could have a large ball of modelling clay, paper and crayons. These should keep him 'properly creative' as earnest educationalists say, or 'keep his idle fingers out of Satan's way', as our grandparents would have preferred to put it.

'Is Ern capable of looking after the children while Minnie's away?' I asked. Ern, Minnie's husband, appears to me to be at about the same stage of efficiency as Minnie.

'Not really. Ern don't like children.'

As he had five of his own when he married Minnie, and took on her three as well, it seemed odd that he did not like children. Unless, of course, the eight offspring had been the cause of his dislike.

'How long does she expect to be in hospital?'

'Not long. The doctor said it was her Salopian tubes.'

Confused images of underground trains hurtling through Shropshire vanished when I surmised that Mrs Pringle meant Fallopian tubes, but I did not intend to enquire further. I know virtually nothing about my own, or anyone else's internal organs, and am content to remain ignorant.

Once I had been foolish enough to ask my doctor what he proposed to do to a minor leg injury. He was a painstaking fellow, and after his explicit and conscientious account of the proceedings to be undergone, I vowed never to be enlightened again. On the rare occasions when I have had to go to hospital, I have said: 'Put me out, watch your work, and don't wake me up until all the blood's gone!'

So I did not press Mrs Pringle for details, though I might have guessed that she was more than keen to give them.

'Oh, it only takes a day or two. It's a job that's got to be done if you wants any more babies.'

I was about to ask if Minnie, with eight children already, really hankered for more, when Mrs Pringle continued.

'They just blows them out. They takes one of them instruments –'

'Good heavens,' I cried, 'is that the time? I must get the children in.' I rushed away, and Mrs Pringle, deeply umbraged, limped after me.

Later I went into the infants' class to borrow some simple jigsaws for Basil. The modelling clay had inspired him sufficiently to roll out a worm-like object which he had seemed content to leave at that. My suggestions that he could coil it round and make a flat dish or, even more ambitiously, a small vase, was met with a stubborn shake of the head.

The crayons were not a great success either, and after I had discovered him crunching a particularly virulent-looking green one, I decided that his activities needed to be channelled into another direction.

'Would you like me to have him in here?' inquired my noble assistant, but I could not accept such self-sacrifice.

'Of course,' she went on, 'if we had all Minnie's school-age children, we shouldn't need to worry about the school closing. Besides,' she added hopefully, 'she might have more. She's no age, is she?'

I thought of the Salopian tubes, and agreed that there was every possibility of Minnie's family increasing over the years.

'But strictly speaking,' I told her, 'they are living in the Beech Green area. It's only because Mrs Pringle is taking on the three youngest that we can claim Basil – and then he's not on the roll, of course.'

At that moment, Joseph Coggs appeared in the doorway to announce that our visitor had 'gone to the lavatory'.

As was quite apparent when I returned to deal with the puddle, that was exactly what Basil had not done.

Dolly Clare's cottage, for so I always thought of it, was not neglected. Mrs John went in several times a week to air it, do a little dusting, and generally tidy up, and I went over each weekend, and sometimes during the week after school.

I asked Wayne Richards to come and have a look at it for any signs of immediate repairs which might be needed.

His verdict was favourable on the whole. 'It's pretty sound inside, though there's a nasty damp patch on the kitchen wall. Probably had a tub with brine in it years ago, for salting the pork, and the salt's leaked in. But I could seal that, I think. And there's woodworm up in the loft but there again I could treat it.'

'What about the roof?' I asked.

'You'll have to face having that roof re-thatched in three or four years' time, but it'll do a few winters yet.'

I was glad to hear it. Now that I was a property owner, I knew that I should have to use my meagre savings to put the place in order and I looked forward to doing it. Nevertheless, I could not face such a major job as re-thatching which, I knew from other cottage owners, could run into thousands of pounds.

'I thought of having it redecorated inside,' I said. 'Dolly could not face the upheaval in the last few years, but it really should be done. Could you do it?'

'No problem. Except time. I could give it a good doing with emulsion paint on the walls, and some good hard gloss on the woodwork. That'd do you for years.'

'You'd better give me an estimate for that and the other odd jobs,' I told him, 'and then we'll see what's urgent, and how soon you can start.'

'Right. You thinking of keeping it all white inside?'

'Yes. It looks fresh and cottagey. Besides, all the carpets and curtains go well with it.'

He laughed, and drove off, leaving me to lock up and return to Fairacre. But before I set off I wandered round the garden which Dolly had enjoyed all her years.

It was not as big as my own, and the fruit trees were not as healthy or as prolific. Sometime in the past a knowledgeable headmaster had stocked the school-house garden, and I was well supplied with plum and apple trees, an espalier pear by the garden shed, and gooseberry and black and red-currant bushes.

At times I cursed the bounty of my garden when I returned tired from school duties and was faced by an abundance of red and blackcurrants, all needing to be picked, stripped, washed, bottled, frozen or made into jelly or jam. But my friends were always glad to help me out, and Alice and Bob Willet made good use of my surplus.

With the exception of a sturdy old Bramley apple tree,

Dolly's fruit trees were past their prime, and I resolved to get Bob Willet's advice about replacing them in the autumn. The vegetable plot too, I decided, should be halved. Room for a few lettuces, some new potatoes, spinach and runner beans would suffice. There are several first-class market gardens nearby and in any case I am given no end of fresh vegetables in the autumn and winter, from friends and neighbours who have enjoyed my surplus fruit during the summer.

The flower border too looked in need of attention, and would need a good load of manure later on after I had divided some of the perennials. There were one or two particular favourites of mine in the school-house garden which I proposed to bring over, phlox and penstemon and various pinks.

There was a lot to do; the paths needed weeding, the hawthorn hedges needed a trim, and the laburnum tree by the gate was almost split in two with advanced age and the rigours of many downland winters, but I surveyed my inheritance with love and pride. I hoped to keep Dolly's cottage as well as she had done, and hoped too that I should be lucky enough to have many happy years there, as she had.

Perhaps, too, I should be as fortunate in my end, surrounded by my garden and the distant downs, and sheltered by my own thatched roof.

I was rather touched to receive a visit from Minnie Pringle one evening.

'Come to say thank you,' she said, 'for having our Basil. Auntie don't get on with Basil ever since he spat in the jam she was making. She's funny that way.'

For once, Mrs Pringle had all my sympathy, but it seemed best not to comment on this disclosure.

'Well, it's good to see you up and about again,' I said. 'Would you like some coffee?'

She followed me into the kitchen and I saw her eyeing a bowl of blackcurrants awaiting attention on the table.

'Those are to spare,' I told her, hoping to be let off a tedious job, 'if you would like them.'

She said that she would, and I gave her a bag and let her scrabble away while I filled our mugs.

'Basil wasn't much bother,' I said, nobly squashing the memory of constant sniffing, complete absence of interest in his surroundings, and the regrettable puddle on the floor.

'He liked it,' said Minnie, with her mad grin. 'I wish they could all come here, but they has to go to Beech Green. Ever so strict that Mr Annett is! Give our Billy the cane once.'

'Why?'

'Well, he shut one of the other's fingers in the door. Could've been an accident, I told Mr Annett when I went to complain.'

'And was it?'

'Not really. Billy got some other boy to hold the first one while he slammed the door.'

I changed the subject. Despite my dwindling numbers, I did not feel inclined to welcome any more of the Pringle tribe to Fairacre school.

'And how's Ern?'

'He's a bit cross with me.'

This I knew might well be construed as being violent. Ern is not above attacking Minnie when he disapproves of her behaviour.

'It's Bert, see,' she went on. 'Bert come up the hospital to see me, and Ern didn't like it.'

As Bert has been an admirer of Minnie's for many years and, according to local gossip, the father of two of her young children, it is hardly surprising that Ern views his attentions to Minnie with great disfavour. The two men have come to blows in their time, and Minnie appears to be rather proud of the fact.

'Bert brought me some roses and the nurse put 'em in a vase by my bed, and Ern wanted to know where they'd come from. So I told him. He was that wild!'

Minnie smiled happily at the memory.

'Why did you tell him?'

'He asked didn't 'e? All I done was tell 'im the truth.'

'So what happened?'

'Ern went down 'The Spotted Cow' in Caxley that night, and had a real old turn-up with poor Bert. Blacked his eye, and knocked a tooth out, and made his nose bleed somethin' terrible, Bert said.'

'Bert told you?'

'Yes. He came up to see me the next night with some carnations. I was ever so sorry for Bert.'

I began to feel ever so sorry for poor Ern, but kept quiet.

'Best be getting back,' she said, rising briskly. 'I've left the kids with Auntie, and there's Ern's tea to get. He gets a bit nasty if he has to wait for his tea. Thanks ever so for these currants.'

She bustled off to the door.

'I hope Ern is looking after you properly,' I ventured.

'Nice as pie,' she replied. 'Never laid a finger on me since I come back from hospital. The doctor had a few words with him, see. Mind you, once I'm really better I shouldn't be surprised if he turned nasty about Bert. Funny really, I keep tellin' 'im I knew Bert long before I knew him, so why shouldn't we be friends? But he's real funny that way.'

She skipped off down the path to collect her offspring

from Mrs Pringle's. A stranger, seeing her for the first time, might have guessed her age at twelve or thirteen.

Mentally and morally, I thought, she was a good deal less than that, but it was nice of her to come and thank me, I decided charitably, as I went to get Tibby's evening meal.

Later that week I had another visitor. It was Amy, elegant in a cream trouser suit, and I hastened to brush down the sofa before she sat on it.

'I was stripping redcurrants an hour ago,' I told her, 'and I don't want you to sit on any stray ones.'

'But surely you do that in the kitchen?'

'Not when there's an old film of Fred Astaire's on,' I told her, lifting up a glossy report of some unknown firm which was at one end of the sofa.

Amy settled herself and turned the pages idly. 'I didn't know you had shares in this. James is one of its directors.'

'Aunt Clara left them to me,' I explained, 'with her seed pearls, and a nest of occasional tables which I handed on to one of my god-daughters.'

I saw her studying a page of photographs at the beginning of the booklet.

'I can't think why they put those in,' I said, peering over her shoulder. 'Far better to leave their shareholders in ignorance. It may be the fault of the photographer, of course, but at a quick glance, would you trust any of those with five bob?'

'There's James,' said Amy, pointing to one of the photographs.

I peered more closely. 'So it is. Well, he's certainly the best looking by a long way.'

'Of course,' agreed Amy smugly. 'Now sit down, and I'll tell you why I've come. You haven't a spot of sherry, I suppose? Not that stuff you won at our raffle, I mean.'

'I've got some Croft's.'

'Perfect.'

I poured out two glasses.

'I've been thinking,' said Amy, after an approving sip.

'Oh, Amy,' I wailed. 'Not another prospective husband for me? I've got such a load of trouble already.'

'No, no, no!' tutted Amy. 'How you do harp on *MEN!*'

I was too taken aback by this unjustified aspersion to retaliate, and she continued unchecked.

'It's really about James and his trip to Scotland. He's flying up, a few days before he planned, to meet this fellow.'

She tapped a finger on one of the photographs on the open page beside her.

'They're going house-hunting together before the main meeting.'

'House-hunting? You're not leaving Bent?'

'Nothing like that. They're both on the board of some charity trust for orphans, and they want to start up a home there for the Scottish lot. The point is this. I shall be driving up a little later, and hope you will come with me. James knows a lovely quiet hotel on the Tweed. Lots of salmon on the menu. What about it?'

'Oh, Amy! You are sweet to think of it, but I ought not –'

'My treat,' said Amy swiftly. 'My shares are doing well, and James wants you to keep me company as he'll be so tied up with business affairs. Do say you'll come. We'll take two days to go up, and two back, and have two there. It would do you good after all you've had to do these past weeks.'

She looked at me with such concern, almost tearfully, that I weakened at once.

'It sounds heavenly. Tell me more.'

She proceeded to give me details. A night in the Peak District on our way north. A leisurely drive along the A7 towards Kelso the next day. Visits to Mellerstain House and Floors Castle. It was apparent that Amy had been very busy working out routes, planning little treats such as these visits to lovely houses, and generally becoming acquainted with all that the neighbourhood had to offer.

'Then, yes please,' I said, 'I'd love to come. But I can't let you pay for me, Amy. It's too much.'

'If it makes you feel any better,' said my old friend, 'you can pay for the petrol, and any odd ice-creams.'

'Willingly,' I told her, 'but let –'

'But I warn you,' she said, 'my car is a thirsty one, and I have a great weakness for cornets and wafers.'

'As though I didn't know,' I told her, 'after all these years together.'

9   Holiday with Amy

IT is wonderfully exhilarating to set off on holiday. The days before, of course, and particularly the one immediately preceding departure, are fraught with as much anxiety as anticipation. Have you stopped the milk, the papers, the laundryman? Have you left enough cat food for Tibby? Should you switch off the electricity at the mains? If so, what about the fridge and the light that comes on automatically after dark? There is no end to the household problems.

Personal packing is comparatively easy. I have long given up trying to compete with other hotel visitors in the realms of sartorial chic. To be clean and decent, and not to shame dear Amy, is the limit of my ambitions these days.

Nevertheless, there are decisions to be made. The weather may be hot. It may be cold. Cotton frocks and a thick cardigan may be the basis for one's wardrobe, but it is necessary to have a little more flexibility.

Then there is the problem of underclothes. Should you take enough to ensure a change every day, and possibly an extra outfit in the unlikely event of falling into a Scottish burn or being soaked to the skin in a Scotch mist? Or would it be safe to hope that the hotel bathroom would have one of those clothes lines that pull out from the wall – and sag dangerously when a pair of tights is slung over it?

And what about a mackintosh? Should it be the heavy raincoat just back from the cleaners? The cost of its recent reproofing makes one feel it should be housed in a glass case rather than bundled into a suitcase or the boot of

Amy's car. Perhaps the thin bedraggled one hanging on the peg behind the kitchen door might fit the bill?

But when one is actually in the car, cases stowed behind, keys and telephone number left with the neighbours, and handbag safely on one's lap, then the pleasure begins.

A certain recklessness takes over. What if one *has* forgotten toothbrush, handkerchieves, sun spectacles or talcum powder? Presumably all these can be bought in Scotland.

And what if I have forgotten to leave out the tin opener for Tibby's meal tins, or the bottles for the milkman, or that old piece of bread which I intended to throw out for the birds? Dear Alice and Bob Willet would see to it all.

'Amy,' I said, snuggling back into my luxurious seat, 'I am so happy!'

'That's the whole idea,' she responded, putting her foot down on the accelerator.

We sped northward in great spirits.

By lunchtime we were in the neighbourhood of Warwick, and I was beginning to look out hopefully for a café.

'Don't bother,' said Amy. 'I've brought a picnic. Just keep your eyes skinned for a leafy lane to the left.'

We soon found it, a lovely lane with ferns growing from the banks, and some pink campions among the cow parsley, and we got out thankfully. Even a car as large and magnificent as Amy's cannot quite overcome the stiffening of the human frame.

Amy produced one of those splendid wicker hampers that I always associate with Glyndebourne or glorious Goodwood. There were plates and glasses and cutlery and even two large linen napkins. We sat on the bank amidst the verdure with this splendid object between us. Amy had made smoked-salmon brown sandwiches, and egg and cress white ones. Lettuce hearts nestled in a plastic box. Pears and peaches supplied dessert, and two flasks contained coffee and hot milk respectively. There was even a bottle of sparkling wine to go with the smoked salmon.

I thought of my own slapdash picnics, comprising cut bread with crusts left on, and the contents usually hanging out in a ragged manner, followed by a banana or an apple from the garden. I was lucky if I remembered to put in a piece of paper torn from the kitchen roll at the last minute.

'This is superb,' I said, trying not to make my napkin too disgusting with peach juice. 'How do you manage to do everything so elegantly?'

'My mother taught me,' she answered. 'She was terribly strict about standards. One of her favourite maxims was: "Never let yourself *go*!" And she lived up to it too. I don't think I ever saw her untidy, even in her last illness. She really was remarkable.'

'You take after her,' I told her. 'She would be proud of you.'

'Mind you,' said Amy, packing away plates and boxes briskly, 'she was very bossy with it.'

My private thought was that dear old Amy took after her mother in that too, but it would have been churlish to say so after consuming such a memorable meal.

'Thank you for that marvellous lunch,' I said instead.

We were in the Peak District for our one night stop in time for a refreshing cup of tea, before unpacking.

Then we walked along the path by the River Dove which had remarkably few visitors just then. We stopped to hang over the rail of a wooden bridge, and fell companionably silent as we watched the bright water cascading over the boulders beneath us.

What a benison water is, I thought, watching a wagtail enjoying the spray. Whether we drink it, wash in it, swim in it or simply stand and stare at it, as we were doing now, it has the power to refresh, to soothe, and to exhilarate. It has much the same beneficial properties as sleep, I thought, remembering Macbeth's tributes to that panacea. Certainly, gazing downward with the waters of the Dove below, and listening to the rustle of the Dovedale foliage above me, I could feel the pain of Dolly's absence, and the many petty domestic and school frustrations and worries ebbing away from me. Amy had been absolutely right. I needed to get away from Fairacre now and again.

It was Amy who returned first to the present. 'Let's go on. We haven't worked up an appetite for a four-course dinner yet.'

'Speak for yourself,' I retorted. But we went on all the same, and peace went with us.

The hotel in Scotland was old and grey, and full of years and tranquillity. It stood amid acres of grass dotted here and there with clumps of fir trees. The flowerbeds close to the house were bright with freshly-planted annuals, and some climbing roses, pink and white and red, nodded against the stone walls.

James and Amy had a bedroom on the first floor and from their windows they could see to the nearby valley where the river Tweed ran its course eastward to Berwick-on-Tweed.

I had a room on the ground floor which overlooked a particularly pretty part of the garden, with a bird bath and flowering shrubs, a private small garden of my own, it seemed, adjoining the larger grounds.

James joined us in time for dinner, and was good company. James is one of those fortunate people who really loves his neighbour, and likes to hear all about that neighbour's affairs. I have rarely seen him tired or depressed despite the busy life he leads, and tonight he looked as dashing as ever.

I told him about the photographs of his fellow directors in the only shares brochure which falls through my letter-box, and how he was by far the most handsome. Needless to say, he fairly glowed at the compliment. How vain men are!

'And Ted and I came across two decent little houses at the end of a terrace on the outskirts of Glasgow. I think something could be done with them, and we've asked the architect to see if they could house six children.'

'Who looks after them?' I inquired.

'There will be two foster parents. That's the principle of this charity – family units, not too big, in a smallish house. So far it seems to work. Now, tell me about the journey. Were you very long on the M6? It's quick but tedious, I find.'

Our meal was delicious, and afterwards we strolled in the grounds watching a number of thrushes stabbing the lawns to find their supper. At Fairacre, thrushes are in short supply these days, and it was good to see that they flourished here in the Border country.

I said my goodnights early, for I could hardly keep awake. It was seven o'clock when I woke to a fine sunny morning, and I reckoned that I had slept solidly for nine hours.

That day, James returned to his labours while Amy and I explored the market town of Kelso, some three miles away. We admired its fine square, its friendly shop keepers and, above all, the cleanliness of its streets.

We noticed this throughout our visiting. North of the Border, it seemed, people liked to see things clean and tidy. Caxley streets these days are littered with rubbish thrown down by the people too idle to walk six steps to a nearby litter bin. In the lanes around Fairacre I frequently pick up Coke tins, bottles, crisp packets, cigarette cartons and other detritus which the consumers have simply cast out of their car windows, careless of the damage these things can do to animals and plants, as well as making the countryside hideous.

We went on to visit Floors Castle standing close to the ubiquitous river Tweed which we crossed and recrossed dozens of times during our stay. It was magnificent, and Amy and I coveted the Dresden and Meissen porcelain more than anything else in that delectable array of pictures and furniture.

However, the next day we decided to visit Mellerstain, not far away, and its Adam elegance won us completely.

'"Comparisons,"' quoted Amy, as we gazed upwards at the superbly decorated ceilings, '"are odious," but I think I'd rather live here.'

'Either,' I said, 'would suit me.'

The Border country was gently rolling, with plenty of

cattle enjoying grass far lusher than that which grows on our downs. We drove across to the Northumberland coast, and were refreshed by the salt winds blowing over the North Sea and a good lunch at Bamburgh, where the great castle dominates the little town.

By the end of our break together, my face was glowing as if I had spent days on the beach. I slept solidly both nights, ate the hotel's lovely food as if I were starving, and altogether felt a new woman as we set off for home.

James drove, and our first idea of spending a night in the Peak District on our way back was abandoned.

'Let's get on,' said James. 'I can't wait to get home.'

Sitting in the back of the car, thinking of the places we were now leaving behind, and occasionally snoozing, I realized how much good this holiday had done me. It had put things in perspective. To see those beautiful old houses, their contents, their well-kept gardens, all so enriching to the spirit, had made my own worries seem fleeting. It had also made me deeply conscious of the simple future pleasures I should enjoy at Dolly's cottage, and my good fortune in having friends as dear and generous as Dolly and Amy.

I returned to a host of minor irritations, and a pile of letters. The minor irritations included a leaking tap, a broken saucer of Tibby's, and a colossal branch ripped from the plum tree, its plentiful but unripe fruit scattered on the lawn.

The post included a fair amount of material for the waste paper basket. 'Had I thought of the best way to invest my savings?' (What savings?) 'Would I help a child?' (I already helped twenty-one, and would be glad to have those numbers increased, but under my school roof.) 'Had I considered a fun-filled fortnight on the exotic beaches of Florida?' (Well, no!)

Such missives were easily disposed of, but some heavy-looking correspondence from the office would need my attention, and several more welcome letters from friends. I put the lot aside to greet Bob Willet who hove in sight.

'My word, you look ten years younger,' he greeted me. 'Time you had that break. You was looking real white and spiteful.'

'Thanks,' I said. 'And proper thanks to you and Alice. Did you have much trouble?'

'No. Old Tib bolted the grub, as if starved, as usual. The only thing that went wrong was me droppin' the saucer. And, what's more, the mower's on the blink.'

'Oh dear! And you can't mend it?'

Usually, Mr Willet can cope indoors with anything from light bulbs to domestic plumbing, and outside, of course, he can turn his hand to anything growing, and the maintenance of my simple gardening equipment.

'I reckon it's had its time. We could get someone to see if spares here or there'd be the answer, but it's that old I doubt if anyone's seen 'em.'

'You mean, I shall have to buy a new one?'

'Looks like it to me, but you get someone else's opinion, afore you lash out on a new one.'

This was grim news, but I guessed it was probably the answer.

Bob Willet waved to the battered plum tree.

'That happened the night afore last. Had a sort of mini hurricane. Barmy, it was. Like a whirlwind. Took half the thatch off of Mr Roberts's barn, and flattened a field of barley down Springbourne way. Josh Pringle said three of his bantams was tossed up in the air like shuttle-cocks. But, mind you, you don't want to believe all Josh Pringle tells you. Still, it was pretty nasty while it lasted.'

'Did it do any damage to your garden?'

'Blew a bit of felting off my shed roof, but I got that back next day. And I heard as our Maud Pringle got hit on the head by a bit of guttering as blew off of her house, but no doubt you'll hear plenty about that when she turns up.'

'Coming in for a drink?'

'No thanks. I promised the vicar I'd have a look at his garage roof. He thinks a tile or two's come off, and he's like a new-born babe when it comes to anything like that. Still, he do give a good sermon, and I suppose we all has different talents.'

I watched him stump off down the path, and felt grateful, as I so often do, for Bob Willet's particular and practical talents.

One Saturday morning, soon after my holiday, I bumped into Miriam Baker in Caxley High Street.

I had just emerged from Marks and Spencer's with a bagful of goodies from the food counter, and was on my way back to the car.

'Hello, and what are you up to?'

'Wondering if I have the strength to seek out another cotton frock. Gerard's away with the cameraman for a television programme, looking at a possible site, and I thought it might be a good opportunity.'

'Good hunting then.'

'Oh, I've given up the idea already. My shopping threshold, if that's the term, is pretty low.'

'Then come back to Fairacre with me, and have a Marks and Spencer's lunch.'

'No, really,' she protested, but not very convincingly, and I had no difficulty in steering her towards the car park.

'We haven't seen each other for ages,' I said, stowing parcels in the boot. 'Not since our lunch with the Winters.'

We set off for home, and as we passed through Beech Green I pointed out Dolly's house.

'I heard about that,' said Miriam, 'and we were both so glad it's to be yours.'

'When I'm really settled there you and Gerard must come and see me.'

'Lovely! And when are you moving from the school house?'

'I may go towards the end of the school holidays, if the builders have finished, and it is ready for me.'

'Will you miss it? The school house, I mean?'

I pondered the questions. They had been rattling about in my own mind for some time now.

'Yes,' I told her soberly. 'I shall miss it very much. Some of my happiest years have been spent under that roof, but I should have to face leaving it sometime, and thanks to dear Dolly I have somewhere of my own now to end my days.'

'But what will happen to it?'

'It will be sold, I expect. The church owns the property, and if the school has to close, which seems horribly likely at the moment, I expect my house would be sold too.'

Miriam shuddered. 'I don't like to think of changes at Fairacre.'

'Neither do I,' I replied, swinging into my drive, 'but I'm afraid I've got to face them.'

We both agreed that the grilled plaice stuffed with shrimp sauce, with salad from the garden, was just what we had needed, and coffee cups in hand we sat on the garden seat to enjoy the summer sunshine.

'And now tell me your news,' I said. 'Still regretting leaving Sir Barnabas?'

'Not really, but I've other plans afoot.'

'Tell me.'

'Well, I don't know if I'm an oddity, but I find that

being married is all very nice, but not quite enough for me.'

'You get bored on your own?'

'No. I just miss the job. I suppose I've always been geared to work, and marrying late it's harder to give up the routine. All the youngsters who take the plunge at nineteen or twenty seem delighted to settle down to home-making and babies and such –'

'I thought they had to go on working to pay for the mortgage,' I broke in. 'Bob Willet calls them "tinkers".'

'I didn't find that so when I was at the office. We were always looking out for new girls to replace those who had left. Which brings me to my plan.'

'And what's that?'

'I'm starting an agency, mainly for supplying office staff. As a matter of fact, the only one in Caxley is about to be sold. The proprietor is retiring, and to be truthful it never operated very efficiently, as Barney and I discovered on many occasions when we were desperate for staff. I should thoroughly enjoy it and, though I don't want to boast, I really can sum up people's ability pretty quickly, and also what the employer wants. For instance, nothing would annoy a man like Barney more than one of those motherly types for ever bringing in cups of tea when he was telephoning. On the other hand, you get bosses who just love that sort of attention.'

'You'll be marvellous at it,' I told her. 'What does Gerard think?'

'He's all for it. He has to be away such a lot, and I think he soon realized I was getting fed up with kicking my heels. He's pretty astute.'

'So when do you start?'

'With luck, in the autumn. It means married women with children at school will have more chance to take on part-time jobs. There's been an enormous increase in part-time work as firms have come to see that this is the sensible way of organizing offices. Matching bosses to applicants will be just what I like, and honestly Caxley is in real need of a service like that.'

'Well, the best of luck,' I said. 'I'm sure it will be a wild success, and your name will be blessed by all the Caxley folk.'

'We'll see,' she said, looking at her watch.

'You don't have to hurry back, do you? Is Gerard due back soon?'

'Not till the evening. He's doing a series of documentaries about inland waterways, and is giving the Kennet and Avon canal a thorough scrutiny further west.'

'It sounds pleasant enough.'

'So I imagined, but Gerard says there are an awful lot of snags, like fishermen, and people tramping along the tow path, not to mention mosquitoes and the occasional hostile swan.'

'But surely all those creatures have a right to the canal?'

'Not according to Gerard and his cameraman,' said Miriam.

10   Flower Show and Fête

THE month of July every year in Fairacre is domi-
nated by the village Flower Show. It is held in the
village hall, and the funds raised go to two good
causes – the Fairacre Horticultural Society and to repairing
whichever portion of the church is in most urgent need of
attention.

At one time there was also a village fête, held in the
vicarage garden, but latterly the two functions have
combined and a few stalls outside the village hall, and
sports events in the field around it, now take the place of
the earlier fête whilst the gardeners hold sway inside the
hall itself.

Naturally, this sensible combination took years to ac-
complish. It had been the vicar's idea, and of course some
people thought it was because he did not like to see his
lawns spiked with high heels nor his borders damaged by
wooden balls bowled erratically in 'Bowling For The Pig'.
Those more kindly disposed thought that it was far better
to use the village field for the fête side of the occasion.

'Stands to reason,' said Bob Willet, 'folks feel freer on
their own patch, and who wants *two* summer dos? There
ain't the money about for it, for one thing, with cornets
the price they is.'

Personally, I thought it was a much more practical arrangement.

I have spent several fête afternoons sheltering with dozens
of others in the vicarage summer-house or barn, with the
rain lashing across the stalls, watching the crêpe paper

dripping coloured rivulets on to the sodden grass, while tea trays were being rushed into the house for protection.

Under the present scheme we could at least bundle into the hall, even if it did mean enduring the disgruntled comments of the gardening community jealous for the welfare of their produce and lush displays set out on black velvet.

The entrants for the many classes for fruit, flowers and vegetables, had obviously worked for months beforehand to produce their bounty. But the rest of us were busy, too.

As always, there was a cake stall, and a produce stall, and to these I had promised to contribute. Why is it, I wondered, surveying my lop-sided Victoria sponge sandwich, that the cakes one dashes off for home consumption rise splendidly, stay risen, and supply most satisfactory eating? And why, when one hopes to achieve something memorable for public display, does the wretched thing burn, or sink in the middle, or refuse to rise at all?

My first attempt went into my own cake tin, and I turned to a tried and true recipe for almond cake for my contribution to the cake stall. Two pots of gooseberry jelly were to go to the produce stall, with half a dozen Tom Thumb lettuces. More I could not do.

A notice had been put in *The Caxley Chronicle*, and various posters decorated the village and its environs. All that remained to ensure success was a fine afternoon.

It has always been a source of wonder to me that so many English occasions are planned as outdoor events, with not even a tent in sight for shelter from the rain which is liable to appear at any time. It says much for the hope and confidence of organizers. I only know that if I plan some public display at Fairacre school, and the playground is the main venue, I am glad to be able to make a rush for the ancient building with my flock and the visitors when the heavens open. The fact that we shall have to face the wrath of Mrs Pringle is of secondary importance compared with a heavy summer storm.

The combined fête and show was to take place on a Saturday, and the weather forecast was delightfully vague. A band of rain affecting the north west *might* reach our area by midday, followed by brighter fresher weather with increasing winds. The forecaster prudently promised un-settled weather, with a likelihood of showers, but possibly some fine spells. As you were, in fact.

Summer clothes, then, I decided, accompanied by stout shoes for the (possibly) wet grass, and a cardigan and an all-enveloping mackintosh.

In an unguarded moment, I had offered to help Mrs Partridge on the cake stall. This, as everyone connected with fêtes knows, is a veritable magnet for keen shoppers or, if not actual buyers, then astute spectators happy to assess the cooking abilities, or better still, the frailties of those whose products are publicly displayed.

As a vicar's wife, Mrs Partridge takes a firm stand about not opening her stall until after the local celebrity has formally declared the fête open. Of this I entirely approve. When I have assisted at jumble sales, I have often been appalled by the number of articles 'put aside' or 'bought in' in advance by the persons preparing for the event. If not checked, this can result in anything attractive being extracted beforehand, leaving the poor stuff to be sold when the doors open to admit the customers.

I arrived at my station by Mrs Partridge's side some ten minutes before Basil Bradley, our local novelist, was due to open the fête.

'No, no!' Mrs Partridge was saying firmly to a question-ing buyer. 'I can't serve anything until we are officially open. But do wait here, and we shall start selling as soon as Mr Bradley has made his speech.'

It was somewhat of a surprise to me when I bent down to tie my shoe lace, to see half a dozen cakes in polythene bags resting on a tea towel in the grass beneath our stall. Clean sheets had been spread over our stall, and hung down to the ground concealing the booty from public gaze, and my faith in Mrs Partridge's integrity was severely shaken.

The vicar rang the school handbell lent by me for the afternoon, and most of the conversation ceased.

He introduced Basil Bradley as 'our old friend, the famous author', and led the clapping as Basil advanced to the microphone. After some alarming cracklings and whistlings, the machine calmed down, and Basil gave his usual charming speech saying how delighted he was to be present, and exhorting us to spend freely in supporting this good cause. I had a strong suspicion that he had no idea where the funds were going. Church roof? Organ fund? New

hassocks? Upkeep of village hall? Never mind, he carried out his duties with great charm and elegance, and did not forget to conclude with the magic words:

'I declare this show and fête OPEN!'

This was the sign for a rush to the stalls, and pudding basins, plastic boxes and ancient Oxo tins began to fill with coins and notes.

Activity on our cake stall was frenzied. It was easy enough to pass over a sturdy fruit cake wrapped in its plastic bag with the price displayed on top. It was quite another matter to manipulate inexpertly a large plastic pair of tongs, in the interest of hygiene, and to insert three, or five, or six, according to demand, small sticky cakes into a paper bag.

Alice Willet's jam sponge sandwiches, and her large batch of fruit scones soon vanished, bought by knowledge-able customers, but an ornate chocolate cake decorated with chocolate icing and beautiful curlicues of chocolate on top of that, remained unbought.

'Too rich, dear,' pronounced the vicar's wife, when I inquired why. 'And it was sent by the owner of that cake place in Caxley. I think people are suspicious of it, and it is really rather expensive.'

At that moment, Basil Bradley arrived on his dutiful tour of the stalls. He was clutching a golliwog, a lettuce, two pots of chutney and a plastic vase which he had just won at the hoop-la stall, and he was followed by Joseph Coggs.

'If that gorgeous cake is not already bespoke, can I buy it?' he asked, after his affectionate greetings to us both.

'You can certainly have it,' said Mrs Partridge, 'and I shall give you a large cardboard box for all your pur-chases.'

Hard behind, the lurking Joseph was given the task of

carrying Basil's box of goodies to the car, which he did with a beaming smile. It was not hard to guess that Basil would reward him handsomely when the time came.

Our stall gradually cleared, leaving only some shortbread fingers and a lumpy-looking bran loaf. I broached the subject of the hidden treasures under our stall.

Our vicar's wife was not discomfited in the least.

'Yes, dear, I know it looks bad, but there are exceptions to every rule. Two of those cakes were put by for Miss Young and Mrs Ellis, both great supporters of the fête, but unable to be here as they are poorly.'

I nodded.

'Miss Young,' continued Mrs Partridge, 'makes those delightful soft toys for the handiwork stall, and Mrs Ellis always makes a most generous donation. The other cakes were set aside for those helpers who couldn't leave their own stalls during the initial crush.'

I said that seemed fair.

'I noticed you looking highly disapproving,' she went on. 'Quite rightly so, of course, but there are times when one must be *flexible*!'

I felt suitably chastened, but not entirely satisfied. However, there was nothing to be said.

'Now we are so slack,' said Mrs Partridge, 'why don't you run along and have a look round? Perhaps have a cup of tea? I'll go when you come back.'

And so I set off to see what the fête and flower show offered, first making my way into the hall to see all the exhibits.

The din was appalling. Somehow one expected a reverent hush among all this beautifully arranged provender, but one might have been standing in Paddington Station, except that it smelt more pleasantly rural. There were wonderful whiffs from the vases of sweet peas and roses, so I went to look at the flower exhibits first. I was not surprised to see that Bob Willet had first prize for six magnificent cream sweet peas. Josh Pringle, the black sheep of the Pringle family, was surprisingly second. I guessed that his wife had done most of the nurturing of his six mauve beauties.

Several of my children had red or blue tickets against their flower arrangements in the Under-Twelves class, including Joseph Coggs. Each would receive a modest monetary reward, and I only hoped that Joe would conceal his from his father, otherwise The Beetle and Wedge would swallow up Joe's prize.

But it was the vegetable tables which really were stunning. Mr Lamb from the Post Office had carried off quite a few of the first tickets. I stood to admire six splendid carrots, almost a foot in length and a good three or four inches round the top, lying straight and true as swords on their black velvet background.

'Grows 'em in one of them oil drums,' I heard one man say glumly to his neighbour. 'Seen 'em there. Plenty of sandy soil and enough slurry from the pigs to feed a field of taters. It ain't natural.'

'Well, he don't do that with his onions,' replied his friend fairly. 'Look at 'em! As big as footballs, nearly!'

'Terrible coarse eating,' sniffed his companion. 'If my missus dished 'em up, I'd throw 'em on the floor, that I would.'

Passions are easily aroused at these exhibitions, as I knew from experience. There would be little rejoicing over Mr Lamb's success, and the tongues would wag tonight in the pub, and not with much goodwill.

I decided to take Mrs Partridge's advice and find a cup of tea. The tea tent was as noisy as the hall, and it was difficult to find a chair which would stand squarely on the tussocky grass floor.

I had just collected my cup of tea and a rock cake when I was hailed by the Winters who were at a table nearby.

'Come and sit with us,' called Jane. 'We're getting our strength up for the men's tug-of-war.'

'Have you had any luck with your flower entries?' I asked, as I knew she was going to put a vase of annuals in the show.

'No luck at all, I'm afraid. And as for my cheese and asparagus quiche which I entered in the cookery section, it was dismissed out of hand as it was baked in a fluted dish.'

'What nonsense!' I said.

'Exactly. But the judge was some terrible old battle-axe from the cookery department of the Caxley Tech so there was no gainsaying her dictum. Anyway, it all helped to swell the number of entries,' she added tolerantly.

'I think this must be the first time we've had a quiche class in the show,' I said. 'How Fairacre is changing! I'm sure we never had anything more dashing than a class for scones and fruit cake in my early days here.'

'It's the same with the vegetables,' agreed Jane. 'All those courgettes and dark red lettuces would have been giant marrows and cos at my mother's horticultural show, if you follow me.'

An ear-splitting crackling shook the tent, and a voice boomed out unintelligible messages.

'The tug-of-war,' cried Jane to her husband, and they struggled to their feet. 'Come along and see what the head of the Winters can do.'

It was half past six by the time Mrs Partridge and I had cleared our stall and packed up all the paraphernalia. We had also done some general tidying, carrying chairs from the tea tent into their usual place in the hall, and retrieving teacups and teaspoons from the grass. These activities, of course, were interspersed with lengthy conversations with other workers, but despite these breaks in our labours, I was dead-beat when at last I arrived home.

It was good to lie on my sofa with only the gentle purring of Tibby in the room. I decided it was the noise rather than the press of people and the physical activity which I found most tiring.

I must have fallen asleep for it was almost eight-thirty when I looked at the clock, and the sun was reddish-gold in the west. It seemed a good idea to make myself a cup of coffee and I went into the kitchen which was still bathed in warm sunlight.

Through the window, beyond my garden, I could see a figure walking round the edge of the field which was already thick with corn. As the man came closer, I saw that it was our vicar, with Honey, his yellow Labrador bitch, following behind him.

I went out to speak to him over the hedge. He often exercised Honey in this field, safe from traffic and other more belligerent dogs, for Honey was somewhat timid as well as being almost soppily affectionate.

'Wonderful day,' he called as he approached, 'and Henry Mawne has already counted five hundred pounds, and more to come!'

I expressed my gratification.

'I'm just making coffee,' I added. 'Come and join me.'

I have a useful gap in the hedge, for which Mr Willet is constantly offering me 'some nice stout thorns' or 'a few real tough old holly bushes'. He cannot understand how I can put up with the gap, but I tell him it saves me walking all round the house to get into the field, and he simply puffs out his moustache with disgust, and says no more.

The vicar entered through the shameful gap, and we

were soon sipping our coffee, with Honey lying at our feet. Tibby had left home in high dudgeon but would doubtless be back in time for a bedtime snack.

'I intended to call on you next week,' said Mr Partridge.

'About end of term?'

'Well, no, not exactly.'

He looked a little uncomfortable and I began to wonder if I had failed in my duties in some way. Perhaps he simply wanted me to play the organ while George Annett was on holiday? Or was I going to be asked to organize some school event for next term?

'Are you happy here?' he asked surprisingly.

'Very, why?'

'In this house, I mean. You haven't thought of moving?'

I felt on firmer ground. 'As you know, I think, I hope to move to Miss Clare's cottage before long.'

'Yes, yes. You had apprised me of that very kindly.'

He leant down and began to fondle Honey's ears. He was rather pink in the face, but whether from his stooping, or my coffee, or simple embarrassment it was difficult to say.

'You see,' he went on, straightening up, 'I met that nice fellow from the education office when I was at a committee meeting in Caxley. Salisbury or Winchester, I can never remember his name. And he rather delicately, I thought, wondered if you would be needing this house much longer. He seemed to have heard about your good fortune with the house at Beech Green.'

'Who hasn't?' I said.

'It's very difficult for me to talk about this,' he said sighing, 'but as the school is now so small, I really think we shall have to accept closure before long, unless something extraordinarily felicitous turns up. What is in the committee's mind, I think, is the sale of your school house, and if it comes to it, the sale of the school building itself if the children are transferred to Beech Green. Of course, both are church property, and it is the church which would benefit from the sale.'

'I had realized that,' I told him, 'but is there any urgency? I had begun to make plans to move before the end of the summer holidays, but nothing's really settled.'

The vicar began to look more agitated than ever, and dropped his custard cream biscuit on the floor. He bent to retrieve it with a shaking hand, but Honey kindly cleared it away for him.

'No, no! Of course there is absolutely no urgency. You can stay here as long as you wish. It was simply that happening to meet dear Rochester he asked if I knew your plans. You know I should give you every support if you decided to stay on here and, say, let your Beech Green property until you wanted it for yourself.'

'I know I should never be homeless,' I told him. 'You've reassured me about that on several occasions, and I'm eternally grateful. But I really do want to live in Dolly's cottage. It was what she wanted too, and I think I can safely say that I hope to move sometime before the winter – possibly before the beginning of term, if the alterations are done by then.'

Mr Partridge rose, looking mightily relieved, and – much to my surprise – gave me a vicarish kiss on the cheek.

'And now Honey and I must be on our way,' he said, making for the door. 'Thank you for that excellent coffee, and for being so understanding. I really have been so worried about broaching the subject.'

'Well, there's no need to worry any more,' I told him, making my way with him to the useful gap in the hedge. 'I'm glad we've spoken about it.'

'I shall sleep more easily tonight,' said he soberly.

'And so shall I,' I assured him.

PART TWO
BEECH GREEN

11   A Family Survivor

THE last day of term, and of the school year, was its usual muddle of clearing up and general euphoria.

Only one child was leaving to go to Beech Green school under George Annett's care. He had a sister there already and was happy about his future. To my delight there would be one new admission to the infants' class in the next term, so our numbers would remain unchanged. Mr Roberts's new farm worker had a son of five years old. He would be warmly welcomed by all those at Fairacre School.

As usual, the vicar called to wish everyone a happy holiday, exhorting them to help their mothers and fathers and to remember the date on which the new term began.

He turned anxiously to me. 'Could you remind me again?'

'September the fifth.'

'Ah yes! Of course!'

He picked up the chalk and wrote the date on the blackboard, looking triumphant as he dusted his hands afterwards.

'Just read it out,' he urged the children.

They chanted it obediently. Was there a touch of indulging-an-old-man, I wondered? But there were no smiles, and they stood politely, without my prompting, as Gerald Partridge departed.

I was particularly glad to start the summer holidays. Wayne Richards, husband of my assistant teacher and owner of a local building firm, had asked 'if I minded' his men making an early start in Dolly's house.

So dumbfounded was I by this unusual request that I simply gazed at him speechless.

'You see,' he explained, 'what with things being so bad in the trade, I'd be glad to see the two chaps I had in mind for your little problem, getting some work. I don't want to stand anyone off, though I reckon it'll come to it before long.'

'Is it really as bad as that?' I managed to say, when I had got over the initial shock of a real live builder wanting to come *earlier* than arranged.

'Things are tight. Even the big firms are feeling the pinch. People can't afford to move. Can't afford to have repairs done, for that matter.' He looked at me speculatively.

'You won't have to wait for your money on my little job,' I promised him. 'I've put aside the amount in your estimate.'

He hastened to assure me that he had never had any doubts on that score, but I thought that he looked relieved, as well he might if more prosperous firms than his were already suffering.

'The company that built these new places in Fairacre is going bust, so I heard last night. Nobody's buying, see, with mortgage rates as they are. They'll have to bring the price down to get rid of those two that are left.'

'They have already reduced the price,' I said. 'So the Winters told me.'

'I bet they're cursing they bought when they did,' he replied. There was a touch of contentment in his expression. How often other people's misfortune gives gratification, I thought!

'Well, do start as soon as you like,' I told him. 'I shall be glad to move in during these holidays.'

Heaven alone knows, I thought after his departure, it will take weeks to sort out my present abode, even the goods and chattels in the rooms themselves. What the cupboards, the loft, the garage and the glory-hole under the stairs would bring forth, I shuddered to think.

Time, and back-breaking work, would tell.

A day or two after this, Amy called in unexpectedly, accompanied, to my surprise, by Brian Horner.

After our greetings, we sat in the garden and I told Amy about my move, possibly in a few weeks' time.

'Splendid!' said Amy. 'Once you've made up your mind it's best to get cracking. No point in drifting along as you so often do.'

'Oh, come!' I protested. 'I'm not quite as bad as that. I'm always telling myself that "procrastination is the thief of time". What a marvellous phrase, incidentally.'

'Not quite as reverberating as that one in our *Handbook for Teachers*,' Amy reminisced. 'Something about teachers in dreary city schools "directing the children's attention to the ever changing panorama of the heavens".'

'I can go one better than that,' I told her, still smarting from her remarks about *drifting*. 'In some scriptural commentary or other, I read once that "Job had often to suffer the opprobrium of anti-patriotism." What about that?'

'I think I can top both those reverberating phrases,' broke in Brian. 'It was said by Dr Thompson, Master of Trinity College, Cambridge from 1866 to 1886, about Richard Jebb: "The time that Mr Jebb can spare from the adornment of his person, he devotes to the neglect of his duties." How's that?'

'Perfect,' we agreed. Brian's final two words emboldened me to ask if he was called 'Basher' because of his cricketing ability.

'Only partly. My full name, I'm sorry to say, is Brian Arthur Seymour Horner, and naturally boys soon called me 'Basher'. What a lot parents have to answer for when they name their children.'

'Excuse me,' I said. 'I must look at my oven. I'm cooking a chicken.'

Amy followed me into the house while Brian meandered about the garden admiring, I hoped, my flower borders.

'I thought he was safely in Bristol,' I said to Amy, in the privacy of the kitchen.

'So did I,' she responded, 'but he has to go to head-quarters with James tomorrow, and so he's spending this weekend with us. I'm quite sorry for him. He misses his wife and home so much. He fairly jumped at the chance of coming to see you.'

'Well, I'm not particularly sorry for him,' I said, slamming the oven door, 'and I've got quite enough to think about without taking on an estranged husband.'

'You're a hard woman,' said Amy, giving me a loving pat, and we returned to the garden.

I was pottering about that evening wondering if Amy would ever be free of Brian Horner. Would James's hero worship survive all the strain that was being put upon it? To my mind, Brian was a mediocre little man, full of self-pity, and I should like to have heard his wife's side of the tale. Still, I told myself more charitably, both James and Amy came very well out of the present situation: generous, and good-hearted. I only hoped that their faith in their friend would remain unclouded.

The telephone bell aroused me from my conjectures, and I was surprised to hear a strange woman's voice announcing herself as 'Dolly Clare's niece, Mary.'

'Well,' I said, 'I *am* delighted to hear from you. Where are you?'

'In Caxley for a few days. My husband – my *second* husband, that is – is over from the States on business, so I came with him to visit some old friends here. They told me about Aunt Dolly.'

'Would you like to come and see the cottage?'

'Indeed I should.'

I went on to tell her about Dolly Clare's legacy to me, but naturally she knew about that from her Caxley friends. I arranged to pick her up two days ahead, and to take her to Beech Green.

'I didn't see as much of Aunt Dolly as I should have liked,' she told me. 'She and mother became somewhat estranged in later life. To be truthful, I think my mother was jealous of Dolly's friend, Emily Davis.'

'What a pity!'

'It certainly was. Anyway, I should like to see the little house again, and perhaps you could spare something of hers as a little keepsake?'

'Of course, I'm sure we can find something,' I told her, and we went on to arrange the time of our meeting.

Later, I began to wonder what could be offered to Dolly's niece. As she had stated in her will, all her trinkets, as she called them, were to go to Isobel Annett who had been such a staunch friend, and this request had been met.

There were several nice pieces of china, and some silver spoons; also a pretty little clock which had graced Dolly's bedroom mantelpiece. Perhaps Mary would prefer some of her aunt's linen, embellished with hand-made crochetwork? In any case, I thought, I was glad to be able to offer a selection of mementoes. She seemed to be the only living tie with Dolly.

I had given several things to people who had been close to my old friend, such as Mrs John, Alice and Bob Willet and various neighbours who had looked after her during her long life. I only hoped that there would be something suitable for Mary to take back.

I suddenly remembered an occasion many years ago when I met an elderly Austrian man and admired a magnificent set of eight mahogany dining-room chairs in his home. His eyes had filled with tears as he said: 'Ah, my dear friend Wilhelm! When he died his good wife asked me to choose a little keepsake. So I chose these chairs.' I had often wondered what that poor widow thought.

I only hoped that Mary would not take a fancy to the cottage staircase or Dolly's kitchen dresser. It was some comfort to remember that she had to transport her choice to the United States eventually, and weight would have to be considered.

Mary Linkenhorn turned out to be a middle-aged, cheerful woman with absolutely nothing in her appearance to connect her with Dolly Clare.

She was beautifully dressed with many fine rings and a three-row string of pearls. Her expensive crocodile shoes had high heels and matched an enormous handbag. I felt that she was perhaps a little too exquisitely turned out for a morning visit to a cottage where possibly Wayne Richards's employees were messing about with plaster and emulsion paint. However, I liked her at once. She was friendly and unaffected, and obviously delighted to be going to see Dolly's house. She chattered about her early memories of the place, and of her affection for her Aunt Dolly.

'My mother, I'm sorry to say, rather looked down on her, you know. She was a bit of a social climber, my mother, I mean, and she felt that she couldn't invite Dolly to meet some of her affluent Caxley friends.'

'Dolly Clare,' I said, 'would have been welcomed in any society.'

'I agree, but mother didn't think so. To tell the truth, my brother and I fell out with her when we were old enough to leave home. We visited her, of course, and always kept in touch by letters when we left England, but there wasn't much love lost. She was a headstrong woman, and we were better apart.'

'What happened to your brother?'

'He went sheep farming in New Zealand, and did very well, but he contracted cancer some three years ago, and died last Christmas.'

We drew in to the side of the lane outside Dolly's cottage, and I switched off the engine.

Mary sat, silently gazing at the little thatched house. I was rather relieved to see that no builders were at work this morning. We should have the house to ourselves.

It was very quiet in the lane, and we were both content to sit there in silence. A lark was singing overhead, high above the great whale-back of the downs behind the village. A young pheasant crossed the road a few yards from the car, stepping haughtily from one grass verge to the other, and ignoring a small animal, shrew or vole, which streaked across the road within yards of the bird. There was a fragrance in the air compounded of cut grass, wild flowers and, above all, the pungent scent of a nearby elder bush heavy with creamy flowers.

Mary broke the silence first.

'It's so small,' she said.

'Actually,' I told her, 'it has been enlarged since your time. Dolly had the sitting-room made wider, and the kitchen too. But I agree, it is a little house. I think that's why I like it so much.'

We climbed out of the car, and I unlocked the front door. The familiar smell greeted me of ancient wood, slight dampness, and the faint smell of dried lavender which

Dolly had never failed to keep in china bowls in each room.

The furniture remained much as Dolly had left it. Some if it would have to go later to the Caxley auctioneers; I had removed anything portable of value to my school house for safety. Beech Green may look idyllic to the passing stranger, but it has its share of villains, as well as a few marauders from elsewhere who take advantage of the nearby motorway to steal anything which will bring them a few pounds, and then make a hasty getaway. It was this hoard which I proposed to display to Mary when we returned to my house for lunch, so that she could choose her keepsake; and this I told her.

Her face was transfixed with pleasure and wonder as she stood inside the sitting-room: 'It still smells the same. Isn't it strange how strongly smells evoke memories? Far more so than sight.'

She crossed to the window and looked across the little garden, now in sore need of attention I noticed guiltily, to the sweep of the downs beyond.

'And the view's exactly the same. What a relief!'

She sat down suddenly, as though everything was too much for her.

'You know,' she said after a while, 'my friends in Caxley dissuaded me from going to visit a place near the town where we used to picnic as children. There seemed to be every wild flower imaginable there – cowslips, scabious, bee orchids and early purple orchids, and lots of that yellow ladies' slipper. They told me it has all gone. A new estate has been built there, and all the trees cut down "Cherish your memories," they said to me, and I'm sure they are right.'

She looked about the room.

'But this has changed so little, and I'm glad you've brought me. Can we see the rest?'

We wandered into the kitchen, and Mary ran her fingers over the old scrubbed kitchen table, ridged with years of service. She peered excitedly into the larder with its slate shelves, and the massive pottery bread crock on the brick floor.

'It's all as I remember it,' she said delightedly. 'Will you keep things as they are?'

'I shall do my best,' I assured her, as we mounted the stairs.

It was plain that work was in progress here, though not at the moment. Dust sheets draped the beds and the rest of the furniture which had been put into the middle of the rooms. Paint pots and brushes stood on newspaper on the window sills, and there was a smell of fresh paint.

Mary gazed out of the window. It did me good to see how much she relished her visit here after so many years, and I was glad that so little had changed for her. It was right, as her friends had said, 'to cherish her memories'. But how much better to find that some of those memories, at least, were still reality.

She was very quiet as we drove back from Beech Green to Fairacre and, I guessed, much moved by all she had seen. I was careful not to break the silence until we had stopped the car outside my home, when Mary seemed to return to this world with a cry of delight.

'But this is a lovely house!' She turned to me, looking perplexed. 'It is so much better than Aunt Dolly's! Can you bear to move away?'

I laughed, and led her into the house.

As we sipped our glasses of sherry, I explained that the school house was virtually a tied cottage, something that went with the job, and when I retired I should have had to have found another abode. That was why Dolly's wonderful legacy to me had been so deeply appreciated. Her house would be my haven in the future.

'But won't you mind what happens to this place when you go?'

'Of course, I shall. I've always loved it, and I think the school authorities would let me buy it if the school were closed down. But that's out of the question. The property will be sold, I've no doubt, and if the school closes, then that will be sold too. It could make a splendid house with care and money spent on it.'

'I hope that never happens,' said my guest.

'So do I,' I assured her, 'but things don't look very promising at the moment. Now, come and have some lunch.'

Afterwards, I broached the subject of a memento and told her about Dolly's valuables which I had stored upstairs.

We went up to inspect them, and I spread out Dolly's

things on the bed for Mary's inspection. She fingered the beautiful old linen, and picked up the pieces of ancient china with great care.

'It's all so lovely, and so difficult to choose. I love this little china cream jug, but I think I'll settle for one of Dolly's tablecloths, if that suits you?'

'Take both,' I said. 'I know Dolly would love to have seen them in family hands.'

She made her selection from the pile of linen. The chosen cloth had a deep edging of hand-made crochet, done years ago, I felt sure, by Dolly's mother Mary, after whom the present Mary had been named.

'I shall use it on very special days, like Christmas,' Mary said.

Later I drove my new friend to Caxley. Only three days remained before she and her husband returned to America, and I was much touched when she invited me to go and stay with them, and have a holiday there.

'Perhaps next summer?' she pressed, as I stopped outside at her friends' home.

'There's nothing I should like more,' I told her, 'but I shall have to think about it.'

We parted with a kiss, and I drove back thinking how good it had been to have contact with this last link with Dolly's family.

Should I ever go to the United States, I wondered? A lot would depend on the future of Fairacre School. Would it still be there? For that matter, would I still be there?

I had plenty to think about in the time ahead, but I was enormously glad to have met Mary and to have been able to give her the mementoes she liked. And at least she had not put me in the position of poor Wilhelm's widow when those Austrian dining-room chairs had been appropriated.

* * *

At the Post office the next day, I was surprised to see Mrs Lamb standing behind the grille in place of her husband.

'He's down at the surgery,' she said, in reply to my enquiry. 'Got a bad back, picking gooseberries yesterday, and anyone would think he was at death's door. You know what men are.'

'Well, I hope it soon gets better. Backs are so painful. Just six air letters, please, and a book of stamps.'

She busied herself in a drawer. 'Have you heard any more about the school closing?' she asked.

Mrs Lamb has been a manager, or *governor*, as I have to remember to call them now, for several years, in company with other good villagers such as Mr Roberts and Mrs Mawne, wife of our local ornithologist, Henry.

'Nothing definite,' I said. 'As you know, we are now down to about twenty on roll, but I have had no word from the office about closure so I'm keeping my fingers crossed.'

'Well, we've trounced the idea before, and we'll do it again,' said Mrs Lamb, slapping down my purchases in a militant manner. 'There's not a soul in Fairacre who wants the school to close. That must count for something.'

I said that I hoped so.

'You don't think,' she went on, a note of doubt now in her voice, 'that you leaving for Dolly Clare's place might make them think of shutting the school?'

The thought had never occurred to me, and although I did not think that my removal a few miles distant would affect the authority's decision, I was somewhat taken aback.

'I don't imagine it will make the slightest difference,' I said, trying to sound reassuring. 'After all, I spent several weeks commuting from Dolly's house to school during her last illness.'

'That's what I said to Maud Pringle when she came in yesterday. There's a fair amount of gossip about the school at the moment.'

This I could well believe, and I made my way homeward with all the old familiar worries buzzing in my head like a swarm of bees.

It really looked as though the school might close. It would not be just yet, as we should have had fair warning if such a step were imminent. I remembered the vicar's blackboard message about the dates of the coming term, and felt a faint comfort.

But I really ought to give some serious thought to my own future. My departure from the school house would probably mean that it would be put on the market. That I had already faced. But what should I do if the school closed? I felt sure that I would be offered another post in the area, possibly at Beech Green School if there were a suitable vacancy. There were a dozen or so schools in Caxley and nearby which might employ me. But did I want to go elsewhere? I certainly did not.

I could, I supposed, take early retirement, but could I afford to? And wasn't I still an active person, wanting to work and, though I said it myself, able, healthy and experienced? I should soon be bored, kicking around at home, and I remembered Miriam Baker's remark about 'being geared to work'. Like most people when working, I professed to loathing it, but deprived of it I should probably be far less content.

As I came towards the church, I saw that Bob Willet was busy digging a grave, and I went across to speak to him. He looked hot with his labours, and pushed his cap to the back of his head.

'Fair bit of clay over the chalk in this 'ere graveyard,' he said, clambering out and taking a seat on a conveniently placed horizontal grave stone over the tomb of Josiah Drummond Gent. He nodded towards his work. 'Poor old Bert Tanner. Went last week.'

I made to sit beside him, and he dusted a place with his rough old hand.

'Bit damp, you know. Don't want to get piles. Nasty things, piles.'

'I shan't hurt,' I said. 'I'm pretty tough.'

'You needs to be these days,' he observed, and a companionable silence fell between us as we let the peace of the place envelop us. A country churchyard is a very soothing spot among all our 'rude forefathers', including Josiah Drummond Gent, whose last resting place was providing us with a comfortable, if chilly, seat.

'Heard any more about our school shutting?' he said at last, breaking the silence.

'Not a thing. I don't think there's any cause to worry just yet.'

'Looks as though it's bound to come, though. I hates all this 'ere change. New houses, new people, that dratted motorway, you moving out before long. It's *unsettling*, that's what it is.'

'I shan't be going far,' I pointed out. 'In a way I shall only be carrying on where dear old Dolly left off. So there's a nice comforting piece of continuity for you.'

Mr Willet sighed.

'I s'pose you could look at it like that. There's still plenty that stays the same. Digging graves, for instance, and them downs up there. They won't change, thank God.'

The stone was beginning to strike some chill through my summer skirt, and I rose to go. Mr Willet heaved himself to his feet, and grasped his spade again.

'Ah well! My old ma used to say: "Do what's to hand

and the Lord will look after the rest." I'd best get on digging.'

He jumped neatly into the mottled clay and chalk hole of his making, and I went to embark on what my own hand should be doing.

12   Relief by Telephone

I WENT to Beech Green on most days during the summer holidays, to see how the refurbishing was getting on, and to take over a few pieces of furniture, china and so on from the school house.

Wayne Richards was doing me proud, I felt, and the basic decorating was done within two weeks, and rejuvenated the whole place. I felt immensely pleased with my new home.

I had got our local electrician to inspect all the wiring, and the plumber to check his work in the cottage. To my relief all was in good repair. It looked as though I should be able to move in before term started, unless any unforeseen problems cropped up.

The biggest headache was the state of the garden, and I took Bob Willet with me one hot day, to get his advice on it. He mooched about it in a thoughtful mood, taking particular note of the ancient fruit trees.

'Almost all have had their day,' he told me. He stood by an ancient plum tree. Brown beads of resin decorated the trunk, and some of the topmost branches were already dead.

Bob's brown hand slapped the wrinkled bark.

'You thinkin' of replacing any of 'em?'

'Is it so bad?'

'In my opinion, yes. The only tree here as is worth its salt is that old Bramley and the yew tree. They'll be good for another fifty years, but these 'ere fruit trees should be out before they falls down.'

I nodded my agreement.

'I think I'd like a new plum tree – one of the gage type, if possible – and perhaps a couple of new apple trees. But I agree there's no need for more.'

'Come early autumn I'll bring a lad up with me and we'll get this lot down.'

He moved on to a James Grieve apple tree which was already leaning over at an alarming angle.

'Tell you what, Miss Read, these 'ere trees'll give you a nice lot of firewood for the winter.'

He turned his attention to the neglected border, and shook his head.

'Hopeless?' I hazarded.

'Best to dig up the lot and start afresh,' was his verdict. 'It's that full of twitch and ground elder nothing won't grow well there.'

And so it went on as we did our tour of inspection. Only the soft fruit bushes, black and redcurrant and gooseberry bushes passed his ruthless inspection. Even they, it

seemed, could do with 'a good old spray against the bugs'.

We went into the house to arrange matters. As always, Bob had some practical advice.

'I've got a young lad in mind, nephew of Alice's over Springbourne way. He's a good worker, when he gets the chance. Just been stood off from one of those Caxley firms as has gone bust. Tip top gardener he is. Shall I get him over?'

'Yes, please. I suppose we could make a start on that border?'

'The sooner the better,' said my old friend forthrightly, as he rose to go home.

August seemed to hurry by at an alarming pace with so many things to do in both my abodes. Luckily there were no urgent maintenance jobs to be done at the school house, as the upstairs rooms were now in pristine condition and, apart from getting new mats for the kitchen floor sometime, I felt that I could sit back.

In any case, I did not propose to do any more to my present home. The outside maintenance was the responsibility of the school authorities, and I was only responsible for things inside; I felt that I had done my duty honourably throughout the years. With the possible closure of the school hanging over me, it seemed prudent to postpone any long-term decisions for my domestic arrangements at the school house.

My social life during the holidays was limited to a few outings to friends, a short trip to Dorset to see an aged aunt, and entertaining my cousin Ruth for three nights at the school house – 'probably,' I told her, 'for the last time.'

'It's sad. I shall miss it,' she said. 'Will you?'

'Naturally, but I should be far more upset if the school were to close. As it is, I have Dolly's house to enjoy, and all the fun of new neighbours at Beech Green with the continuing of life as the village school teacher here.'

I took her to see my new property. The work was well on the way to completion, and privately I reckoned to be in by the end of August.

Ruth was enchanted with it, and it was good to have her whole-hearted approval. She is a wise woman, and I have always respected her judgement.

'Well, the next time you come,' I told her, 'you will be sleeping under that thatched roof.'

We were blessed with warm sunshine while she was with me, and we had several picnics, and two visits to nearby National Trust properties. August is not my favourite month: there is an end-of-summer look about the countryside, shabby and worn, before the glory of autumn transforms it.

But the verges of our lanes were still bright with cranesbill, and the tall grass was dusted with minute purple flowers. The lime trees had shed their yellow bracts, but the remains of the flowers still fluttered moth-like among the foliage.

I was sorry when Ruth had to go. There are times when I realize how much I miss family ties. This was one of them as I drove her to Caxley station.

'Come again soon,' I urged her. 'Come for Christmas in the new house.'

'Nothing I'd like more, but I'll have to let you know,' she replied, and with that I had to be content.

That evening I was surprised to get a call on the telephone from Mr Salisbury. He is the representative from the local education office who attends our school governors' meetings, and acts as the line of communication between the local schools and the education authority. He performs his rôle admirably, being kind and tactful. I wondered why he should be ringing me personally, presumably on a school matter.

After polite inquiries about my state of health, he began to approach the purpose of his call.

'I happened to meet Gerald Partridge recently,' he said smoothly, 'and he mentioned the fact that there was a little disquiet in the village about Fairacre School.'

This is it, I thought, feeling slightly sick. He is going to warn me about closing the place before the next governors' meeting.

'I do want to put your mind at rest, Miss Read. There is no suggestion of closing the school in the near future.'

I sat down abruptly on the chair by the telephone. My legs did not seem capable of supporting me.

'That's good news,' I croaked. 'Naturally, I've been anxious as the numbers are so low.'

'They are indeed,' he agreed, 'but they may pick up before the next school year. In any case, that side of the matter will be kept under review, and you would be apprised of any official decision in good time.'

'I was sure of that,' I told him.

'No. The other matter was rather more personal.'

He cleared his throat while I thought, now what? Had I forgotten to return some vital forms? Had an angry parent complained about me? Was I about to get the sack for some unknown misdemeanour?

'It's really about your tenancy of the school house,' he went on. 'I gathered from Gerald Partridge's remarks that you were proposing to live at Beech Green sometime in the future. Is that correct?'

'Yes, indeed,' I replied, and went on to explain my plans as far as I knew them myself. 'I was going to bring this up at the next governors' meeting,' I added. 'I realize I have to give a month's notice.'

'There is absolutely no hurry on our side for you to leave the school house, you know. You have been a model tenant, and we should all be very sorry to see you go. I only rang so that I could get matters straight before anything official was put into writing.'

I said that I appreciated the courtesy, and felt that perhaps I should have mentioned my plans earlier.

'Indeed no! There's nothing to blame yourself for, but I am delighted to have had this little talk.'

He went on to more general subjects such as the traffic congestion that morning in Caxley, the early harvest this year, and ended up with his hopes for more children at Fairacre before long.

I agreed fervently, and with mutual compliments the conversation closed.

As the end of August approached, the school house began to look pathetically bare. My future abode, on the other hand, was in danger of getting seriously overcrowded, although I was happy and excited at the prospect of moving in.

Amy came over one morning to help me pack books, a formidable task, and a particularly dirty one as it happened. We swathed ourselves in overalls against the dust of years which was being blown off, or slapped off, the contents of my book shelves.

'I should have thought you could have got Mrs Pringle to dust these now and again,' observed Amy.

'Mrs Pringle,' I told her, 'doesn't hold with books. If I'd let her have her way, she would have had a bonfire of the lot in the garden. She maintains that *reading* keeps decent folk from *proper work* like polishing and scrubbing and dusting book shelves. By the way, Mrs Pringle insists on "doing me" at my new home on a Wednesday afternoon.'

'Well, I'm glad to hear it,' said Amy. 'Do you really want to keep this *Historic Houses and Gardens Guide for 1978?*'

She held it up by one corner, looking fastidious. Her usually well-kept hands were filthy, I noticed guiltily.

'Throw it in the junk box,' I said, 'and let's have some coffee.'

We washed our filthy hands at the kitchen sink, and sat down exhausted with our coffee cups.

I had switched on the television to catch the news on the hour, but we'd found ourselves confronted with an old black and white film. The heroine, wearing a black satin suit with aggressive shoulder pads, and a minute pill-box hat with sequins and an ostrich plume was sobbing noisily on a settee. At the other end sat Cary Grant, ebony-haired and looking greatly concerned.

'Aw, kid,' he said, 'don't take on so,' and produced a beautifully laundered handkerchief which he pressed upon his weeping companion.

She proceeded to mop her cheeks, being careful not to touch her mascara.

'Gee, you're so kind,' she gulped. 'I bin silly.'

I switched them off.

'I wonder,' said Amy meditatively, 'why weeping women in films never have a handkerchief? I don't know about you, my dear, but I can truthfully say that I *always* have a hanky on me, thanks to my mother's training. Although I did know two sisters who *shared* one when they went out to parties. I remember one saying to the other: "Have you got *the handkerchief?*" I was appalled.'

'And quite rightly so,' I said. 'D'you want more coffee or shall we get on?'

We returned to our labours, and later that day took the books, a box of china and some garden chairs over to

Beech Green. Our load needed both cars, and Amy arrived before I did. I found her sunning herself on an old bench under the thatch at the back of Dolly's cottage.

'If ever you want to part with this,' she said dreamily, eyes still closed, 'let me know.'

'Not a hope,' I told her. 'I intend to stay here, like dear Dolly, until I'm summoned hence.'

I unlocked the door, and we manhandled our heavy loads into the house.

The books went into the new shelves without much bother, but it was quite apparent that cupboard space was beginning to run short. I could see that Wayne Richards would have to be prevailed upon again, but not until the Christmas holidays, I hoped.

When we had done all that we could, we sat down to recover. The sun was shining into the sitting-room, and I thought of the many times I had sat here with Dolly, enjoying her company and the peace of her home.

I looked at Amy with renewed affection. It was good to have an old friend under my new roof. I began to tell her about the telephone call from Mr Salisbury, and the relief I felt at knowing the closure of Fairacre School was not imminent.

'That's marvellous,' agreed Amy, 'but what hopes are there of new pupils?'

'Not too bright immediately,' I told her, 'but we are waiting to see if two large families come to live in the new houses.'

'Or in your school house,' observed Amy. 'I take it that it will be on the market sometime?'

'I suppose so,' I said, and was surprised to find the idea distinctly upsetting. Somehow, *other people* in *my* house, was an unpleasant prospect.

Amy was studying me with some concern. 'You must worry,' she remarked.

I have no secrets from Amy. We have known each other too long for dissembling.

'I do,' I said truthfully. 'I worry about the school itself, that dear shabby old building which has seen generations of Fairacre folk under its roof. I worry about the children, and the parents, and grandparents.'

'But what about *you*?' pressed Amy.

'Funnily enough, not so desperately. I should probably be worrying far more if Dolly had not been so generous to me. But I'm pretty sure I would be offered another post locally, or I could contemplate early retirement, I suppose.'

'Would you like that?'

'Half of me fairly leaps at the idea, but the other half wonders if I should get restive after the first few months of euphoria. Like Miriam Baker,' I added, and began to tell her about Miriam's plans.

After this we parted, Amy driving off southwards to Bent, while I locked up the house and then drove in the opposite direction to Fairacre.

The village seemed deserted, and nothing stirred near St Patrick's and its churchyard. It was a golden evening of great calm, the kind of post-harvest lull when the stubble is still in the fields reflecting a warm September effulgence.

I remembered that I needed some of the children's readers to check an order list I was sending to the office, and went to the school before going home across the playground.

The brickwork threw out considerable warmth, and I could smell the drying paint round the window panes. Mrs Pringle had 'bottomed' the place at the end of the summer term, and would be up again in a day or two to see that all was ready for our opening again soon.

Meanwhile, the school had remained locked. A few dead leaves whispered on the porch floor, as I inserted the massive key into the Victorian lock. The woodwork was warm against my hand, and I suddenly noticed that the crack of the door was sealed with a criss-cross of gossamer threads, spun by a host of small creatures who had been undisturbed for weeks.

I stood numb with shock, the key motionless in my hand. This, I suddenly realized, would be the state of this well-loved school for ever, should its doors finally close. Dust, cobwebs, flaking paint, a few dead leaves, an overall acceptance of time's ravages and the onslaught of the seasons.

It must have been several minutes before I could find the strength to twist that key and return to the present. But as the gossamer threads broke, and the familiar scent of the old schoolroom assailed me, I found my eyes were wet.

13   Two Homes

I MADE the move into Dolly's cottage before the end of the summer holidays, as I had planned. But only by the skin of my teeth.

As everyone who has moved house knows, there are always *snags*. The day before the move, I returned to the school house from the Post Office to find a roll of stair carpet in the porch. This was supposed to have been delivered to Dolly's house where Mrs John was awaiting it. I rang the firm who expressed surprise and said: 'I'd better hang on to it, didn't I?' as the men could pick it up with my other 'bits and bobs' the next morning. And yes, yes, they'd certainly be at my place (School House wasn't it now, at Beech Green?) by nine o'clock prompt.

I straightened out that one, rang Mrs John to apologize for keeping her waiting all the afternoon, hauled the unwieldy package further into the porch in case it rained, and hoped for the best.

At ten o'clock the next morning, I rang the removal firm again. The same man answered. I recognized his adenoidal symptoms.

'That's funny! The chaps as left that stair carpet had a note for you.'

'It's not here.'

'Well, we're working you in with a party at Cirencester.'

'How do you mean? "Being worked in"?'

'Well, there's a full load going to Cirencester, see, and a half-load being picked up there, and the chaps will call at yours for your bits to fill up the space, see, and drop it off at Beech Green on the way home, see. Save you all a lot of trouble.'

'There's quite enough here to be getting on with,' I said tartly. 'So when can I expect this half-empty van from Cirencester?'

'About midday.'

'So I should hope.'

'With luck, that is,' said Adenoids. 'This way you save quite a bit of money, you know.'

'It doesn't save my time and temper,' I snapped back, crashing down the receiver.

It was perhaps fortunate that I had been unable to catch Tibby earlier. That astute animal had seen the cat basket which I had attempted to hide in the cupboard, recognized it at once as the carriage which conveyed animals to the vet, and had made for open country. Luckily, just before twelve, Tibby appeared, accepted the last of the milk, and was corralled in mid-sip, poor thing. Together we sat, awaiting the van's return from the party in Cirencester.

In the quiet, denuded room, I had plenty of time to look back over the years I had spent beneath this roof. They had been happy ones, busy with worthwhile work and enriched by Fairacre friends. Should I feel as secure at Beech Green, I wondered? Time would tell.

By one o'clock Tibby and I were still waiting, and both hungry. Tibby had some rather unpopular cat biscuits in the cat basket, and I dined on two somewhat fluffy wine gums from the bottom of my handbag.

At two o'clock the van appeared, loaded up the last of my removables and took off for Beech Green.

Tibby was put on the front seat of my car, protesting loudly at this indignity, and I drove away to our new home.

* * *

Later that night, I climbed the stairs at Beech Green, weary
with all the day's activities. Tibby was settled in the kitchen
below, the doors were locked and the empty milk bottles
stood on the doorstep.

Everything was quiet. I leant out of the bedroom
window and smelt the cool fragrance of a summer's night.
Far away, across Hundred Acre field, an owl hooted. Below
me, in the flowerbed, a small nocturnal animal rustled
leaves in its search for food.

A great feeling of peace crept over me. The tranquillity
of Dolly's old abode and my new one enveloped me. I
knew then that I had come home at last.

My link with the school house was not entirely broken.

At the governors' meeting the matter was discussed with
all the sympathy I knew would be shown. Mr Salisbury,
from the office, was among those who sat in some dis-
comfort in the schoolroom after the children had gone
home.

I explained my position, knowing full well, of course,
that my move to Dolly's cottage was known to all present,
but these formalities must be observed. I ended by saying
that I proposed to vacate the school house at Michaelmas,
the end of the present month, so that it could be put on the
market if that was, in fact, to be its fate.

Here Mr Salisbury intervened. He was empowered, he
told us, to make quite clear that there was absolutely no
hurry in this matter. It would be perfectly in order for me
to stay at the school house until the end of the year, giving
me more time to see to my affairs. Any decision about the
house's future would be taken then.

I was truly grateful for this gesture. It meant that I now
had ample time to clear up my domestic matters.

The rest of the business went much as usual. The school

log book was produced and handed round. The punishment book, its pages unsullied, was also scrutinized. The chairman, the vicar, thanked us all for coming, and the meeting dispersed into the September sunshine.

Although almost everything of mine was now installed at Beech Green, I had left one bed and a chair beside it, in my old bedroom. This I had done for two reasons. Firstly, I might need to stay overnight if school affairs kept me late during this interim period, or if some unexpected weather hazard made it difficult to get home. Secondly, I had always used the school house in any emergency with the children. A sick child would be taken over there to lie down whilst help was fetched and parents informed. Somehow I felt safer in keeping a place of refuge close to the school in case of sudden need. Naturally, when the end of the year came I should have to face making other contingency plans, but it was good to know that these temporary arrangements had the blessing of the school authorities.

I went home to Beech Green that day, very much happier in mind.

The golden weather continued, and people were looking for blackberries along the hedges. It was plain that we were going to have a bumper crop of apples, and even the farmers could find little to deplore after an unusually good harvest.

'Want a marrow or two?' asked Mr Willet. 'A *proper* marrow, I mean, not these 'ere soppy little runts what gets cooked whole. Courgiettes, or some such name. I reckon it's pandering to women as is too idle to cut the skin off a decent marrow. I fair hates to see a dish of them little 'uns, like a lot of chopped-up eels, and my Alice knows better than to serve 'em up.'

I refused the marrow – or marrows – as kindly as I could. A lone woman simply cannot cope with a full-sized marrow, and Mr Willet's were mammoth.

'I thought you might like to make a bit of jam,' he said, looking hurt.

'I don't eat much jam.' I said apologetically.

'There's always bazaars as could do with it,' pointed out Bob. 'Good causes. Charity. All that.'

'Well,' I began weakly.

'I'll bring you up a couple,' he said swiftly. 'Put a nice bit of ginger and lemon with it, and it'll sell like hot cakes. Mrs Partridge has made twenty-five pounds of it with the marrows I took up to the vicarage last week.'

This looked to me as if the local market for marrow jam would be overloaded already, but Mr Willet's undoubted dismay at my reluctance to accept his bounty had to be assuaged.

'I'm sure I could cope with one of your lovely marrows,' I said bravely. 'It's just that, living alone, you know – '

'Well, that could be righted,' observed Bob sturdily, 'if you wasn't so picky about chaps.'

He turned to go, leaving me speechless.

'I'll look you out a couple of beauties,' he promised, stumping away.

Those 'couple of beauties', I told myself ruefully, would probably make another twenty-five pounds of marrow jam to add to Fairacre's surplus.

One Saturday morning, soon after receiving four massive marrows from Bob Willet, I went into Caxley to buy a pair of shoes. I tried on about sixteen pairs which were either too tight or too loose, the wrong colour or design, and finally settled for the pair which hurt least, looked un-obtrusive, and hoped for the best.

Still in a state of shock at the price asked for the shoes I took myself to the store's restaurant and ordered coffee. At that moment I was hailed by Horace and Eve Umbleditch at a nearby table, and I was invited to join my old friends.

'Just the girl we wanted to see,' cried Horace. 'We've been hearing about your move, and wondered if your school house was going to be put on the market.'

I told them my story up to date, and that a decision about the house would be taken in the New Year, but it looked highly likely that it would be for sale then.

'But not if the school stays open, surely?' asked Eve. 'Won't the house be kept in case the next head teacher wants it?'

I explained that the school had been reprieved for the time being, but in any case the chances were that anyone appointed after I had retired, sometime in the future, would probably want to live elsewhere.

'When I came years ago,' I told them, 'cars were not so abundant. I was jolly glad to have the school house on top of my job, so to speak. But nowadays the head of Fairacre School could live anywhere within striking distance by car. In any case, the school house is really only suitable for a single person.'

'Any hope of building on?' said Horace, stirring his coffee thoughtfully. 'Eve and I were wondering if it would suit us. We're in the same position as you were – living in a tied house virtually – and it's high time we found a place of our own.'

'It might suit you very well,' I answered. 'You have seen it, I know, but if you really are considering buying, do come over at anytime and have a good look at it. I love the place dearly, and it would be lovely to think of you there. But don't forget, you are cheek by jowl with the school, and all the noise that causes.'

'We've thought about that. But after all, we should be away at our own school when your children are there, and we have long holidays when Fairacre School would be empty too. It might work out very comfortably.'

The conversation then turned to the past school holidays which they had spent in France, and to my own spell in Scotland with Amy.

We parted with renewed promises about their visiting the house, and I drove back to my new home at Beech Green wondering if my old house would one day see the Umbleditchs happily settled there.

I must say, I liked the idea.

The garden at Dolly's was beginning to look tidier, thanks largely to Bob Willet's efforts. He cycled over from Fairacre when he could spare the time, and did a stout job on the neglected borders, sometimes assisted by Alice Willet's nephew.

Under his direction I too did my stint, and on some days I was assisted by Joseph Coggs who was always willing to come back with me in the car, eat a substantial tea, pitch into digging and weeding, hedge-trimming or tending a bonfire, and earning a modest sum in payment.

I enjoyed his company. He was never going to be an academic person. His parents' distrust of 'book-learning' was partly shared by all the Coggs' family. But he loved natural things, flowers, birds, curiously-shaped stones, the evolution of tadpoles into frogs – in fact, anything which involved the living world and its past in the countryside around him. He had an enquiring mind retentive of all that really appealed to him. Moreover, the sense of wonder, which so often fades as a child grows older, remained as keen as ever, and we spent many happy hours together restoring the old garden.

'The next real job,' said Bob Willet when the three of us were sitting on the bench under the thatch surveying the result of our back-breaking labours, 'is them old trees.'

He was looking with great disapproval at the ancient fruit trees which were looking decidedly sick.

'That old Bramley will do a few years yet,' said Bob, 'but I'd have them two plums and that pear and greengage out as soon as they've dropped their leaves. Riddled with canker, I'll lay. Best put in some new stuff – bush type, I'd say so as you can pick 'em easy.'

I agreed to all his wise advice. When the time came, I knew that Mr John and George Annett would give a hand in getting the trees down. Meanwhile, Joe and I were content to obey our mentor, and went on with our humble weeding and other unskilled labour under his watchful eye.

The spare bed in the near-empty school house was used only twice during the next few weeks. One of Mrs

Richards's little boys looked flushed and was tearful. On investigation, we discovered an ominous rash on his chest, and whipped him across to the school house before the rest of the infants showed the same symptoms. As it turned out, our fears of measles or chickenpox were groundless. A new jersey, desperately tickly, had irritated the poor child's chest, and he was back in school within two days.

On the second occasion, I occupied the bed myself after a long evening of gardening. I was splitting up the roots of my favourite perennials to take over to the Beech Green garden, and found that my back was in such a parlous condition that driving was next to impossible.

An early night under the old familiar roof eased the pain, and I was able to nip over to Beech Green to feed Tibby before breakfast. The poor animal had missed supper, and I was greeted coldly.

After friends had been given any particular object of their choice, surplus furniture from my old house, and from Dolly's had been sent to the auctioneers and had brought in a tidy sum. Dolly, I felt, would have approved.

The thatched roof insulated the cottage well, keeping it snug in winter and cool in summer. The ceilings were low, so that the rooms soon warmed up when the electric fire was on, and I found the staircase easier to negotiate than the rather steep one at the school house.

I relished my new home, and looked forward to returning to it after each day at school. I began to realize that a few miles between one's place of work and place of home made all the difference to one's relaxation. Hitherto I had gone between house and school many times between dawn and dusk. In truth, I was always on duty, and fair game for any parent or governor who wished to drop in and discuss school matters. Now I was less vulnerable, and I appreciated this change in my life.

Tibby too seemed to enjoy an environment without children, and explored the new hedges, trees and ditches with fresh energy.

We settled into this different routine with great satisfaction, now that the worries of the move and the clearing-up of Dolly's affairs were over, though nothing could take away the sharp sense of loss which overcame me now and again. The pungent scent of southernwood by the back door, the photograph of Dolly which hung over her desk, and the sight of the bright rug she had made for the landing, all sent a pang of loneliness through me. How potent such inanimate things are!

Horace and Eve Umbleditch came to see me one Saturday soon after our encounter in Caxley, and we drove over to Fairacre to see the school house.

'It doesn't look at it's best unfurnished,' I warned them, 'but at least it is all newly decorated upstairs, and you'll get some idea of size and outlook.'

It was a balmy afternoon, and the school-house garden was looking tidy. I still had the key, of course, by courtesy of the school governors, and water and electricity were still available. Our footsteps echoed hollowly on the bare boards and the uncarpeted stairs.

'This looks very monastic,' observed Horace in my old bedroom. He was looking at my lone bed, chair and electric heater. There were no curtains at the windows and no covering on the floor. Somehow it looked even more bleak than the completely bare rooms elsewhere, I realized.

I explained about the emergency arrangements.

'But I really think it's time to get the removal men to take these few things to the sale room. With luck, I'm not likely to need them again before the end of term, and anyway I must make other plans after that.'

After they had looked at the house, we sat on the grass in the sunny garden. A bold pair of chaffinches came close, hoping for peanuts. A lark sang high above us, and in the distance we could hear the bleating of Mr Roberts's sheep.

'It's a blissful spot,' said Eve.

'It is indeed,' agreed Horace, chewing a piece of grass lazily. 'It would be worth waiting for if you think it will really find its way on to the market.'

'Not for me to say,' I responded. 'But all the signs point that way. Sometime in the New Year, I imagine.'

We returned to Beech Green for tea. They were both very quiet on the journey there, obviously mulling over all that they had seen.

'And what's the village like?' enquired Horace when I had poured the tea. 'I suppose we should be looked upon as newcomers, and not really accepted.'

'That would depend on you,' I said. 'If you really want to join in, I've no doubt you would soon find yourselves president of this, and secretary to that, sidesman at the church, umpire at cricket matches, and a dozen other offices.'

'Well, we *would* like to join in,' said Eve roundly. 'I was brought up in a village, and it's one of the reasons we should like to make our home in one.'

'The only snag is,' added Horace, 'we should obviously have to be away most of the day, just like the rest of the village commuters. I suppose you have such bodies in Fairacre?'

'We do indeed. It's one of the more obvious changes in the village, and I really don't see what can be done about it. When I look back to my early days at the school, I can remember how close-knit the families were. I suppose Mr Roberts and his neighbouring farmer were the two main employers in the village, and I know there were the old familiar names on my school register which were in the log book almost a century ago.'

'And aren't there now?'

'A few. Nothing to speak of. So many have moved away, and when the cottages have become empty they have been sold for far more than the original village people could afford. It's happening everywhere. On the other hand, you can understand people wanting to bring up their children in the country, and if they have the money to pay for a suitable piece of property, and are game to have miles of travelling each day to work, who can blame them for buying village houses?'

'Like us,' commented Horace.

'The only objection I have,' I added, 'is that the children don't come to my school!'

'Take heart,' said Eve. 'They may come yet. After all, it's not going to close, is it? You told us that the other day.'

'It will be a miracle if it survives for another few years,' I replied soberly. 'I sometimes wonder if the authorities are waiting to see how low the numbers will fall, and if perhaps the whole property – school, school house and the ground – will then be put on the market. It would be a valuable property if that happened.'

'I noticed a shop in the village,' said Eve. 'Do you use it?'

'Indeed I do. It's the Post Office as well, and I suppose I do almost all my weekly shopping at Mr Lamb's, and get stamps and post things at the same time. Now and again I have to trundle into Caxley, mainly for clothes and the like, but I go as little as possible, parking gets worse and worse.'

'And is that the only shop?'

'Afraid so. Years ago things were different. Bob Willet

was telling me the other day that when he was a boy there was a thriving blacksmith at the forge, a baker, a carpenter, a cobbler, a man called Quick – who was extremely slow – who was the carrier between local villages and Caxley. Fairacre must have been a busy place, and quite noisy too with plenty of horses about and the forge clanging away.'

'Sad, really.'

'The saddest part for Bob Willet was the demise of the old lady who used to keep the Post Office when he was young. She sold a few sweets, and home-made toffee was twopence a quarter. Guaranteed to pull out any loose teeth, too, in a far more enjoyable way than a trip to the dentist.'

'My favourites were gob-stoppers,' said Horace reminiscently. 'The sort that changed colour as you sucked them.'

'And mine were licorice strips,' continued Eve. 'My mother wouldn't let us have gob-stoppers. She said they were *common*!'

'Not common enough for my liking,' said Horace, 'on threepence a week pocket-money, I never got enough of them.'

And with such sweet-talk, the question of house-buying was shelved for the rest of the afternoon.

14   A Mighty Rushing Wind

AS we entered October the weather became very unsettled. There were squally showers, the wind shifted its direction day by day, and Mrs Pringle began to complain about the leaves which were making her lobby floor untidy.

Her complaints became even more strident when I proposed that the two tortoise stoves would have to be lighted.

'What? In this 'ere mild spell? I'd say the Office'll have a thing or two to say, if we starts using coke this early. It's tax-payer's money – yours and mine, Miss Read – as pays for the coke.'

'Children can't work in chilly conditions,' I retorted.

'Chilly?' shrieked Mrs Pringle. 'They'll be passing out with heat stroke, more like.'

Nevertheless, the stoves were roaring away the next day, and we were all the better for it. Except, of course, Mrs Pringle, whose bad leg definitely took a turn for the worse.

Bob Willet, who much enjoys our little fights at a safe distance, approved of the stoves being lit.

'We're in for a funny old spell,' he forecast. 'You noticed how early the swallows went this year? They knows a thing or two. And them dratted starlings is ganging-up already. Flocks of 'em in them woods down Springbourne way, messing all over they are, doin' a bit of no good to the trees.'

'Well, what does that mean?'

'Something nasty in the weather to come. That's what

all that means. Birds know what to expect before we do.
I'll lay fifty to one – that is if I was a betting man, which
I'm not, as you well knows – as we'll have a rough day or
two before long.'

I always take note of Bob Willet's prognostications. He
is often right. But apart from the veering weathercock on
St Patrick's church, all seemed reasonably normal on the
weather front.

Or it seemed to be until midday on a fateful Wednesday.
The dinner lady appeared, bearing a stack of steaming tins,
and looking wind-blown.

'Coming over the downs was pretty rough,' she said.
'The wind's getting up. I heard a gale warning on the van
radio.'

'I shouldn't take a lot of notice of that,' I said. 'Ever
since that really dreadful gale two or three years ago, the
weathermen have been only too anxious to give us gale
warnings, and half the time they never materialize.'

'Well, we'll have to see. I know I'm going to be glad to get home today,' she replied, bustling away to her next port of call.

As the children tucked into macaroni cheese and sliced tomatoes, followed by apple tart and custard, the wind began to drum against the windows. Half an hour later, the gusts increased in intensity, and when I went across to the school house to see if all the doors were secure, I was blown bodily against my gate, and could barely get my breath.

It was at this stage that I saw the door of the boys' lavatory wrenched from its hinges and hurled towards the vicarage garden wall. I had a brief inspection of the school house exterior, decided that it was as safe as it could be in the circumstances, and struggled back to the school. Somehow the children must be evacuated to their homes before flying tiles and torn branches endangered us all.

Mrs Richards and I held a council of war as the windows rattled, and leaves and twigs spattered the panes.

Those who had a parent at home were dispatched at once, with strict instructions to run to safety and then to stay indoors. One or two others had telephones in their homes, and these we could forewarn about their children's early return. Several of them offered to pass on the message and mind neighbours' children with their own, until they returned from work.

It was lucky that the telephone lines were still intact, and I rang Mr Lamb at the Post Office to tell him that I was closing the school, and would he pass on the news.

'You're doing the right thing,' he assured me. 'I've just seen Roberts's tarpaulin blow off a straw stack across the road. Might have been a handkerchief the way it floated up!'

I also rang the vicar who said he would come at once

with his car, and house any odd children (I had plenty of those, I thought) until their parents could collect them. Looking at the school clock, I said that I hoped I had not brought him from his lunch.

'Only from banana blancmange,' he said, 'and I don't like that anyway.'

Poor Mr Partridge, I thought replacing the receiver. I should have liked to have offered him a slice of our own excellent apple tart, but as usual it had all been polished off.

By a quarter to two, almost all our little flock had departed, and I said that I would run Joseph Coggs and his two younger sisters to their house before I made my way home to Beech Green. It had not been possible to get in touch with the Coggs' parents, but Joe assured me that Dad was off work (no surprise, this) and Mum got back from helping out at Mrs Mawne's at two o'clock.

Before I locked up, I put things to rights at the school, windows and doors secured, and tortoise stoves battened down, and saw Mrs Richards off towards her home.

The car was quite difficult to handle when the gusts hit it on my way through the village, but I deposited my passengers as Arthur Coggs opened the door himself.

He thanked me civilly, and although there was a strong smell of beer, past and present, he seemed comparatively sober, and I left my charges with a clear conscience. I then battled my way to Mrs Pringle's and told that lady not to attempt to go up to the school.

'It can all wait,' I shouted to her outraged face at the kitchen window.

'But what about them stoves? We should never have lit 'em.'

'I've damped them down.'

'And the washing-up?'

'Stacked on the draining board. That'll keep. Just *don't go out!'*

At this stage the window was all but wrenched from her grip. She gave a gasp, slammed it to, and I returned to the car to make my way home.

It was a frightening journey. The road was strewn with leaves and quite large branches from the trees, which were bowing and bending in an alarming way. There was an ominous drumming in the air which I had never heard before, and it was as much as I could do to drive a steady course along a road lashed with this hurricane-force wind.

About halfway home, I rounded a bend to encounter a damaged car, two others and an ambulance whose lights were flashing in warning. Two men were just sliding a stretcher into the shelter of the ambulance, and when it moved off towards Caxley, I saw how badly damaged the small car was.

The branch of a beech tree, thicker than a man's leg, had obviously been torn from the trunk and landed on the unfortunate driver's Fiesta. The two men had manhandled the branch to the side of the road, but although cars could just about pass, it was going to cause a hazard, especially when darkness came.

I wound down my window to shout any offer of help, but the two men assured me that the garage men were on their way.

I had hardly driven another quarter of a mile when I found a fully grown tree straddling the road, blocking it completely. Panic began to seize me. What now?

It was beginning to get eerily dark which added to my uneasiness. Could I get down the little road to Spring-bourne, I wondered, and make a detour to my cottage?

It was a narrow lane, little used except by walkers, but I knew it well from my ambles with Miss Clare in earlier days. I turned the car, and made for the lane. It came out near the village of Springbourne, and from here I could take a similar narrow lane up the side of the downs beside a spinney which I hoped would shelter me from the worst of the wind.

I was in luck, but the screaming of the wind in the little wood was unnerving, and I was horrified to see that already quite large trees had been uprooted and were lying at all angles among the others. How the damage could ever be sorted out was going to be a sore problem, and how many small animals had already lost their homes, one could only guess.

I emerged into Beech Green half a mile from my home, and was thankful to see it again. After putting the car away, I stood in the shelter of the house to see what damage had occurred in the garden.

A lilac bush was already upended, and roofing felt on the garden shed was flapping dangerously. No doubt it would be ripped off completely before long, but I was too exhausted to bother much about it.

Miss Clare's ancient fruit trees, which Bob Willet proposed to take down, were swaying so violently that I doubted if they would survive another hour of this onslaught.

I struggled indoors, and looked for Tibby. There was no sign of him, and I was beginning to fear that he was outside somewhere in the maelstrom, when he emerged from under an armchair, attempting to look at ease. It was plain to see that Tibby was just as scared as I was, and it was good to have a fellow coward to keep me company.

I rang Mrs John, one of my nearest neighbours, to see if she and the children were safe, and although she sounded as frightened as I was she assured me that all was well.

'Mr Annett's closed his school as well,' she told me.

'The school buses came early, and let's hope everyone's got home.'

It was amazing to me that the telephone was still in order, but how long, I wondered, before the power cables came down and we should be without electricity?

I switched on the kettle while the going was good, and prudently looked out my old Primus stove, a torch and some candles. I checked that I had stocks of kindling wood, coal and logs in my house, and felt that I could do no more.

It seemed worse when darkness fell, and during the night I feared that the thatch might be ripped from its rafters, and the rattling windows might be torn out.

It was the incessant noise that was hardest to bear. The wind screamed and howled. It drummed and throbbed. Every now and again there would be a strange thump as something heavy, such as the wooden bird table hit the side of the house. Or there would be a metallic clanging as some unknown object, such as a dustbin or part of a corrugated iron roof collided with another.

I cowered beneath the bed clothes, glad to have Tibby at the end of the bed. What on earth would daylight show?

It showed chaos on a scale I could never have envisaged. Five of the condemned fruit trees were completely uprooted displaying great circles of chalky roots. The sixth leant at a dangerous angle. Only the old Bramley apple tree remained, and a sycamore and two lime trees. The border which Bob and Joseph had so carefully prepared was strewn with twigs and leaves, not to mention an upturned bucket and part of the shed roof.

It was hardly surprising to find that the electricity had gone, so I soon had my Primus going.

'Cornflakes for me,' I told Tibby, 'and Pussi-luv for you.'

Thus fortified, I rang the highways department to see if there was any chance of getting to school. A harassed individual told me that all roads within six or seven miles of Caxley were impassable, and 'to stay where you are, my duck'.

I rang Mr Partridge who sounded distraught and begged me not to venture out, and then Mr Lamb.

Although the wind had somewhat abated, it was still difficult to hear clearly as the line crackled. But Mr Lamb gave me more news of Fairacre damage.

'Tiles everywhere. Dozens off the church roof and the school, and your house, Miss Read, has had the chimney through the roof. You be thankful you weren't there. One of the big trees fell clean on it. Bob Willet's been up to have a look, and he's fair shaken, I can tell you. He's rigged up a tarpaulin to keep the worst of the weather out.'

He promised to let as many people as possible know that school would be closed until further notice, and Bob Willet had offered to put a notice on the school door if anyone should have managed to fight their way there. We could do no more, but I was desperately worried.

I spent the rest of the day trying to get some order out of the chaos outside, as the wind gradually died down.

Luckily the thatch had weathered the storm, and the house had stood up sturdily to the battering. The garden was such a shambles that I could do little there but rescue buckets, flower pots and even a water-butt which had all been shifted from their rightful homes.

It was not cold, but I lit a fire for comfort. Tibby and I both needed it.

As soon as possible, I intended to get over to Fairacre to see my school and the school house. I was very much worried by Mr Lamb's message. But at least the children should be safe. I dreaded to think what could have befallen them if the hurricane had arrived earlier.

Meanwhile, I rang friends and neighbours who all had hair-raising tales to tell, and then finally, Amy, at Bent.

To my surprise it was James who answered, and he sounded breathless.

'I thought it was the hospital,' he said.

'The hospital?'

'Amy's there. I thought there might be news of her.'

My heart sank. The sight of that battered car and the stretcher being put into the ambulance came back to me with devastating clarity.

'Tell me what's happened?' I quavered. I sat down. Somehow my legs had suddenly ceased to support me.

'She went into Caxley just before things really got too fierce, to take a load of clothes to the Red Cross shop. She packed the car in that side road, and struggled round with her parcel, but by that time things were getting pretty hairy.'

'So she wasn't in the car when whatever it is happened?'

The memory of yesterday's smashed car began to fade slightly, but what horrors would take its place?

'Tiles were sliding off roofs, and poor dear Amy caught one on the side of the head. Laid her out, of course, but the Red Cross ladies saw it happen and carried her into the shop, and did some much needed first-aid. They managed to get her to hospital, still unconscious, and bleeding like a stuck pig.'

'And how serious is it?'

'Not sure yet. They've stitched her ear on again.'

My inside, never really up to this sort of thing as a squeamish woman, gave a disconcerting somersault.

'But you haven't seen her yet?'

'I'm just off now, as a matter of fact. She came round last night, but our lane's blocked and we've a couple of trees down in front of the garage. I'm going to walk across the fields to the main road, and a friend there says he'll take me into Caxley. They've managed to clear the main road evidently, which is a stout effort, but I can't see how we're going to get Amy home until things are easier for travelling.'

'Well, I won't hold you up,' I said. 'My love as always to poor Amy, and I'll see her as soon as possible.'

'I'll keep you posted,' promised James. 'Now I must get into my wellingtons.'

This news, of course, haunted me for the rest of the day. Would pretty Amy be scarred? That she would face any affliction with enormous courage, I was well aware, but I hoped that nothing permanent would remain. A head wound, I gathered, could have some nasty consequences.

The wind had now died down, and across the south of England the gigantic task of clearing up was beginning. The highways' staff had worked heroically, and a great many of the main roads were clear enough to allow at least one-line traffic to proceed. There was still no electricity in our immediate area, but mercifully the telephones still seemed to be in order. I did my best to pull the worst of the debris in my garden to one side, and also walked among the rubble to see how the village of Beech Green had fared.

It was a sorry sight. Mr Annett's school roof had a dozen or so tiles gone, and someone's chicken house had been blown into the playground. The churchyard, where dear Dolly was buried, was almost covered with two fallen trees and scattered leaves and branches. The church itself, apart from a smashed window, appeared unscathed.

People were in a state of shock, scarcely able to believe what had happened in the space of twenty-four hours. But luckily there seemed to have been no casualties. George Annett had sent his pupils home early, as I had done, and the damage to his school had occurred during the night.

Tibby and I relied on the Primus stove for our cooking, and the open fire for warmth and comfort. But reading was impossible, I found, and I wondered yet again how people managed to read and write by candlelight years ago. Even my ancient Aladdin lamp scarcely threw enough light for reading, and I found myself listening to my battery-run radio for hours on end, before going early to bed. It was clear that our part of the country had suffered severely.

I rang the hospital the next morning to be told that Amy was 'as well as could be expected and quite comfortable'. (With an ear newly sewn on?) She was due to go home during the day, so obviously their lane at Bent was now passable.

To my relief, I found out too that it was now possible to get along our own road from Beech Green to Fairacre, but beyond that it was still blocked.

I got out the car and set off. The devastation on each side of the road was shocking. Fully-grown trees, mainly the beeches, had been plucked from the ground and lay with their roots, in great circles of chalk, pointing upward and outward. Where they had fallen they had brought other trees crashing down, and the work of restoring these woods to normality could not be imagined. Most of the fallen timber would have to remain where it was.

The thatch had been badly ripped away on a pair of cottages, and a corn stack had collapsed and the bales scattered for yards around. Garden fences seemed to have suffered most, for almost all lay flat on the ground. The insurance firms would be busy, I reflected. Thank goodness my new home was covered.

I drove into my old driveway, stopped the car and sat for a moment surveying the wreckage. One of the tall fir trees behind the house had fallen right across the roof and there was no sign of the substantial chimney. A gaping hole midway across the ridge of the roof, however, gave evidence that the missing chimney was somewhere inside the house.

The school building appeared to be only slightly damaged. Again, as in Beech Green school's case, a few tiles lay shattered in the playground, and I could see that the glass of the skylight was broken. But the lavatories across the playground were in a bad way. The doors had been ripped off and one or two of the china lavatory bowls were smashed.

I got out of the car to examine things more closely, and was surprised to see Bob Willet and two other young men emerge from the back door of the school house.

'Ah, I reckoned you'd be along soon,' said Bob. 'Fair old bluster, weren't it? You want to see inside? I've got the key here, but you'll have to watch your step. One of the stairs is busted.'

I followed him inside, and up the old familiar staircase. There was a large puddle on the landing, and my bedroom door leant at a drunken angle.

I stopped in the doorway and surveyed the chaos. The chimney, which indoors looked enormous, had crashed on to my bed, splintering it and the chair by it into matchwood. Soot had tumbled and blown everywhere, and the new paintwork was ruined. Rain had added to the damage, and my heart sank at the sight.

It was only when Bob Willet spoke again, that I realized how lucky I was to be alive.

'Good thing you moved to Beech Green,' he said. He nodded towards the crushed bed and its rags of filthy bedclothes. 'You wouldn't have stood much chance under that lot.'

I agreed, much shaken.

Bob studied me closely.

'We was just going back home for a cup of coffee. Alice has kept the Rayburn in all this time. Come and join us.'

I accompanied him thankfully.

15   Harvest and Havoc

I WENT to see how Mrs Pringle had fared, and found that lady had taken the onslaught of the elements as a personal affront.

'Washing blown clean off the line,' she told me. 'Mrs-Next-Door picked up some of it, but I'm still missing two pillow slips.'

She paused, and dropped her voice to a confidential whisper. 'But the worst of it is I've lost a pair of bloomers. Good winter ones, too, and I don't care to think of 'em being picked up by *some man*.'

'I don't suppose it would worry him,' I said cheerfully.

Mrs Pringle bridled. 'It's not his feelings I'm bothered about, it's mine. What do I say to him if a *man* brings them back?'

'Just thank him and leave it at that,' I said, rising to go.

Something looked different about her garden, I thought, looking through the kitchen window.

'Fred's workshop's gorn,' she said, following my gaze. 'Proper fussed he is. We found some bits of it round the back of Mr Roberts's barn. It was insured, but all his craftwork's gorn.'

I felt very sorry for Fred Pringle. The little shed at the end of the garden was really his haven from his wife. In it he found pleasure in constructing models made with matchsticks. The smell of glue, cardboard and thick paper always clung about Fred Pringle. His thick fingers had made hundreds of objects over the years, ranging from a model of St Patrick's church to innumerable calendars which always hung fire at the local bazaars, as not everyone wants a Swiss chalet, rather askew, or a rustic bridge, slightly uphill, adorning their walls for a whole year. Nevertheless, Fred continued to turn out dozens of articles, which might appear useless to others, but which provided hen-pecked Fred with pleasure and privacy. Now all that had gone, blown away by that mighty rushing wind which had shattered so many homes as well as hopes.

'I hear as you might have been killed in your bed,' said Mrs Pringle conversationally, as we went to the door. 'Bob Willet said as it was all struck to kindling wood.' She spoke with relish.

'That's so,' I replied. 'The chimney fell through the roof.'

'I never did hold with that bed being where it was,' continued the lady primly. 'For one thing, anyone could see you if they'd a mind, being in full view of the window.'

'Well, it only overlooked the playground,' I pointed out. 'By the time the children arrived I was downstairs anyway.'

'There's such a thing as Peeping Toms,' said she darkly.

Her manner changed as she opened the door. 'Ah well! That's the end of that worry, isn't it?'

For once she sounded almost cheerful, and I made my way to the gate.

News of the devastation became more general as roads were cleared slowly, and people started to put things to rights.

We seemed to have caught the severest onslaught, unlike the earlier hurricane which had done most damage in the counties south of us. Now we were all in need of builders, electricians and plumbers, as well as haulage contractors, timber merchants and any company, in fact, which owned heavy shifting machinery.

The great landed estate which surrounded and included

the village of Springbourne, and was renowned for its splendid collection of trees, had lost eight hundred of them in the two days of violent weather. The ancient cedar tree in Fairacre's vicarage garden, under which so many tea parties, bazaar functions and the like had taken place, was now stretched across the lawns and flowerbeds. Nearby the vicar's greenhouse lay in ruins, and his newly-potted geranium and fuchsia cuttings lay among the shattered glass.

There were horrific tales of people trapped in their homes, cattle and sheep mutilated by flying debris, or stampeding panic-stricken into distant parts.

But, it seemed, the travellers had the worst of it. Cars had been crushed by falling timber, roads blocked, and electricity cables and telephone wires brought down. It was impossible, as I knew from my own short but nerve-racking journey home from school, to get to one's destination directly, and a good many traffic accidents had occurred through frightened drivers trying to get through impossibly narrow lanes, or even cart tracks, in order to get home.

Abandoned cars were everywhere, adding to the chaos, and it was amazing that there were so few outright fatalities. As it was, the casualty departments of the local hospitals had worked overtime, patching up the stream of people with cuts, bruises, broken limbs and head wounds.

That afternoon I took out my car, and drove through the wrecked countryside to see Amy who was now on her way to recovery in her own home.

I found her sitting on the sofa wearing a very fetching white turban of bandages. It was at a rather rakish angle and, as usual, she looked quite stunning, although rather paler than usual.

We greeted each other affectionately, and she assured me that she was practically back to normal.

'And there won't be much of a scar,' she added. 'I've been experimenting with my hair style, and I can cover the one by my hair-line, and the ear bit will be invisible any way.'

I asked, somewhat tentatively, if it had healed properly.

She began to laugh. 'I don't intend to harrow you by displaying my wounds like some Indian beggar. I expect James gave you some horrific description which upset you for hours. I know you so well.'

'I was a bit shattered to hear you had had your ear sewn on again,' I admitted.

'Too bad of James to put it like that,' she said severely. 'He knows what a coward you are. Actually, it was really not much more than a nick at the top, and only needed four or five stitches. A very neat little job someone did, and I'm eternally grateful.'

We spent a pleasant hour or so comparing notes on our respective horror stories, and she was suitably impressed by my tale of the roof damage at Fairacre school house.

'Does this mean that it will be a total loss? Will it be worth repairing?'

'Oh, I should think so. I know Wayne Richards has been asked to come and look at the job, though when that will be, heaven alone knows. He's up to his eyes in emergency jobs, but he's promised to make good the lavatories so that school can open again. I imagine he'll inspect the school house then.'

'Heavens, you were lucky!'

'I know it. I have a lot to thank dear Dolly for, and now she has virtually saved my life. The thing that really irks me is the thought of all that wasted time and energy in decorating upstairs earlier this year.'

I told her about Eve and Horace's interest in the little house, and she looked thoughtful.

'Why don't they try for one of those new ones if they really want to live in Fairacre?'

'Too expensive for them. And too large too, I expect. After all, they have no family.'

'Well, they could soon put that right if they got a move on,' said Amy. 'Mind you, they must be fortyish, so there isn't a lot of time to spare. These professional women do run it a bit fine these days when it comes to babies.'

'Two incomes no kids,' I said quoting Bob Willet.

Amy sighed. 'I wish I'd had the sort of inside that coped with a nice string of babies, but there you are. So *unfair*, isn't it?'

'We live in an unfair world,' I told her. 'Shall I make us a cup of tea to cheer us up?'

'A splendid idea,' said Amy.

It was ten days before Fairacre School could open again, and I spent the time trying to tidy my own house and garden at Beech Green, and visiting the school to see how the repairs were getting on.

Wayne Richards had done a mammoth job on the school

itself, coping with roof tiles, the smashed skylight and damage to the porch. But the biggest job was putting the lavatories to rights, and work was held up by trying to get new lavatory pans which appeared to be in short supply.

'Lord knows why,' said Wayne, sounding exasperated. 'I can't believe the gale smashed many lavatory pans. It's my belief the plumbers at Caxley are finding it a fine excuse for shilly-shallying.'

'We can't start school until they are there,' I pointed out.

'Don't you worry. You'll get the first I can lay my hands on, and that's a promise.'

His assessment of the damage to the school house roof was less bad than we had imagined, much to the vicar's and the other governors' relief. Horrific though the damage looked, the rafters could be replaced, and a rather less massive chimney erected above the repaired roof. The decorating would have to be done all over again, but I was told that it would not involve me in any more expense, for which I was relieved.

The repairs would take some time, but as there was no one living there now, it was not considered such an emergency job as so many others. A stout tarpaulin was fixed over my poor little home for so many years, and it had to wait its turn in the repair queue.

'It will definitely be put on the market then,' the vicar told me. 'And as for the school –' His voice died away.

'That's going on, full steam ahead,' I told him, with a conviction I did not wholly feel.

'Of course,' he agreed, rallying slightly. 'Why, of course!'

We had hardly got back into school routine, it seemed to me, when half-term was upon us.

Of course, I had to hear the children's accounts of the great tempest, some so hair-raising that I was forced to conclude that many of my flock had more imagination than I had realized.

However, as a resourceful teacher, I made good use of all this stimulating material; and essays, illustrations and even a long poem had 'The Storm' as subject matter. The fact that one of Mr Roberts's cows had been lifted from its field and deposited in John Todd's bedroom, and that one of the young Coggs twins had seen God sitting on a cloud directing the whirlwind had to be put in perspective, but Ernest's account of finding washing from someone's line entangled on the hedge near his garden sounded plausible. The fact that a pair of lady's bloomers was among these items made me uneasily aware that they could have been Mrs Pringle's.

Ernest's house certainly lay in the path of any wind blowing from the Pringle domain, but I thought it prudent to keep my suspicions to myself.

Luckily, no one had been hurt, although the cat from 'The Beetle and Wedge' had vanished, and Patrick reckoned it was 'stone-dead under that barn door as blew off what Mr Roberts should have lifted, but never done it'.

I was about to unravel this sentence when arguments arose around the class giving various heated conjectures about the fate of the unfortunate cat, and I let the grammar lesson go. There is a limit to a teacher's endurance.

The day before we broke up for half-term, we went over to the church to take part in dressing it ready for Harvest Festival. This is an annual pleasure, and we share the work with experienced ladies from the floral society, and such stalwarts as Mrs Partridge and Mrs Mawne who do their best to keep everyone in order.

The more ambitious floral ladies are given to making

arrangements with little tickets on them saying such things as: 'The Earth's Bounty' or 'From a Thankful Heart'. These are usually set out in rustic baskets with a lot of cornstalks and highly-polished apples and, although to the layman's eye they look much of a muchness, there is a great deal of unladylike jostling for major positions in the church.

Fortunately, the school children know their place, and traditionally keep to such modest decorating as a row of carrots and turnips along one window sill, a tasteful display of upended marrows round the base of the lectern, and a giant pumpkin which is allowed pride of place in the church porch when the ladies have lined the stone bench there with moss and finished adorning it with such sophisticated articles as wreaths of bryony, sprays of blackberries, and corn dollies.

The vicar was doing his duty by commending all the work. I caught him looking doubtfully at one of the floral ladies' efforts which consisted of a basin of flour, some wheat ears and some sprays of oats, and which bore the label 'Our Daily Bread'.

'My grandpa,' said one of the children, grandson of a local baker, 'could have given you a *real loaf* to put there.'

The vicar looked as though he heartily agreed with this sensible suggestion, but as the floral lady was within earshot he contented himself with a smile, and a kindly pat on the boy's head.

The church had got off lightly in the storm, although one of the stained-glass windows had been damaged. It had been put up about 1860 in honour of some local worthy, and I had never liked it. The colours reminded me of those in the paint-box of my childhood, Crimson Lake, Prussian Blue and Gamboge. Furthermore, it made that side of the church very dark, and I had often thought how much more suitable a clear window would have been.

'I suppose we shall have to repair it,' said the vicar sadly, 'but they are having difficulty in matching the glass.'

'Perhaps it could be replaced by a plain glass window,' I said daringly.

'That would be a *very* nice idea,' said the vicar beaming, 'but it might offend the family.'

'Are there any about?'

'A step-grandson, I believe, in Papua, New Guinea.'

'Is he likely to worry?'

The vicar sighed. 'I'm afraid we can't risk it. We must restore this one as best we can.'

He gave me a conspiratorial smile, and I went to inspect the children's artistic endeavours.

On Sunday the church looked magnificent. All the harvest decorations glowed against the ancient stone of the walls. The brass lectern shone with extra-zealous rubbing, and the silver on the altar shone in a ray of sunlight from the south windows.

Even more heartening was the size of the congregation. We country folk enjoy Harvest Festivals. For us it is the culmination of the year, when we can see, smell, touch and taste the fruits of the twelve months' labour. It is significant that St Patrick's church is even fuller for this festival than at Easter or Christmas. The hymns too are well known and loved, and we sing them lustily, our eyes on the marrows and apples from cottage gardens, and the grapes and peaches from the greenhouses of local wealthy families.

We all joined robustly in singing our favourite harvest hymn:

> We plough the fields and scatter
> The good seed on the land,
> But it is fed and wor-hor-tered
> By God's almighty hand.

Looking around the congregation it occurred to me that there were probably only half a dozen or so among us who had really ploughed a field. There might be rather more who had scattered seeds, if only a few sprinklings of hardy annuals in the flower border, or even some mustard and cress on a wet piece of flannel in a saucer.

No matter, we enjoyed our singing, although when I heard Mr Roberts behind me booming out the line, 'The winds and waves obey Him', I wondered if he questioned the obedience of the elements after all we had suffered so recently.

The vicar gave his usual homely address about being thankful for the fruits of the earth, and the satisfaction of seeing the results of our labours, which would be going to the local hospital in the next few days, and we all streamed out into the autumn sunshine after the closing hymn and blessing, mightily content.

It was one of those autumn days, crisp and clear, when the sky has a pellucid quality which is rarely seen in other seasons. The hedge maple had turned a brilliant yellow and the beech trees above the hedges were a deeper gold. A few hardy summer wild flowers such as knapweed, yarrow, and cranesbill still starred the verges and banks, brave survivors of summer heat and the ferocity of the recent storm.

Reminders of it still littered the countryside, and no doubt would continue to do so for many months to come. Some of the copses were criss-crossed with fallen trees and would be impossible to clear. Fine avenues of beeches and lime trees showed sad gaps where full-grown trees had toppled like nine-pins, and loved landmarks, like the vicar's ancient cedar tree, were now no more.

But despite the wreckage, the autumn scene on this vivid Sunday was beautiful. It gave one comfort and hope

to see the modest flowers, the blazing autumn woods, and
to hear the lark singing above the immemorial downs.

There may be many changes in Fairacre, I thought, but
the seasons come round in their appointed time, steadfast
and heartening to us all.

It so happened that it was one of the few bright days we
had that autumn.

November wound along in its gloomy way, and the
tortoise stoves at the school were certainly needed to keep
out the chilly dampness.

In no time at all, it seemed, Christmas loomed. Mrs
Richards insisted on coaching her class in the mid-European
dances which she so enjoyed. The sound of hand-clapping
and foot-stamping, never entirely co-ordinated, nearly
drove me mad, but I managed to refrain from outright com-
plaint.

'Makes a lot of *dust*,' said Mrs Pringle gloomily, 'all that
banging about on them floorboards. They're not up to it
after a hundred years. Besides, there's some as says there's
a well under that room.'

'A *well?* There can't be!'

Mrs Pringle drew in two of her chins, folded her arms
and looked portentious.

'Bob Willet's uncle, dead now of the quinsy, always
maintained the school had a well. This 'ere room of yours
was the only schoolroom then, and the children used to get
their water from the well just next door. When they built
on the infants', they covered it up.'

'But that's nonsense,' I protested. 'Both rooms were
built at the same time, and in any case, why cover up the
well if it was in use? There was plenty of space to build an
adjoining room elsewhere.'

'I'm simply telling you what Bob Willet's old uncle said,

and a more truthful God-fearing man you couldn't wish to meet in a day's march. Went to chapel twice on Sundays regular, and played in the Salvation Army band in Caxley if they was a cornet player short.'

'I'm not doubting his morals,' I replied, 'but I think he was mistaken, that's all. I just can't believe it.'

'Of course, if you're calling me a *liar* –' began Mrs Pringle, getting very red in the face.

'Don't be silly –' I broke in. 'It's not you I'm criticizing, it's just so obvious that this present building was all done at the same time. You can see that by the foundations and footings, and if there had been a well, then it would have been filled in, that is if they had been so stupid as to want to build over it.'

Mrs Pringle began to limp heavily about the room giving sharp little slaps at the partition with her duster. I let her get on with it. Sometimes she sees fit to change the subject when she is getting the worst of it.

Today was a case in point.

'Our Minnie,' she said, in a slightly less belligerent tone, 'left Ern last week.'

'Good heavens! For good? How will she manage with all those children?'

'That's her headache, not mine,' said my old adversary, sinking heavily on to a front desk. 'She had a bit of a turn-up with him last week over some papers the kids had crayoned on. Seems it was something about the poll tax he had to answer. He took his belt to Basil, and Minnie flew at him.'

'Oh dear! What happened then?'

'Well, you know she's never really broke with that Bert of hers, and she caught the next bus to Caxley to say she'd settle in with him, as he's always been so loving and that.'

'What about Basil and the younger ones?'

'She took 'em too, and a bit of money Ern always puts by regular for the electric and that, in a tobacco tin. Bert was out when she got there, and when he got back about nine he wasn't best pleased to see that lot on his doorstep.'

I could understand it.

'He took 'em in overnight, but told Minnie she couldn't stop with him. They had a blazing row, I gather, and our Minnie said she dursn't go back to Ern because of nicking the money, as well as not really liking the fellow much.'

'But she *married* him!' I interrupted.

'Well, yes, I suppose she did, but girls do funny things and then live to regret it. Our Minnie's never been what you'd call *steady*.'

That I could thoroughly endorse, but held my tongue.

'So there she was,' continued Mrs Pringle, 'on the streets of Caxley with them three kids next morning when Bert went off to work. At her wits' end she was.'

And that would not take long was my private comment, but I let Mrs Pringle, now in her stride, continue with the saga.

'Give Bert his due, he did let them have breakfast there, egg and bacon too, before he locked the door on 'em all, and left them to fend for themselves.'

'So she's back home again?' I said, one eye on the school clock, and one ear on a lot of shouting in the playground. I should have to stop this enthralling tale very soon.

'She went to the police,' said Mrs Pringle, seeing through my endeavours to hurry up the narrative. 'They was uncommon nice for policemen, and took her back to Springbourne, and had a word with Ern before he set off for work. He's got a few odd jobs to do these days. Not much, mind you, but it all helps.'

'What did the police say?'

'That,' said Mrs Pringle primly, 'is not for me to say.

But I *gather*, only *gather*, mark you, that they pointed out that Minnie was his wife, and that they didn't want to have to come out again to sort out any domestic disputes, and the courts had quite enough trouble as it was, so he'd better let bygones be bygones. And with that they left.'

'So all's well?'

'Not really. As I say, she's liable to fly off the handle any time as far as I can make out, which is why I told you.'

'Oh?'

'It's quite on the cards that our Minnie will be coming to ask you for a job at your house, and I think you should be warned.'

'Thank you,' I said, my heart sinking. 'It was good of you to warn me.'

'Of course, whether you believe what I've told you, or not, is your affair, Miss Read. I've been called a liar once this morning, so I'll say no more.'

Before I could get my breath she made for the lobby – and there was no hint of a limp on this occasion.

16   Gloomy Days

THE end of the Christmas term is always hectic. As well as our Christmas concert, it is traditional to invite parents and friends to tea in the schoolroom, and the children enjoy acting as hosts and hostesses on this occasion.

Alice Willet made her usual enormous Christmas cake, presents were distributed from the Christmas tree, carols sung, and we all streamed home after the vicar's customary blessing.

To say that I was tired, as I went back to the haven of my new home, is an understatement. Advancing age, I told myself, as I went up to bed before nine o'clock.

But, on comparing notes with others during the welcome holiday, I found that this exhaustion was general, and we started to blame the aftermath of the recent hurricane as well as the short dark days, for our lassitude. 'Delayed shock', we told each other, and felt all the better for finding a solution, even if it were a wrong one, for our inertia.

I spent a few days with my cousin Ruth, who could not travel to Beech Green as her car was laid up, leaving Tibby in the care of Mrs John. I looked out some redundant clothing for a future jumble sale, made marmalade, re-read some of Trollope's Barchester novels, and had one or two modest tea parties.

During this gently recuperative period Amy came over from Bent. She had quickly recovered from her injuries, and had no scars which were visible, but she too looked tired.

'I'm a bit worried about James,' she said, when I inquired after her health. 'Mind you, he's often rather low after Christmas. I think he suddenly realizes he's spent too much money.'

'Well, that goes for all of us, doesn't it?'

'He's so idiotically generous. He always buys me a piece of jewellery, for one thing, and I dread to think what this year's wrist watch cost. And the office people always get fantastic presents as well as their usual bonus.'

'And what news of Brian?'

'That's funny. We invited him for Christmas Day, but he rang to say he couldn't manage it. No reason given. James seemed very upset, and was quite sharp with me. Had I written a *really welcoming* letter? Could I have offended him in some way? And then a lot of guff about how sensitive Brian was, and how humiliated he felt about his broken marriage, and so on. Really, at times I could *slap* James, he's so childish.'

'We're not allowed to slap children these days,' I observed, 'although John Todd had a fourpenny one from me on the last day of term, when I found him picking at the icing on the Christmas cake.'

'I should have given him an eightpenny one,' said Amy approvingly.

We turned to other topics.

'I saw Horace and Eve over Christmas, and they were devastated to hear about the school house. Any news?'

'Not yet. It is still sheltering beneath its tarpaulin, and a dreadful noise that makes too when the wind gets round the south-west. It flaps and rumbles. Quite alarming, I think, but Wayne Richards assures me it is as safe as houses – which seems an unfortunate comparison in the circumstances.'

'Any more Fairacre excitements?'

'Jane Winter is expecting, and not too pleased about it. Sir Barnabas has begged Miriam to return to the office while Jane's away, but Miriam's already in the throes of getting her new agency going, so she has had to refuse.'

'And my friend Mrs Pringle?'

'Flourishing like a green bay tree,' I told her, and added the news of Minnie Pringle's domestic troubles for good measure.

'Has Minnie asked for a job here yet?'

'Fingers crossed,' I replied, '*no*!' And if she does my heart will be as flint.'

'What a tough old woman you are!' laughed Amy. 'When you are dead and gone you will be remembered as the Stony-hearted Spinster of Fairacre.'

'I may not be remembered at all,' I pointed out.

Amy looked serious. 'Do you ever think about such things? About dying, and so on?'

'Frequently. Particularly since Dolly went. She's one of those that will be remembered, that's for sure.'

'I suppose so. It's one of the things that being childless upsets me. After all, you live on in your children, really. And the work you leave behind, I suppose. It must be a great comfort to artists and furniture-makers and so on to know that people will enjoy their work and remember them for years. I shall leave no children, and mighty little worth remembering in the way of work.'

'Cheer up, Amy,' I rallied her. 'You'll leave lots of happy memories among your friends. Me, for one!'

'Thanks,' said Amy. 'I presume that you imagine I shall pop off before you. I tell you here and now that my relatives, on both sides, totter on to their nineties, and my Uncle Benjamin stuck it out to a hundred and one and got his telegram from the Queen.'

'Good for him. And for you, of course.'

'Tell you what, though,' continued Amy, 'we all seem to go deaf after ninety.'

'Never mind. That's a long way ahead, and they do the most marvellous things with hearing aids these days. Do you think a cup of coffee would keep you going?'

'Definitely,' said Amy.

Term began with grey skies and a wicked wind from the east. Even Mrs Pringle agreed that the tortoise stoves were needed, and a great comfort they were as the draughts from the skylight and under the ancient doors whistled around the schoolroom.

Mrs Richards had a very heavy cold, and was accompanied everywhere with a box of tissues. I had earache, no doubt from the malevolent skylight above my head, and most of the children seemed to have coughs or colds or both.

'January,' I told Mrs Richards at playtime, 'should be done away with. Christmas well behind us, and only gloomy months ahead.'

'I agree,' she said, 'but Bob Willet says it will get warmer once the snow comes.'

'Is that his forecast?'

'That's right. He told me we'll get a fall before the week's out.'

'Well, I hope he's wrong this time,' I replied.

But of course he was not.

By Friday afternoon the first flakes began to fall, much to the delight of the children who were up and down like jacks-in-boxes to catch a glimpse of the weather through the high windows.

By playtime the flakes were whirling fast, and it was impossible to see the school house across the playground, so thickly were the snowflakes descending. The coke pile was covered in a mantle of white. The branches of the trees were beginning to sag with their burden, and the fence tops and hedges looked as though they had been decorated with sugar icing.

I closed school early and went into the lobby to see that each child was well wrapped up before going out into the elements. Most of them were well protected in anoraks and woolly scarves, but as always the Coggs children were poorly shod and had no gloves to protect their hands.

'I'll run you home,' I said, surveying their shabby shoes which would soak up snow within three minutes. They exchanged happy smiles as I saw off the others, and then locked up.

As I packed them into the car, I looked up at my old home. The tarpaulin was invisible below its covering of snow. The downstairs windows were plastered with the enshrouding whiteness, and the scene was enough to wring the heart. Never had I seen the little house looking so forlorn and neglected. Could it ever be repaired and made into a home again, I wondered?

My journey home, after dropping the Coggs children was uneventful, although the snow was still falling heavily. One thing, I told myself, tomorrow was blessed Saturday, and there would be no need to face an early journey to school.

I set about my usual preparations for bad weather while the light remained, bringing in extra coal and logs, looking out candles and my trusty Primus stove, in case we had a power cut. I left a spade in the porch in case I had to dig my way out the next morning, and I went early to bed.

It was good to get between the sheets, nicely warmed with a hot bottle, and the fact that the wind had started to howl round the cottage only emphasized the snugness of my bedroom beneath the thatched roof.

Let the elements rage, I thought drowsily, as I nestled deeper beneath the bedclothes!

I ought not to have been so complacent. When morning light came, I was appalled at the amount of snow which surrounded my home, and stretched in billowing waves and whorls of whiteness, as far as the eye could see.

The wind had whipped the snow into enormous drifts. Hedges had disappeared. Garden walls and gates were engulfed, and against some of the nearby houses the snow was so deep that it was within a few feet of the upstairs windows in places. There must have been a fearsome blizzard during the night, and I hastened downstairs to see how my house had fared.

I was fortunate in that the wind had piled the snow at the side of my home, and with the help of the spade I could clear a way out of both front and back doors, although I doubted if I should ever be able to dig a path to my gate.

An eerie light flooded the house, partly reflected from the snow, and partly from those windows which were plastered with it and filtered the morning light.

I soon had my kettle on, and was thankful that the electricity had not failed. But I was perplexed that Tibby had not appeared. Surely that comfort-loving animal had not ventured out during the night?

The weather men gave gloomy forecasts of more snow to come although the northern half of the kingdom would come off worst, evidently. As it was, I found my own attempts at snow-clearing later that morning were quite exhausting enough.

I remembered Dolly telling me about a very old man she had known as a child at Beech Green. He was the grandfather of her close friend Emily Davis, and had been caught in the great blizzard of 1881. By the time he was discovered, many hours later, he was suffering from severe frost-bite and lost some fingers. Ever afterwards, Dolly told me, he wore a black leather glove on the maimed hand, and it was this that fascinated her. I only hoped that we were not in for the same length of horrific conditions as that memorable winter.

It was good to see the snow plough chugging along during the morning. There was something to be said for mechanized transport, I thought, waving to the men as they passed by slowly. In 1881, even the stout shire horses had to remain in their stables while the weather was at its worst. Today, a poor benighted traveller trapped in the snow, as Emily's grandfather had been so long ago, would be rescued by a helicopter, and whisked into hospital. Change, I thought, was often deplored. In these conditions it was welcome.

By mid-morning, there was still no sign of Tibby and I began to get alarmed. There were no tell-tale footprints around the house, but then they would soon have been obliterated in last night's conditions.

I rang the Annetts and also Mrs John in the hope that they had seen him, but there was no help there. I called until I was hoarse, hoping to hear an answering mew from some over-looked shelter, but nothing happened. I had gloomy visions of the poor animal entombed beneath the blanket of snow like John Ridd's sheep in *Lorna Doone*. How long could a cat survive without food in such a situation? One thing, Tibby had plenty of surplus fat to live on, as Bob Willet was fond of pointing out, but would the cold kill him?

I began to get more and more agitated as the hours passed, and remembered all the captivating ways of my truant, and how much his companionship meant to me. By the time early evening began to cast its shadows, I was near despair. At that moment, the lights began to flicker ominously, and I decided that it would be as well to delve into the recesses of the cupboard under the stairs to find the ancient Aladdin lamp stored there.

I undid the door, and bent double to locate the lamp in the gloom. A lazy chirruping sound met me, and Tibby emerged sleepily and greeted me with much affection. Relief overcame my initial irritation with the maddening animal. Why had there been no response to my anguished cries? Why, last night of all nights, had he decided to sleep in that cupboard? I suppose I must have left the door ajar on my first visit there for candles, and then automatically shut it in passing later on. In any case, it was good to see my old friend, and a double portion of Pussi-luv vanished in a twinkling.

Snow fell again that night, and the paths so exhaustingly cleared were white again. The roads from most of the villages into Caxley were partially open, but around Fair-acre itself, I gathered, the drifts were still deep. It looked as though, yet again, my school would have to remain closed.

I rang the office first thing on Monday morning to get an overall picture. It was not very encouraging.

'All schools closed for the next three days,' I was told. 'The school buses and the dinner vans are going to have great difficulty in getting around. Some can't even get out of the depot yet. We'll be in touch on Wednesday, and simply hope that the thaw will have come by then.'

I talked to Mr Lamb and the vicar on the telephone, and they assured me that everyone possible would be told the position.

Gerald Partridge sounded unusually despondent. Snow had seeped into his beloved church and ruined a pile of new hymn books. Even worse, the organ was found to be thoroughly damp from some hitherto unsuspected leak from the roof, and repairs to it could cost a fortune.

'And what about the school and the school house?' I asked him, hoping to deflect him from his own worries.

'I'm afraid I haven't been into the school. Bob Willet has been unable to get up to it yet, there is such a great snow drift in the lane, but I struggled out with Honey to just behind your old home and it looks none the worse for the snow. The tarpaulin has stood up wonderfully against the weather.'

I said I was relieved to hear it.

'Incidentally,' he continued, 'the diocese has definitely decided to put it on the market as soon as it is habitable again. It should be ready by about Easter, if all goes well.'

'Well, it's a dear little house as I know. It should sell, I think.'

'One wonders. Or will it be the *third* empty house in Fairacre? I hear that the price of those two new ones has dropped again. It is definitely not the time to try and sell one's property.'

'A buyer's market. Isn't that the expression?'

'I believe so. But there seem to be no buyers about. I suppose they can't *buy*, until they have *sold* their own.'

'There are such people as first-time buyers,' I told him, thinking of Horace and Eve. 'Perhaps they'll turn up in time.'

'One can only hope,' agreed the vicar. But he sounded very unhopeful as I rang off.

We were closed for a week. It was a frustrating time for everyone. Two days of the seven we were without electricity, and I found that half a day coping with oil stoves, candles and matches, was quite enough for the small amount of pioneering spirit I possessed, especially as the only source of hot water was a kettle lodged on the Primus stove which took forever, it seemed, to come to the boil.

After that, I was heartily fed up with automatically and vainly switching on in every room I entered, only to be frustrated yet again.

The snow plough had made me thankful for mechanized transport, and now I realized all too clearly how much we took for granted in our all-electric houses. It was probably salutory to be reminded of our dependence on this source of power, but it did nothing to improve our tempers.

I found myself using methods of cooking, lighting and heating which Dolly's mother had used daily in this self-same cottage years before. The open fire had to be kept going with coal and logs, and I left the sitting-room door open at night so that some heat would penetrate into the chilly bedrooms.

The lamps had to be trimmed and filled, and the candles replaced. I even rolled up an old rug to stuff against the bottom of the outside door to keep out the wicked draughts, and wished I had the straw-filled sausage of Victorian times to do the job, as Dolly had described.

When at last the power returned, we were all mightily grateful to those men who had restored it, and we counted our blessings with thankful hearts.

It was quite a relief to return to school.

Bob Willet had done a magnificent job in clearing the playground, and Mrs Pringle gave me a graphic account of the state of her beloved tortoise stoves after a week's neglect.

'They was that damp and mildewy you could've written your name on 'em. And all down one side there was the beginning of rust where the water had run along a beam from that dratted skylight, and dropped down on to my poor stove. We'll have to get another load of blacklead

from the Office, and if they gives you any hanky-panky, Miss Read, just let me speak to them.'

I promised to do that, rather looking forward to such an encounter. Mrs Pringle, in defence of her stoves, is a formidable figure, and I trembled for any of the staff at the Caxley Education Office who questioned her demands. What can they know of blacklead, who only red tape know?

The children were full of tall stories about the snow and the havoc it had caused. Patrick told us that his little brother fell in a drift near Mr Mawne's and they only found him because he was wearing a red bobble hat and the bobble stuck up from the snow.

Ernest then capped this with a long rigmarole about his father's bike which was hidden for days by the front gate. But when John Todd tried to make us believe that he had rescued Mr Roberts's house cow single-handed from a snow drift in a neighbouring field, I thought it was time to put a stop to matters. Imagination is one thing; downright lying is another.

'To your desks,' I ordered briskly. 'We'll have a really stiff mental arithmetic test.'

I was not popular.

17   Minnie Pringle Lends a Hand

W E were all very thankful to tear off JANUARY from our calendars and to look hopefully at FEBRUARY.

The days were now perceptibly longer, and I took my first walk-after-tea of the year, in the light. The catkins were a cheerful sight, fluttering from the bare hedgerows, and the bulbs in the garden were poking through. A clump of early yellow irises were already in flower. I had given the tiny bulbs to Dolly some years earlier, and she had planted them under the shelter of the thatch where they thrived.

The birds were busy, bustling about, full of self-importance as they scurried about their courting.

Life was beginning to look more hopeful after all we had endured from gales, snow and flooding.

The children's coughs and colds faded. At playtime they could get into the playground for exercise and fresh air, and altogether I began to enjoy a period of relaxation and to make plans for a variety of outdoor pursuits in the months ahead.

Alas for my euphoria!

As one might expect, I was about to have my comfortable rug snatched from under my feet, and of course it was inevitable that Mrs Pringle would do the snatching.

She caught me in the lobby as soon as I arrived. I might have guessed from her unusually cheerful face that something was up.

'My doctor,' she began importantly, 'though a poor tool

in many ways, as well you know, Miss Read, says I'm to have a thorough check-up on my leg, and I've got to go to The Caxley for an X-ray.'

'Oh dear! When?'

'Friday. Not till the afternoon, so I can do the washing-up. But he says I may have to lay up for a bit.'

'Well, there it is. I'm glad you told me. Are you in pain?'

The reply was as expected.

'I'm *always* in pain, as well you know. Not that it stops me doing my duty. Never has! My mother used to say to me: "Maud, you are your own worst enemy with that conscience of yours. Can't you ever *spare* yourself?" And I used to say: "No, mother. I'm just made that way. What needs to be done, I must do, cost what it may in time and trouble." And it's the same today.'

'It does you credit,' I said, paying a tribute to this eulogy of self-satisfaction. 'Let's hope the X-ray shows nothing seriously wrong.'

Mrs Pringle limped about rather more heavily than usual while the hospital mills ground their slow way through her data. The results were that she should rest the leg for a fortnight and then have another examination.

'Don't worry,' I said, on hearing the news, 'we can easily manage for two weeks. I believe Alice Willet might sweep up, and Bob has always been helpful about the stoves in an emergency.'

'If you let Bob Willet lay so much as a finger on my stoves,' said Mrs Pringle, puffing up like an outraged turkey, 'I shall give in my notice.'

I have heard this threat so often that I take it in my stride, but I felt sorry for my old adversary in her present afflictions, and simply said that I'd see Bob only *filled* and did not attempt to *polish* her two idols.

Unfortunately, Alice Willet had promised to go and stay

with a sister who herself was just out of hospital, so it looked as though we should have to muddle along on our own.

'Of course, our Minnie could come,' said Mrs Pringle. She sounded doubtful, and with good reason. We both know Minnie's limitations. 'She's not a bad little cleaner – if watched.'

'Oh, I don't think it's as desperate as that,' I replied, wondering if that could not have been expressed more tactfully. 'I'll look around,' I added hastily.

But in the end, when Mrs Pringle had taken to her bed and sofa for the allotted time, it had to be Minnie who came to provide help and havoc in unequal portions to Fairacre School.

During Mrs Pringle's absence, I took to staying on after school to supervise Minnie's activities, and to protect the more vulnerable of the school's properties from her onslaught.

I discovered that she was comparatively safe with such things as desk tops, window sills and the floors. Anything horizontal presented little difficulty, and I felt she was really getting quite proficient with broom and duster. But vertical surfaces seemed to defeat her. She took to sweeping a broom down the partition between the two rooms, bringing down anything pinned thereon such as the children's artwork, pictures cut from magazines and the like.

'Well, look at that!' she cried in amazement, gazing at the fluttering papers on the floor. I helped to pick them up, and stopped her attacking another wall with her broom.

On one occasion, in my temporary absence, she tried her hand at window-cleaning. She had begun an energetic attack with a rather dirty wet rag, well coated with Vim,

and was fast producing a frosted-glass effect when I arrived back.

She was anxious 'to have a good go', as she put it, 'at Auntie's stoves', but knowing what I should have to face on Auntie's return, I was adamant that she should not touch the stoves. In fact, I did my poor best to clean them myself, knowing the withering scorn which I should receive in due course from Mrs Pringle, but at least that was better than risking Minnie's ministrations with, possibly, more Vim, or even metal polish, which would be impossible to get off.

The fact that Minnie was unable to read complicated matters, as the directions for use on the cleaning packets meant nothing to her. Neither could she tell the time, so she relied on me to see her off the premises before I locked up.

Nevertheless, the hour after school which we spent together at our labours, had its compensations, and I grew daily more fascinated by Minnie's account of her love life which was considerably more interesting than my own.

I had not liked to ask about her marital affairs after Mrs Pringle had given me the account of Minnie's flight to Bert in Caxley, and his refusal to let her stay. But Minnie blithely rattled away as she dashed haphazardly about the school-room with her duster.

'Ern was a bit nasty with me for a time,' she admitted. 'I s'pose he's jealous of Bert.' This was said with some satisfaction.

'Naturally,' I responded. 'You married him. He expects you to live with him.'

'Oh, I don't see why!' said Minnie, standing stock still in her surprise. A troubled look replaced her usual mad grin. 'I knew Bert long afore I met Ern. He bought me some lovely flowers when I was up The Caxley having my Salopians done.'

I decided against correcting Salopian to Fallopian, and to ignore the past use of the verb 'to buy' when it should have been the past tense of the verb 'to bring'. I get quite enough of that sort of thing in school hours, and I did not propose to do overtime.

'But Minnie,' I pointed out, concentrating on the moral issue, 'if you made a solemn contract at your marriage you should keep it. You are Ern's wife, after all. You married him because you wanted to, I take it.'

'Oh, no!' said Minnie, smiling at such a naive suggestion. 'I married Ern because he had a council house, and my Mum was that fed up with us under her feet, so that's *really* why.'

I must say, I found this honesty rather refreshing. Plenty of people with greater advantages, both mental and material, than Minnie, marry for the desire for property rather than passion, and who was I to criticize?

'Mind you,' went on Minnie, taking a swipe at the black-board and nearly knocking it from the easel, 'that council house doesn't half take a bit of cleaning. I really like my Mum's better. Life don't always work out right, do it, Miss Read?'

And I agreed.

Now that the weather had returned to normal, the repairs to the school house went on apace.

Wayne Richards enjoyed visiting his two workmen, and also gave a hand himself. The fact that his wife was close at hand, and that he shared our school tea-breaks seemed to please the young man, and we found him good company.

'Take about three weeks,' he told us, standing with his back to us and looking out at the repair work through the schoolroom window. The mug steamed in his hand, and he did not appear to be in any great hurry to leave us. I began to find that, on the mornings he shared our refreshment, it was I who had to shoo him out so that I could get on with my work.

Every now and again the vicar called to note progress, and the children had to be discouraged from purloining pieces of putty, odd bits of wood and roof tile, and curly wood-shavings which the wags among them used as ringlets fixed over their ears. At least it made a change from the coke pile which was their usual illicit means of finding ex-ercise.

There was a good deal of noise, not only from the workmen themselves, but from vans and lorries which drove up to deliver materials or to remove the vast amount of rubble that this comparatively small job seemed to en-gender.

I was glad that I could leave the scene of battle each day to seek the peace of my new home at Beech Green.

I grew fonder of the cottage as the time passed. It was full of memories for me, not only of dear Dolly herself, but of the people she had told me about, who had lived there before. Her parents, Mary and Francis Clare, her sister Ada whose daughter I had met, her friend Emily Davis who had visited this little house all her life, and had ended it under this roof, as Dolly had done later, all seemed to me to have left something intangible behind them: a sense of happiness, simplicity, courage and order. I am the least psychic of women, and am inclined to suspect those who lay claim to extra-sensory experiences, but there is no doubt about the general reaction most people have to the 'feel' of a house.

Some houses are forbidding, cheerless and indefinably hostile. Others seem to welcome the stranger who steps inside. Dolly Clare's was one such house. I felt that I was heir to a great deal of happiness, and I blessed the shades of those who had lived in and loved this little home, and who had now gone on before me.

One morning, Bob Willet accosted me as I arrived at school.

'Time I come up to do a bit of pruning up yours,' he told me.

'Sunday?' I suggested.

'Best not. My old woman's got these funny ideas about working on Sundays. Anyway, we've got some tricky anthem Mr Annett's trying out at morning church. What about Saturday afternoon? Alice is off to Caxley wasting her money on a new rig-out.'

I said that Saturday afternoon would suit me well.

'Gettin' on with the job all right,' he said, nodding towards the school house. 'Wonder when it'll be up for sale? Vicar tells me the diocese copes with all that business.

Should make a bomb, nice little place like that. That is if it sells at all, the way things are.'

'Well, the new houses are still hanging fire, I gather. I don't see as much of Fairacre these days, but I haven't heard of anyone being interested.'

'There were two blokes looking at them the other day. Shouldn't think they were buyers though. No women folk with 'em. More likely council or summat. Got nice suits on, and clean shoes.'

'That sounds hopeful.'

'No telling. Maybe just looking to see there's no squatters got in. They was definitely *officials*.'

'How can you tell *officials*?'

Bob Willet ran a gnarled thumb round his chin. 'Don't know entirely. But there's a *look* about 'em. Sort of *bossy*, if you takes my meaning. The sort as carries a brief case and talks posh.'

'Well, I hope they don't come to live here,' I said. 'They don't sound very Fairacre-ish to me.'

As luck would have it, that Saturday afternoon was fine and mild. Over near Beech Green church the rooks were busy with their untidy nest-building. They cawed and clattered about, twigs in beaks, energetically thrusting each other away from disputed sites. The sun gleamed on their black satin feathers. Every now and again, one would swoop down into the garden to rescue one or two of Bob Willet's pieces of pruning.

'Dratted birds,' he exclaimed. 'Only fit for a pie.'

He looked at me suspiciously. 'D'you feed 'em?'

'Well,' I began guiltily, 'I put out a few things for the little birds. You know, the chaffinches and robins and so on, and sometimes the rooks come down.'

'You'll get rats,' said Bob flatly. '*Rats* not rooks, and I bet you don't know how to cope with *them*.'

'I should ask your advice,' I said, at an attempt to mollify him. 'In any case, I've probably got rats already. You can't live in the country and imagine you are free from all unpleasantness. I've learnt to take the rough with the smooth.'

'Well, if you wants my advice now, it's stop feeding the birds. Not that you'll take it, I'll lay. You women is all the same, stubborn as mules.'

I have heard this before from Bob, so could afford to laugh.

'That young Mrs Winter's another bird-feeder,' he went on. 'You should see her garden! Peanuts hanging up everywhere. Coconut halves, corn all over the grass. 'Tis no wonder their lawn's taking forever to get growing. The birds eat all the seed.'

'How are the Winters? Really settled in now?'

'She's not too pleased about this new baby on the way, but still sticking to her job until she durn well has to stop. My Alice worries a bit about her, but I tell her it's not her affair.'

He straightened up and looked over the rest of the garden.

'I'll make a start on them straggly roses after tea,' he said. 'That is,' he added, 'if there is any tea?'

'There's always tea,' I assured him, hurrying indoors to get it.

That evening I had a telephone call from Horace Umbleditch. He began by apologizing for disturbing me. 'You must be busy,' he added.

'I'm only looking through the telly programmes,' I told him, 'and wondering if I want a discussion on euthanasia, a film about the victims of famine in Africa, the increase of parasites in the human body, or one of those mindless games where you answer a lot of idiotic questions, and the audience goes berserk with delight when you win a dishwasher you don't want.'

'There's a nice Mozart piano concerto on the Third,' said Horace.

'Thanks for telling me. I'll listen to that and get on with my knitting. What can I do for you?'

'The grapevine has it that your house will soon be ready for the market. We're still interested. Do you know any more about it?'

'Not really. I've no doubt the diocese will be putting it into a local agent's hands before long. Why don't you ring Gerald Partridge and tell him that you are interested? No reason why you shouldn't get first chance at bidding for it.'

'D'you think we've a chance?'

'Definitely. Nothing seems to be moving much in the property market, and you're in the happy position of first-time buyers, not waiting about to sell your own before buying another.'

'That's true. There's another reason really. We're expecting our first. A bit late in the day, but better late than never.'

I expressed my great pleasure.

'So you see, it would be nice to have a home of our own before the baby arrives. How do you like the idea of an infant in your old home?'

'It gives me no end of delight,' I assured him. 'Now, do ring the vicar and tell him all. I know he will help you.'

We rang off, and I savoured this delicious piece of news as I pursued my knitting to the accompaniment of Mozart.

I hoped that my friends would one day live in my old house, and dwelt on the many teachers who had lived there before; Mr and Mrs Hope, Mr Wardle who had trained

Dolly Clare for her teaching career, and his wife, Mrs Wardle, who had been such a stern martinet during needlework lessons.

It was, like Dolly's, a welcoming house, and I sincerely hoped that Horace and Eve would be able to live there, and be as happy as I had been for so many years.

The mild early spring weather continued and raised our spirits.

During this halcyon spell I invited the Bakers to tea one Sunday. Miriam's agency was doing well, and her chief problem at the moment, she told me, was to find a first-class secretary for her old boss, Sir Barnabas Hatch, when Jane Winter took time off for motherhood.

'He rings me at least once a day,' she said, 'imploring me to come back. Sometimes I feel sure that Jane is present and it must be most embarrassing for her. I've told him it is quite impossible, time and time again, but dear old Barney can't believe that he won't get his own way if he keeps at it.'

'Is such a job well paid?' I asked. I thought the amount she told me was astronomical, and wondered why I had taken up teaching.

Gerard, busy toasting crumpets by my fire, added his contribution. He was engaged, it seemed, on a script for a television company, about the changes in agriculture since the 1914–18 war, and at present was studying the wages earned by farm labourers at that time.

'I came across a quotation from A. G. Street,' he said, surveying his crumpet and returning it to the heat. 'He reckoned that a man working a fifty-hour week in the 1920s earned about thirty shillings. That's *real* shillings, of course, now worth our fivepence.'

'But surely they lived rent free?'

'Not always. His argument was that a man who could plough, pitch hay, layer hedges and shear sheep was a skilled worker. Many farm labourers, he maintained, were under-rated and under-paid.'

'Things have improved though?'

'Well, the wages have gone up certainly, but now a man is expected to be a mechanic as well, with all this sophisticated farm machinery. There's more risk of accidents too these days. Mind you, I wouldn't mind ploughing a field sitting in a nicely-warmed cabin with my earphones on, but shouldn't offer to plough behind two or three horses, with only a sack over my head and shoulders to keep out the weather.'

'So, on the whole, you think things have improved?'

'Definitely. But I still think A. G. Street was right. Farm workers are skilled men, even more skilled now than in his time, and I should like to see that recognized.'

'Well, they are a rare breed now in Fairacre. The vicar showed me some parish records the other day, and the number of farm workers came to almost eighty, what with carters, hedgers-and-ditchers, ploughmen, wheelwrights, shepherds or simply "Ag. Labourers". Now Mr Roberts only has two men to help him. What a change!'

'Isn't that progress?' demanded Gerard.

'It doesn't help my school numbers,' I said sadly. 'There used to be nearly a hundred children at Fairacre at one time. Now we've only twenty-one.'

'Cheer up,' said Gerard, blowing the flames from his cookery. 'Have a nice crumpet. Well done, too.'

18   Country Matters

I T was quite a pleasure to welcome Mrs Pringle's return to her duties. I am not really quite as slatternly as she is fond of telling me, but even I could see that the school was looking increasingly shabby under Minnie's haphazard care.

She gasped at the sight of the stoves, but I defended my efforts on their behalf.

'Now, come on,' I told her, 'you know they're not too bad. Why, I used nearly half a tin of that blacklead stuff.'

'That's the trouble,' retorted Mrs Pringle. 'You only needs a *touch* of that, and *plenty* of elbow grease, which these 'ere stoves haven't had in my absence, as is plain to see.'

However, she seemed pleased to get back after her enforced idleness, and even agreed that her leg was 'a trifle – only a trifle, mind', better than it had been. Her doctor's treatment, she admitted, grudgingly, 'could have been worse'. High praise indeed from Mrs Pringle!

It was good to get back to our normal routine, and I was glad to leave school at the usual time and not have to supervise Minnie's ministrations.

She had departed with her wages, a box of shortbread as a parting present from me, incoherent thanks on her side, and secret relief on mine. A little of Minnie Pringle goes a long way, and although I am sorry for the girl, I find that taking responsibility for such a hare-brained person is distinctly exhausting.

Amy called one afternoon just after I had arrived home.

Looking very elegant in a grey suit, she deposited a paper bag on the kitchen table.

'I bought some penny buns on the way here,' she said. 'I guessed I'd be in time for tea.'

'I bet they were more than a penny,' I observed.

She ruminated for a moment. 'Come to think of it, I believe they were about half-a-crown each. Can that be right?'

'I shouldn't be surprised. Very welcome, anyway.'

We munched happily, and Amy told me that she had been to lunch with the widow of one of James's directors.

'He died some months ago. Great pity. He was dear, and very generous with his pots of money. He's left a pile of it to that trust for orphans. He was one of the founders actually. James was very cut up when he went, and still misses him.'

I enquired after James.

'Still worrying about that wretched Brian. He doesn't tell me much, but I don't think that man is settling down very well in Bristol, and of course James won't hear a word against him from the people there. Anyone who plays cricket as well as our Brian must be above reproach, James thinks. All rather trying, I find. However, he is taking me to the opera next week for a treat.'

'What are you seeing?'

'That Mozart one about those two silly girls who are so thick they can't recognize their own fiancés.'

'*Cosi Fan Tutte*,' I told her.

'Ah! thanks for reminding me. At least the music should be lovely, and the sets and the costumes pretty. Unless, of course, the producer sees fit to set it in some back alley of an industrial town, with all the characters in dirty jeans and sweat shirts.'

'Keep your fingers crossed,' I advised. 'Have another

penny bun. I seem to recall that there were even *halfpenny* buns when we were young.'

'There were indeed. And how sad that phrase: "When we were young" sounds! Nearly as sad as: "*If only*" which people are always saying. You know: "*If only* I had known he was about to die. *If only* I had been nicer to my mother. *If only* I hadn't married that man." Terribly sad words.'

'For me,' I said, 'the saddest words I know were put into the mouth of Sir Andrew Aguecheek in *Twelfth Night*.'

'But surely he was just a buffoon?'

'Maybe. But when I hear him say: "I was adored once", it breaks me up.'

Amy surveyed me thoughtfully.

'For such a tough old party,' she said at last, 'you are remarkably vulnerable. Now tell me all the Fairacre news.'

My prime piece of news about the sale of my old home, she had already heard from Horace and Eve, and she speculated about this.

'I told them that I thought they should try for one of those new houses while they are about it. After all, with this baby on the way, and possibly another while Eve is young enough, a larger house than your two-bedroom abode would be much more sensible.'

'What did they say?'

'They saw the point, but it's much too expensive for them to contemplate. So I suppose they will go ahead with an offer as soon as they can.'

I told her about Horace's telephone call, and my advice to have a word with the vicar.

We went on to gossip about Jane Winter's approaching confinement and Miriam Baker's new agency.

'And Gerard is writing a novel,' Amy told me.

'He was working on a script about farm labourers' conditions earlier this century. Has he given that up?'

'I'm sure he hasn't. He's just pottering along with the novel at the same time, but he says it's much harder than he imagined. I think he really started it because he's bought a word-processor and he likes to play with it.'

'But he'll have to think what to put in the word-processor, won't he?'

'That's evidently the trouble. He says that he is very conscious of keeping his readers interested, and he quoted Wilkie Collins's advice to Charles Dickens: "Make 'em laugh, make 'em cry, make 'em wait". He thinks he can make 'em laugh and cry, but making 'em wait is the tricky bit. He's dying to take his readers into the secret right from the start, but then would they want to go on reading?'

'Well, I'm glad to hear he is at least considering his readers. Far too many writers these days seem to write purely to relieve their feelings, and pretty dreary the result is. Good luck to Gerard!'

'If that's the time,' said Amy, looking at her watch, 'I must be off, or it will be baked beans on toast for James tonight.'

The vicar called at the school the next morning, accompanied by his yellow Labrador, Honey.

The vicar is always welcomed by the children with appropriate respect and affection. His dog is welcomed with rapture. Honey reciprocates with much bounding about, slavering, panting and licking any part of a child's anatomy that is available to her.

I am fond of dogs, and Honey is particularly adorable, but one cannot deny the fact that she is a destructive element in the classroom. Work ceases. Pockets are turned out, revealing a surprising amount of contraband delicacies such as bubble gum, toffee, biscuits and chocolate. All these secret hoards are readily raided by their owners for

tit-bits for Honey, who never fails to gulp them down raven-
ously.

Meanwhile, the noise is enormous, and the vicar and I stand
helplessly until, after a few minutes, Honey is put on her
lead and my own charges are hounded back to their desks.

'That nice fellow Umbleditch rang me,' says the vicar, when
partial order has been restored. 'It would be a great pleasure to
have him in the parish. I've told him the position. Somehow I
think the builders have been a little sanguine in thinking that
the house will be ready by Easter. What do you think?'

'Builders are always sanguine. I've yet to meet anyone
who has been able to get into their homes at the time the
builders have forecast. Anyway, Easter's only a few weeks
away. I can't see the job being finished by then.'

'My view entirely, and I think Mr Rochester at the office
feels the same. He is in close touch with the powers-that-be
in the diocese, of course.'

'Well, we can't do much about it, can we? I mean, the
builders have the last word.'

The vicar began to look rather worried, and patted
Honey's head distractedly. 'Mr Rochester, I mean, Mr Winchester – '

'Salisbury,' I broke in.

'Yes, yes, of course, *Salisbury*! He was mentioning the
future of the school again.'

'But that was settled, surely?' I said, feeling alarmed. 'We
were to stay open.'

'Of course. We were told that quite unequivocally. He
was simply wondering if you have any news of fresh pupils
arriving in the coming year.'

I thought of Jane Winter's baby and Eve Umbleditch's,
but they would certainly not be ready for school by September next.

'Not a word,' I said, 'but I live in hope.'

'We must all do that,' said Gerald Partridge resignedly, and departed with Honey who, hopeful to the last, gave backward glances at her generous hosts.

In the week before the school broke up for the Easter holidays, we had a visit from Henry Mawne.

Henry and his wife own the most beautiful house in Fairacre, a Queen Anne building much the same age as the vicarage, but even more splendid.

An ornithologist of some note, we are very proud of Mr Mawne, and look out for his nature notes, and sometimes rather erudite letters, in *The Caxley Chronicle*. He is very good at visiting Fairacre School, and we can usually welcome him about once a term to give us a lecture on birds.

In a school such as ours it is particularly useful to have people dropping in. The children need to see other faces, hear other voices, and generally find stimulation in other people's points of view. Henry Mawne always appears to enjoy his visits, and so do we.

On this occasion he came bearing an armful of rolled illustrations about birds of prey. A band of willing helpers rushed to undo the tapes and to hang the pictures over the blackboard. Henry Mawne bore their enthusiasm with complete patience, but it was some minutes before we could get all the pupils into a receptive frame of mind.

'Anyone fidgeting or interrupting,' I said firmly, 'will spend the next half hour in the lobby.'

Silence reigned.

'How do you do it?' whispered Henry admiringly, his back to the class.

'Years of practice,' I told him. 'And self-preservation, of course.'

He began his talk, and the children listened attentively. Some of the birds of prey were familiar to them. They are quite used to seeing sparrowhawks winging their way along our hedgerows, disturbing the small birds who soon become their victims. The kestrel is another common bird in these parts, hanging motionless in the sky ready to drop like a stone upon any luckless small animal or bird below.

'My dad,' interrupted Ernest, 'don't call it a kestrel. He says it's a wind-hover.'

Henry Mawne embroidered the theme that this alternative name engendered, and then went on to birds which are rarely seen in Fairacre, the smallest hawk, the merlin, and the hobby which has been seen locally during some summers.

But it was the picture of the golden eagle which impressed them most, probably because of its size and its fierce looks.

'It sometimes strikes at a new-born lamb,' said Henry, 'or any other small helpless creature, but it's not nearly as fierce as it looks.'

'Do Mr Roberts know?' quavered Joseph Coggs. 'There's a lot of young lambs on his farm.'

'They're quite safe,' Henry assured him. 'You'll only find golden eagles in Scotland, and then only in the wilder parts.'

The class appeared relieved.

Henry turned to me. 'Would it be possible to take them to that falconry north of Oxford? Perhaps we could get a mini-bus, or arrange a few cars one afternoon?'

These remarks were made very quietly, and expressively to me, but there was a murmur of approval from the front row.

'Would you like to see real birds of prey one day?' I asked the children.

The roar of ecstasy was unanimous, and Henry beamed affectionately at his audience.

'We'll try and fix up the outing next term,' he assured them. 'Miss Read will come too, of course.' He turned to me and added in a conspiratorial whisper: '*To keep order.*'

Henry Mawne was not only generous with his time in encouraging an interest in birds, he also presented the school with a fine wooden bird-table to replace the old one which had been shattered in the autumn storms. The children welcomed this addition to the playground, but Mrs Pringle considered it 'a nasty great object, encouraging all sorts of vermin'.

'We've got enough mice in the handiwork cupboard,' she said darkly, 'without a lot of corn and nuts and that hanging up. There was definitely a mouse in that paper cupboard what you're leaning against.'

I moved hastily away.

'Unless it was a *rat*,' she added, sounding pleased.

'Anyway the bird table is going to stay there. It was exceptionally kind of Mr Mawne to present it to us, and I don't intend to hurt his feelings.'

Mrs Pringle snorted. '*His* feelings indeed! I'll have you know that everyone remembers *your* feelings when he took advantage of you soon after he come here.'

I was taken aback. I know that villagers have long memories, but that little misunderstanding happened years ago and, in any case, it was not I who was expecting a proposal of marriage from the newly-arrived stranger, then, it had seemed, a bachelor, but the village folk themselves who had cast me in the rôle of ageing bride.

And I did not care for Mrs Pringle's use of the phrase: '*took advantage of you*'. It made me sound like some backward fourteen-year-old raped by a sex maniac. I was certainly not the former, and nor was poor Henry Mawne the latter but, as usual Mrs Pringle managed to give a comprehensive clout with her remarks.

I decided to rise above it, and changed the subject. 'Has Fred found his shed yet? He must miss it.'

For two pins I would have added; 'To get away from you,' but I forbore with Christian charity, and hoped my guardian angel was taking note.

'Part of it fetched up by Mr Roberts's cattle shed, and he brought the bits back on his trailer. The vicar said he'd let Fred have what was left of his tool shed after the storm, and Josh Pringle gave him a hand putting it all together.'

'That was good of the vicar,' I observed. 'A case of true practical Christianity.'

'He knew Fred missed somewhere to do his art-work,' said Mrs Pringle.

'And to have a peaceful place of his own,' I felt compelled to add.

I could almost hear my guardian angel scratching out the earlier entry.

'It keeps him from getting under my feet,' replied Mrs Pringle. '*That's* what the vicar really had in mind!'

I might just as well have saved my breath, and have had a rare entry in my angel's credit column, after all.

Easter was early this year, and I was glad to have some time in my little house.

I was beginning to realize with increasing intensity, the expense involved in being a property-owner. When I lived in the school house, all outside work was paid for by the school authorities, and I was responsible only for indoor maintenance.

Now, despite Wayne Richards's earlier repair work, I found that a mysterious damp patch had appeared in the corner of my bedroom ceiling. On investigation, Wayne traced it to the lead flashing at the base of the chimney stack just above the thatch.

'Must've been the gale,' he said, shouting down from the top of his ladder. 'All bent up, it is. That's your trouble, Miss Read. Won't take more than a day to put it right.'

He descended carefully, and brushed a few wisps of straw from his trousers.

'But I thought lead was terribly heavy stuff,' I protested. 'Isn't that what they use for roofs?'

'True, but it's soft too. Once it gets bent, it sort of rolls up under pressure. Why, the parish church in Caxley lost yards of it in the storms. Took six men to get it into the lorry.'

He gave me an estimated price for the job, and I fixed a day for his men to come and see to it. I have no doubt at all that his price was a fair one, but it gave me a shock. My old winter coat would have to wrap me up for another season, I could see that.

Visits from the plumber, the electrician and the telephone people, all took a good slice from my pay packet, and I began to do some careful budgeting for future repairs. At least it was my own property I was maintaining, and this gave me enormous satisfaction. I did not have to notify anyone of things which needed to be done, for it was now my decision, and I could employ whom I wanted, and have the work done when it pleased me.

I knew from experience how frustrated some of the nearby cottagers had been when they had gone to their employers with a list of things needing to be done. Cracked windows, leaking roofs, damp walls and dozens more defects were often met with either downright refusal or grudging agreement to do the minimum.

'He told me what did I expect for ten bob a week,' one man told me, 'and us with a bucket catching the raindrops in the kids' bedroom.'

I had sympathized. There were many many with conscientious landlords, but there were certainly others who seemed callous.

But now that I was a house-owner and realized just how much was needed to keep my own modest home in good repair, I was beginning to feel sympathy with the owners of so many rural homes. Many of these properties in Beech Green and Fairacre were well over a hundred years old, some almost three hundred, and there was something needing to be done to them practically every month. It was hardly surprising that so many were put on the market for others to repair and to spend their money on.

Nor was it surprising that council houses were proliferating, but even these were often too much for country people to afford, and there was a drift to the towns where there was often cheaper property to rent, and also more work available.

I thought of Gerard Baker and his present work on the change in agricultural matters during the present century. He was dealing with general change involving mechanized farming, intensive rearing of animals, the drastic reduction of men needed on a farm these days, and the rise in wages and conditions.

I too, in my small way, could vouch for change. From being a dweller in a tied-house, I was now a property-owner.

Surveying Wayne Richards's written estimate, I thought to myself: 'It's heavy going being a home-owner. But worth every penny.'

Luckily, the weather stayed fine for the holidays, and Wayne was able to get on with the flashing round the chimney. Better still, it was done in one day, as he had promised.

I had made no plans to go away, but took several day

trips to places I enjoy visiting. One was to Great Tew, the renowned Cotswold village which went through a sad period of neglect some time ago, but has now been restored to its former beauty.

Amy came with me on one or two occasions, and we lunched one day at Kingham Mill, and visited some of the lovely Cotswold villages which we knew from experience would be clogged with traffic in the summer but were relatively empty early in the year.

'Isn't it strange,' remarked Amy, 'that so many of these villages appear to have no people around? And all these cultivated fields never seem to have anyone working in them.'

'You'd better listen to Gerard's programme when it's on the telly,' I told her. 'You'll hear all about changes in country life.'

'But there doesn't appear *to be* any country life,' protested Amy. 'That's my point.'

'There's plenty in Fairacre,' I told her, 'particularly in my school. Far too much going on most of the time, especially when Mrs Pringle appears on the scene.'

'But in my youth,' continued Amy, surveying the empty rolling fields around us, 'you would see men ploughing the fields, or layering a hedge, or scything the verges –'

'But it's all done with machinery now.'

'Of course, I know that! But you used to see washing blowing on the line, and women sitting in the sun shelling peas. Where are they now? There must be washing to do, and peas to shell, even now.'

'They're inside with their washing machines and tumble driers. And the peas are in nice clean packets in the freezer. You're harking back to those dear days beyond recall. But think, Amy, would you really want to go back to boiling clothes in a copper, and stirring them about with a copper stick? And then rubbing them on a wash-board?'

Amy laughed. 'Of course not. Not that I ever boiled clothes in a copper, though my dear old granny did, and I used to help her hang them out, using lovely hazelwood pegs the gypsies used to sell. And come to think of it, what's happened to real gypsies who used to sell pegs and paper flowers at the back door?'

'They're all in their fabulous mobile homes,' I told her, 'watching the telly with one eye and the tumble drier with the other.'

'And shelling peas?'

'Not likely.'

'It seems so extraordinary that things have changed so drastically in the country in such a comparatively short time.'

'Gerard will tell you all about that,' I assured her.

19   Problems for Friends

IT was quite a pleasure to return to school after the
Easter holidays. I suppose that it is partly that I am
'geared to work', as Miriam Baker once put it. I
always welcome a break from it, but after a time I begin to
feel uneasy and somewhat guilty.

Then, too, I was now really settled in to the routine of
living at Beech Green, driving the few miles to Fairacre,
and not bobbing back and forth across the playground to
see how things were faring in the school house. In many
ways it was a more ordered existence, and I found it much
to my liking.

After a short spell of cloudy weather, the sun had
returned with all the pleasures of spring. Daffodils were
out in cottage gardens, and primroses starred the banks on
the road from Beech Green to school.

Mr Roberts's lambs were frisking about, untroubled by
golden eagles safely in Scotland, and the dawn chorus of
thrushes, blackbirds, and finches of all kinds, greeted me
when I awoke. The snowdrops had withered, the catkins
which had fluttered so bravely through the winter months
were now tattered, and as frayed as the dying flowers of
the yellow winter jasmine. They had played their part in
keeping hope alive during the darkest days of the year, but
now bowed out to let the larger and more showy flowers
take the stage.

But although I welcomed the spring as rapturously as the
children did, and despite my more settled way of life now

that I had become used to the changed rhythm of my day, I felt a secret unease.

The vicar's remarks last term about the fact that my school might close despite assurances to the contrary had brought back the fear that had always lurked at the back of my mind. I tried to remind myself that this had been faced for years, and that still the school remained open. I told myself that I had been assured that although the school house would be put on the market, the school would continue. But I still worried, and all the old bogeys about my future came back to haunt me.

Should I take early retirement? Could I afford to? The expense of keeping my own small property in good heart had been brought home to me pretty sharply recently, and the thought that old age and general infirmity must be faced one day, with all the added expense that that would bring. In any case, it came back to the fact that I was 'geared to work' and would miss it.

But what about working in someone else's school, the other alternative? I knew myself well enough to know that I should hate it. For too long I had been monarch of all I surveyed, and had my own way in most things. I thought of having to fall in with the wishes of a strange head teacher, undertaking methods of which I probably disapproved, sharing a staffroom with dozens of others, and my spirits quailed. After all this time, I recognized that I should not be an admirable member of a team. Mrs Richards and I worked happily together, but of course it was I who really prevailed as head mistress when it came to the crunch.

No, the thought of teaching in another school, no matter how splendid the building or how angelic the staff, could not be contemplated. I should just have to soldier on as things were at Fairacre, comforting myself with Mr Salisbury's promise, and the slight hope that particularly large families would decide to make their homes in the village before too long.

Horace and Eve came to see the school house one afternoon. By now the roof repairs were done, but the garden still showed signs of the builders' recent activities. There were indentations on the lawn where the ladders had stood, the shrubs and flowerbeds were dusty with the débris from the roof, and there was a battered air about the whole place. Nevertheless, the job itself had been well done, and the new roof tiles matched the old ones admirably.

The estate agent had let them have the key, and they had spent an hour looking over the interior, until I finished the afternoon session.

They followed me to Beech Green for tea, and were full of plans if their offer were accepted.

'One of the things I mentioned to the agent,' said Horace, 'was that we should prefer to do the decoration ourselves. It might mean a lower price, for one thing, and in any case it always seems to me a mistake to re-decorate a house just to sell it. Usually the new owner can't bear the colour scheme, and sets to and repaints as he wants it. Also, it might mean a quicker sale, and everyone would be happy.'

'When do you expect to hear?'

'Heaven alone knows! You know how these matters drag on. The thing is, we've made our offer, and I doubt if many other people will with the market as it is. We'll keep our fingers crossed.'

It was good to see them so hopeful as they drove away, and I only wished that they would see those hopes fulfilled.

* * *

One morning towards the end of April, before the school bell was rung, Mrs Pringle informed me that someone was looking over one of the empty houses.

'Good!' I cried. 'Did they look as though they might have children?'

'Not as far as I could see,' replied Mrs Pringle. 'More like *grandparents*, I'd say.'

'That's right,' agreed Mr Willet who had joined us. 'More like folk from the council again, I reckon. I recognized that old trout from Caxley as is on the District Council. Wonder what's up?'

'Checking on the drains and that perhaps,' surmised Mrs Pringle. 'Don't do to leave a place uninhibited too long.'

'*Uninhabited*,' I corrected automatically.

'Like I said,' agreed Mrs Pringle. 'You don't want no one in it for too long.'

Here was the double negative rearing its ugly head again, but I did not join battle.

'Looked more like buyers wanting a bit added,' said Mr Willet. 'They was looking at the kitchen side. Maybe they want one of these glass-house places stuck on. All the go, them conservatories these days.'

'Perhaps one of those people was a buyer,' I speculated.

'That young woman as is expecting,' continued Mr Willet, 'said she thought they looked at both houses.'

'Definitely drains!' pronounced Mrs Pringle. 'They shares a septic tank no doubt.'

'I never saw them looking at but just the one,' said Bob. 'Mr Annett had us in early for choir practice. Trying out a new anthem, he was, and a right pig's breakfast we made of it, I can tell you. Some modern thing, it is. What's wrong with a nice bit of Stainer, I want to know? So anyway, I never saw as much as Mrs Winter did from her kitchen window.'

He sounded disappointed.

'All I hope,' I told him, nodding to Patrick to ring the bell, 'is that they are building on to accommodate their large families.'

'That's what's called *"wishful thinking"*,' he shouted, above the din, and departed.

I came across Jane Winter myself one dinner hour when I was calling at the Post Office for the school savings' stamps. She looked remarkably well, with that radiance that pregnant women so often show, once the first uncomfortable months are over.

'Yes,' she said, 'I certainly saw those people, and a couple of men have visited the houses once or twice. What's going on?'

'I've no idea. Perhaps two couples – old friends or something – have decided to retire together. It sometimes happens.'

'But the houses are too big for retired folk,' she said.

'Sometimes they have lots of grandchildren who come to stay,' I surmised. 'But honestly, your guess is as good as mine.'

I enquired about the coming baby.

'Not long now, thank heaven. To tell you the truth, we were both a bit miffed about it when we first knew, but now I'm quite looking forward to having a baby in the house again.'

'The old wives' tale is that those that aren't ordered always turn out the best,' I told her.

'That's a consoling thought,' she laughed. 'Perhaps this one will be able to keep us in our old age.'

We walked back towards my school and her home in good spirits.

* * *

Amy rang me one evening soon after my meeting with Jane. She sounded worried, and wanted to know if I could spend the next Friday night, and perhaps Saturday too, with her at Bent.

'James has to be away, and he's heard such a lot about people breaking in that he doesn't like the idea of me being alone. Besides, he still looks upon me as an invalid after that bang on the head.'

'I'd love to come. What time, Amy?'

'Come to tea if you can manage it. If not, soon after. And many thanks. James will be grateful.'

'So shall I. Have you had more than usual robberies in Bent?'

'As a matter of fact, we have. Mrs Drew, our daily, seems to have fresh instances ever time she comes, but at the moment the poor soul is laid up with her back, so I don't get the gossip, good or bad.'

'Anything serious?'

'Just a displaced vertebra somewhere from the sound of it, but you know how painful backs can be. Sometimes –' she broke off. 'Sorry, I forgot how squeamish you are.'

'I don't mind *bones*. It's *insides* I can't take. All those tubes, and squashy bits.'

Amy laughed. 'Well, anyway, I won't curdle your blood with any more horrors. See you on Friday, as soon as you like.'

I must admit that I wondered once or twice why James was so suddenly anxious about leaving Amy alone. He often had to be away from home on business, and surely the fact that there were burglars about could not be the whole story. I looked forward to hearing more.

April was on its way out, and I looked forward to May, to my mind the loveliest of all the months. The hedges were breaking into leaf, and the trees' stark branches were beginning to be clothed in a veil of swelling buds, soon to become a mantle of fresh green.

I drove to Amy's about six o'clock, and found her picking narcissi in her garden.

'Smell those,' she said, thrusting the bunch under my nose, and I sniffed rapturously.

'Bliss!' I told her. 'Now tell me all about James's concern for you. I'm intrigued.'

'Come and have a drink, and I'll tell you as much as I know.'

She dropped the flowers into a jug of water as we passed through the kitchen, and we were soon comfortably settled in the sitting-room, glasses in hand.

'It's a sad story, and to be frank, I'm much more worried about James than he is about me.'

'Is it something to do with Brian?' I ventured.

'It has *everything* to do with Brian,' said Amy, putting her glass down on a side table with a bang. 'The little rat!' she added violently.

I gazed at her speechless. It is not often that I see Amy in a fine temper.

'He's hopped it. Scarpered. Gone to ground. Vamoosed. In short, he's nowhere to be found. And what's upset James so much is the fact that he had arranged an interview for Brian with one of his high-powered city pals – no easy task – and of course that wretched Brian didn't turn up. He'd vanished, and so had the money.'

'Good lord! From the Bristol firm?'

'That's only part of it, and a small part at that evidently. Our Brian has been pinching funds from his various places of employment for years now. They think he plays a fairly minor rôle in a group of wide-boys with nice little bank accounts in various places abroad.'

'I can't believe it. I must admit I always thought that he was a rather mediocre little man, but I should never have credited him with enough savvy to be an international crook. Where is he, I wonder?'

'He could be anywhere. Bolivia or Brazil or one of those islands where people stash their ill-gotten gains. He obviously took a plane from Bristol. Last Thursday I think.'

'But can you fly to Bolivia from Bristol? I thought you could only hop across to nearby places like Paris and Madrid.'

'Presumably you can change planes at Paris and Madrid,' snapped Amy crossly. 'Don't be so pettifogging!'

I apologized meekly. It was quite obvious that Amy was deeply upset. In the silence that followed I turned over the word 'pettifogging' in my mind. I had looked it up recently for a crossword I was doing, and I felt sure it had said something about 'a cavilling lawyer', which could not possibly apply to me. Perhaps Amy meant to use the word 'pernickety'? In any case, this was not the time to discuss such niceties of the English language with my suffering friend, and I put forward a less controversial question.

'Won't Interpol catch him?' I ventured.

'Of course they're doing their stuff, and so too is the fraud squad, I gather, but people like Brian and his dubious friends are always one jump ahead, and poor old James seems to think we'll never see him again.'

'Jolly good thing too! And after all you and James did for him! Makes my blood boil!'

'I think James is dreading the possibility of Brian being brought back to face trial. Although he's furious about being let down over that interview, he still can't bear the idea of having to be a witness against Brian. Frankly, I should enjoy it.'

'Me too. But then women are much tougher than men.'

'You'd think that this business would have turned James

completely against that little horror, but it hasn't. He's had the most terrible shock, his idol with feet of clay, and all that, but he's still besotted. He makes idiotic remarks such as: "Can't hit a man when he's down." "Brian always played a straight bat." "He must be covering for someone." Really, sport has a lot to answer for when it comes to men's thinking.'

'Don't you argue with him?'

'Of course I do, until I'm blue in the face, but then James starts to blame the women in Brian's life. He would have been perfect if his wife hadn't left him. She should have stuck by him. Loyalty should come first, and all that guff. I must say I wonder if she didn't suspect things years ago, and removed herself while there was time.'

'So James is in Bristol now?'

'Yes. He's meeting this old school friend who employed Brian. I expect there'll be a lot of wailing and gnashing of teeth over the fall of their cricket hero. More about that, I'll bet, than the plight of the shareholders.'

'Maybe the employer will be made of sterner stuff.'

'I hope so. The point is that I'm truly worried about James. He looks so wretched and ill. Brian has properly let him down. For a really tough business man, he is extraordinarily soft-hearted, and this really has hit him badly. I wanted to go with him, as I don't think he should be driving when he's so upset, but he and the friend and the firm's accountant are going through the books and will be hours on the job, evidently. Then they've got the other firms to contact, and the police. He'll probably be down there for the whole of the weekend. Can you stay?'

'Of course I can. Poor old James! What a wretched underhand sort of affair it is!'

'Hardly cricket, is it?' agreed Amy, with a wry smile.

* * *

Naturally, it was an anxious weekend. Every time the telephone rang, Amy rushed to answer it, hoping for news from James.

He rang just as we were off to bed on the Saturday night, telling Amy that he would be home on Sunday evening, and to see if all was well.

'How was he?' I asked.

'He sounded very weary, and says there's more to do than any of them realized. No news of Brain, as you might expect, but there's another complication.'

'What's that?'

'One of his erstwhile colleagues, at a previous job he had, has also vanished into thin air. Looks remarkably suspicious according to the police. This other chap's a real hard nut with a record. The police want him for other matters. James reckons he's had a strangle-hold on poor Brian.'

'And nobody's seen Brian or this other fellow getting on a plane?'

'No. They're now beginning to wonder if they are still in this country, lying low.'

'Perhaps it will be easier to pick them up,' I offered, consolingly. I was worried on Amy's behalf. She looked pale and drawn, and I felt that I should really be doing more for her than I was.

'Let's go to bed,' I said. 'You look all in, and James will never let me be a wife-sitter again if he finds you under the weather.'

We made our way upstairs, and I hoped that Amy's exhaustion would let her sleep. As for me, sleep was impossible, and I found myself thinking of idiotic ways of tracking down Brian. It must have been about three o'clock when I hit upon the ruse of attending the coming summer Test matches at Lords and the Oval (school matters allow-ing, of course), when I fell into an uneasy sleep, where I was busy making marrow jam which refused to set, with Bob Willet and Mrs Pringle in the school lobby.

It was quite a relief to wake up.

I left Amy in the early evening, knowing James would be back very soon, and feeling that I must do some school marking, as well as a few household chores before Monday morning.

A white froth of cow parsley lined the verges below the sprouting hedges, and I thought how lucky I was to live in Beech Green.

My own garden looked exceptionally tidy after Bob Willet's pruning and general clearing up, and in the growing dusk I pottered around outside noting the tulips now breaking into flower, and the little knots of tightly-furled buds on the old Bramley apple tree. The wicked storm, the snow, the horrors of winter and all it had brought seemed far away and long ago, and I rejoiced in the summer so soon to come, before going indoors to face my duties.

It is always annoying to me when people think that a single woman's work is over when she comes back from her daily grind. After all, her home needs as much cleaning, her clothes as much laundering, her food as much cooking, her correspondence as much answering, as any other woman who spends her day at home. Added to these domestic chores are the necessary tasks which she brings back from the school or office. In my case, I have a considerable amount of marking and preparing of lessons to face after school hours, and when people point out that I have lovely long holidays, I reply firmly that I need them.

Mrs Pringle comes to Beech Green on Wednesday afternoons on the convenient Caxley bus, and I must admit that she thoroughly 'bottoms' the cottage before I get back to share a pot of tea with her, and run her home to Fairacre. On the few occasions when she has had to miss her stint, the place certainly lacks that extra gloss.

On the Wednesday following my weekend with Amy, we sat in the garden with our mugs. To tell the truth, it was hardly warm enough, but we could just about stand the coolness in the air, and it was good to realize that summer had arrived.

'You been to see them new houses lately?' asked Mrs Pringle. 'Getting on a treat they are with them kitchens.'

'I don't get down that way very often now,' I confessed. 'I miss strolling around Fairacre in the evenings. Somehow I just get in the car and head for here these days.'

'Well, the boards are down, of course, and from what I hear they've both been bought.'

'Must be two retired friends,' I said, repeating my earlier prognostication. 'Or maybe an old couple and a married son or daughter.'

'At that price?' queried Mrs Pringle. 'With that sort of money they could buy Buckingham Palace. No, it's my belief they've been brought by some rich firm for retirement homes, to put their pensioners in.'

'But they couldn't house more than four or six pensioners,' I protested. 'I still plump for two families. Want to make a bet?'

Mrs Pringle bridled, as I knew she would.

'I am not a betting woman, as well you know, and it's a good thing the children aren't here to listen to such a scandalous idea. I should have thought that Arthur Coggs with his betting and swilling would be enough trouble for Fairacre, without the headmistress of the school uttering such wickedness.'

By this time she was red in the face with wrath, and I hastened to apologize. Her feelings were not assuaged by my trying to make amends, and we drove to Fairacre in heavy silence.

She struggled from the car at her gate, and turned to give me a parting message.

'What you said,' she told me, 'is an abomination in the sight of the Lord. Betting indeed!'

With a final snort she turned towards her gate, as always the victor in any of our battles.

20   Good News

MRS Pringle's guesses about the future residents in the new houses were echoed by one or two other people in Fairacre. Mr Lamb favoured my own view that probably two fairly well-off friends had decided to be neighbours.

'If you were retired,' he said, 'you'd like to have someone handy to help you out when you had an accident, wouldn't you? Someone told me that they reckoned they might have been bought by Caxley folk who came from these parts originally. You know, made their pile and now returning to their roots. It happens sometimes.'

Mrs Pringle stuck to her pensioners idea. Bob Willet favoured two families, unknown to each other, who had just happened to buy at the same time.

The children's interest was desultory. Only old people had been seen looking at the premises. Who cared about new folk? It was their own families in Fairacre that really mattered.

The vicar seemed rather guarded in his conjectures, I thought, simply expressing the hope that they would be church-goers.

In any case, there were other and more pressing things to think about. The summer term is always busy. We have the school sports day, weekly trips to Caxley's swimming bath for the older children, the annual outing to the seaside, and the village fête in July.

This particular summer we also had the trip to the falconry arranged by Henry Mawne, and we were lucky to awake to a glorious June morning. Only my class of ten children were making the trip, while Mrs Richards held the fort at school.

We decided to go in three cars. Henry drove his with three excited children as passengers, Mrs Mawne accompanied us in her beautiful Rover, with four more, three in the back, and Ernest in the front passenger seat, full of importance because his aunt lived somewhere near the birds of prey centre, and he assured everyone that he knew the way.

I had Joseph Coggs beside me, with Patrick and John Todd, the two most unreliable boys in my school, in the back. My eagle eye gleamed at them from the mirror, and I had threatened to deposit them on the road *anywhere* if I saw the slightest sign of bad behaviour.

It was a wonderful drive and my three were remarkably appreciative. One would have thought that, country-dwellers as they were, the rolling Cotswold scene would not have affected them. But they noticed the difference in architecture, the honey-coloured stone of the village houses compared with their own native brick and flint with thatch or tile atop.

We had taken picnic lunches with us, and stopped at a quiet spot by the river Windrush, known to Henry from his fishing days. In addition, I had brought enough apples for everyone, and Mrs Mawne had been even more generous with some chocolate apiece, so that it was a very happy and well-fed company that watched the bright water and the willow branches trailing in it.

By half past two we were waiting in the grassy centre for the display to begin. We saw owls, hawks and merlins in all their glory of flight and intermittent obedience to the falconer, and the children were awe-struck.

One at a time they were encouraged to don the leather

gauntlet, and to feed the bird which landed there. Some were rather timid about it, but I was touched by Joseph Coggs's reaction to this new experience. He was entirely without fear, his face rapt, as the great owl swept silently to his outstretched arm to take the bait. Of all my country-bred flock it was Joe who had the strongest link with wildlife. When the other boys were drawing vehicles, it was Joe who was drawing birds and trees, and now this affinity was more than ever apparent. Joe's dark eyes gazed in wonder at the yellow eyes of his new friend. They seemed in complete accord, and I knew that today's experience would mean far more to Joe than to any of the other children.

They were still excited on the way home. Patrick and John in the back boasted about their bravery at the centre. But Joe sat silent, his eyes shining at the memory of all that he had seen.

It was sometime after this that Horace Umbleditch rang to tell me the good news that their offer had been accepted, and the school house would be theirs.

'And when do you expect to be in?' I asked.

'Sometime next term, I think. We'll spend the summer holidays here, decorating and doing the garden –'

He broke off suddenly.

'You won't mind us altering your garden?' he continued.

'Good heavens, no! It's not my garden now, you know, and in any case it's been altered every time a new head teacher took over. I think I inherited Mr Hope's spotted laurels when I came, but they were soon uprooted.'

'Eve will see this term out and has given in her notice. She's remarkably fit, but we both think it's a good idea for what she calls "a geriatric mum" to take things gently.'

'Very wise,' I agreed, and we went on to discuss the

problems to be overcome to make my old home into their new one, until a strange smell began to emanate from the kitchen and I found that a pan of milk had spread itself over not only the stove, but a few square yards of kitchen floor as well.

The vicar enthused about the news when he called in soon afterwards.

'Mr and Mrs Umbleditch called on me, you know, when they were negotiating for the buying of the house. A charming pair. A great asset to the village, and I gather that Mr Umbleditch has a fine tenor voice. He will be much welcomed by Mr Annett. They are both regular church-goers too. All *very* satisfactory.'

I said that I thought they would settle very happily in Fairacre. 'After all,' I went on, 'they have wanted to live here for a very long time.'

'Fairacre is the perfect place to live,' asserted the vicar. 'I have been fortunate to be appointed to this living. I do so hope that all our newcomers will enjoy the village as keenly as we have.'

This was said with some emphasis, and I wondered if he had prior knowledge of other people coming to share our environment.

The children were out at play, and we were alone in my classroom.

'Have you had any news about the two empty houses?' I asked.

He began to look slightly embarrassed. 'Well yes, my dear Miss Read, I have, and I don't know whether it is quite in order to tell you.'

'Then please don't,' I replied. 'There's nothing worse than being told a secret, and having to keep mum when people inquire. Forget about it.'

'No, no. I really can't do that, and I don't suppose for a minute that there is really anything *secret* in the news. It's just that I haven't brought the letter with me.'

This began to get curiouser and curiouser, and I started to feel all the well-known prickles of fear, envisaging a letter to Mr Partridge, as chairman of the school governors, from our old friend Mr Salisbury about the dwindling numbers at Fairacre School.

'Have you heard of the Malory-Hope Foundation?' asked the vicar.

'Never.'

'You have heard of Sir Derek Malory-Hope, I'm sure. He was a well-known –'

But well known for what remained a mystery, for at that moment Mrs Richards appeared with a howling child who was dripping blood from a grazed knee.

I hurried to get the first-aid box.

'Heavens!' exclaimed the vicar, gazing at the great wall-clock. 'Is it really so late? I am due at a meeting in Oxford at four o'clock. I will call tomorrow with the letter.'

We bandaged the knee, provided a boiled sweet as medicine, and comparative peace reigned again.

I forgot about the vicar's visit until after school when I asked Mrs Richards if she had ever heard of someone called Malory-Hope.

'Isn't he that rich man who gave a lot of money to the Soldiers, Sailors and Air Force Association? Wayne's dad had something to do with it when they were raising money for that hall in Caxley.'

'Oh, I've never heard of him, I'm afraid.'

'It was in *The Caxley*,' said my colleague, looking rather shocked, 'with photos. He opened the hall, cut ribbons, and pulled curtains back over plaques – all that stuff. You must have seen it.'

'Sorry, I missed it.'

'He lived somewhere around here. Died some months ago, and there was a big memorial service. That was in *The Caxley* too.'

I had no recollection of that item of news either, but I did not admit it to Mrs Richards. Obviously she read her *Caxley Chronicle* with far more attention than I did. I should just have to wait for the vicar's letter to explain these mysteries.

Bob Willet was scraping up the coke which had dribbled away from the pile in the playground. I put my question to him while it was still fresh in my mind.

'Bob, have you ever heard of someone called Sir Derek Malory-Hope?'

'The chap what died last year? All over the *Caxley*, it was. He was a good bloke, rolling in money. Give a lot of it away though.'

'I must confess I'd never heard of him.'

'What put him in your mind?'

I said that the vicar had mentioned him when I had asked about the empty houses.

'Did he now' said Bob, leaning on his spade. He looked thoughtful. 'Did he now?' he repeated, before returning to his labours.

When I arrived home, *The Caxley Chronicle* was lying on the mat with one or two uninteresting-looking envelopes. I made myself a mug of tea, and took it and the paper into the sitting-room, and made myself comfortable on the sofa. Tibby, unusually affectionate, leapt on to my lap, and we settled down together happily.

There was a rather nice photograph on the front page of an old mill, situated on the River Cax, some miles downstream from our market town. According to the caption, it had been mentioned in the Domesday Book and funds were now being raised for its restoration.

Among the donors I saw that 'The Malory-Hope Foundation' had contributed a substantial sum.

I have noticed before that when a new name, or simply a new word, crops up, it appears again quite soon. Here it was again: a body, unknown to me yesterday, now cropping up in my life twice in one day.

I turned to this week's deaths. Not that I am particularly morbid, but it is as well to check who has fallen off the bough recently, to save one from asking brightly about a husband who has gone before. There was no one I knew personally, but one of the entries was embellished with a verse:

> To Heaven you've gone
> Dear Dad who we love
> To Mother who is waiting
> All glorious above

I set about correcting it.

The first line could stand.

The second line should have 'whom' instead of 'who'.

The third line was frankly disgraceful. Why not have: 'Where Mother is waiting', or if one wanted 'Dear Mum' to match the earlier 'Dear Dad' thus: 'Where dear Mum awaits you'?

As for the last line it was simply lifted wholesale from *Hymns Ancient and Modern* Number 167, and was the second part of the opening line of: 'O worship the King'.

I have often thought of offering my services, 'free, gratis and for nothing', to *The Caxley Chronicle* in order to overhaul their list of these funeral rhymes, which they presumably keep in their offices and from which bereaved families may make their selection. I have never got down to actually approaching the editor; it would need a good deal of tact.

While I was still wondering how one could achieve one's aim, the telephone rang, and I leapt to answer it, catapulting poor Tibby to the floor.

It was Amy.

'Am I interrupting anything?'

'Only the reading of *The Caxley*.'

'Good! I was just wondering –'

'Before I forget,' I broke in. 'Do you know anything about the Malory-Hope Foundation?'

'Of course I do. Derek Malory-Hope started it. He died last year, and James and I went to his memorial service. You must have seen his obituary in *The Caxley*, surely?'

'I seem to have missed it.'

'I had lunch with his widow some time ago. Come to think of it, I called on you on the way back. Remember? Anyway what's the connection?'

'I just saw that the Foundation has given a hefty sum towards repairing an ancient mill near Caxley.'

'That's right. James mentioned it. Not that he has much to do with that side of their work. He's mixed up with the other part, the Hope Trust. You know, the orphan bit.'

'What orphan bit?'

'You must remember,' said Amy impatiently. 'Those houses in Scotland.'

I cast my mind back to our holiday together, and saw again Floors Castle, Mellerstain and Sir Walter Scott's pile. Not an orphan in sight as far as I could recall.

I said as much to Amy.

'*Not us*,' she shouted in a most unladylike manner. 'We didn't visit the houses I'm talking about! James did. In Glasgow. For the orphans up there.'

I said I still did not really understand.

'Let's forget it,' said Amy. 'Anyway, besides the mill

involvement, why are you worrying about the Malory-Hope Foundation?'

'The vicar mentioned it.'

'*The vicar?*' Amy sounded thunderstruck.

After a pause, she resumed in a more normal voice. 'This conversation becomes more surrealistic every second. Let's start again. I really rang to see if you would be in on Saturday afternoon, as James has to go to Fairacre on business and he could drop me off as we come through Beech Green.'

'Perfect. Come to tea, and I'll make some of that sticky gingerbread James likes.'

'You spoil him. Sometimes I think James married the wrong woman.'

'I'm certain he did!' I said, and put the telephone down smartly, before she could reply.

I spent an uneasy night wondering about the vicar's letter, and the information Amy had provided about the Malory-Hope activities. More specifically, I worried about James's part as a busy member of the Hope Trust, or as Amy put it, 'the orphan bit'.

If James, on the Trust's behalf, had bought Fairacre's two empty houses, did Amy have anything to do with it? If so, was I involved? Had I been whining more than usual about lack of pupils? Was it possible that my dwindling numbers had made James look into the possibility of the houses being bought by the Hope Trust, just as the Glasgow ones had been?

If it were so, how would it affect me, and my friends in Fairacre? I began imagining crocodiles of orphans, all clad in a dreary uniform, roaming the village street under the stern eye of their jailers. The mind boggled at this Dickensian scene, though there would hardly be enough orphans to form a crocodile if they only had those two houses as their home.

This brought me to even more conjecture. Surely it would be reasonable to have a much larger establishment to house orphans? It seemed very extravagant to use an ordinary family-sized house for such a project. On the other hand, had not James said something once about 'family units' in connection with his Glasgow excursion?

I tossed and turned until my bedroom clock showed a quarter to four, when I must have fallen into a far from dreamless sleep, for Gerald Partridge and I, accompanied by Mrs Pringle, were busy herding about fifty real crocodiles into Mr Roberts's sheep dip at the foot of the downs, to immunize them against crocodile-tetanus to which, as we all know, reptiles are particularly vulnerable because of their webbed toes –

I was fit for nothing when the alarm went at seven.

Naturally, I was anxious for the vicar's visit the next morning to see if the promised letter would give any further information.

Assembly came and went. Playtime came and went. School dinner came and went, and the vicar was still absent.

Mrs Richards departed with my class for the swimming bath at Caxley, while I took myself into the infants' room for the usual Friday afternoon lessons.

After a short session of modelling tea trays complete with saucers and cups, and such intricate pieces of workmanship as teaspoons and crumpets, I embarked on two short poems by Robert Louis Stevenson. I am a great believer in stuffing young children's heads with worthwhile verse which they will have safely stored away for the rest of their lives.

And so we learnt 'The Cow' and 'Happy Thought' from *A Child's Garden of Verses*, and I felt the afternoon had been profitably spent. I had quite forgotten my worries about the Hope Trust, empty houses and Amy and James, when the vicar arrived, envelope in hand.

It was time for the children to go home, and the vicar obligingly helped me with shoe laces, coat buttons and all the sartorial problems of young children.

Then, when the school was empty, he handed me the large envelope and roamed the classroom while I read.

It was headed The Malory-Hope Foundation, and had an impressive list of directors, among whom, I noticed were James and, to my surprise Sir Barnabas Hatch, erstwhile employer of Miriam Baker.

The letter was extremely polite and pointed out that negotiations had been satisfactorily completed, and that the Hope Trust, part of the above Foundation, was now the owner of the two Fairacre houses. Their local director, Mr James Garfield, would give himself the pleasure of calling upon the vicar, and the chairman of the Parish Council, Mr Lamb, to explain matters in greater detail and to hear local people's views and suggestions.

It was envisaged that each home would house four, or possibly five children, with a house-father and mother to care for them. The children would be of school age, viz: from four and a half years to eleven. A leaflet explaining the aims and work of the Foundation was enclosed, and the same information had been sent to Mr Lamb.

So that was why James was making a visit to Fairacre next Saturday was my first thought. The second was had I got some black treacle for the gingerbread?

I looked across at the beaming face of the vicar, and only then did the true impact of this momentous news hit me. I felt stunned. The room gyrated in the oddest way, and I became conscious of the vicar's face close to mine. The smile had changed to an expression of concern.

'My dear Miss Read, are you all right? It is a shock, I must admit, but a *nice* one, isn't it?'

I pulled myself together. 'It's incredible,' I croaked. 'An answer to a maiden's prayer, definitely.'

'And to a vicar's,' said Gerard Partridge soberly.

Mrs Richards always saw off the children when she returned on Friday afternoons from swimming, and although I was longing to tell her the great news, I was glad to have some time to myself to think it over. I drove home still in a state of shock, but remembered to stop at Beech Green's village shop for the black treacle.

After tea I set about making the gingerbread, and the cottage soon became redolent with the fragrance of cooking. As I went about greasing tins and mixing ingredients, my mind tried to come to terms with this amazing news.

Eight new children! Was I right in thinking that the letter had said from four and a half to eleven years of age? I should have almost thirty in my school, and that would mean that it would remain safe from closure.

I still wondered why our village should have been selected by the Hope Trust for its two new homes. Had James and Amy somehow connived in this happy arrangement, for my especial benefit? If so, it was embarrassing for me, although typical of their generous spirit.

I could only possess my soul in patience until I saw them the next afternoon.

Their car drew up at twenty past two, and Amy, elegant as ever, came in whilst James waved, and went on his way to Fairacre. I should like to have babbled away about all my hopes and fears but managed to appear fairly composed. In fact, it was Amy who made the first reference to our telephone conversation.

'So have you found out any more about the vicar and the two new houses?'

She sounded genuinely interested, and not at all like a conspirator.

'Amy,' I said, 'you'll never believe this.'

She listened attentively, her eyes growing rounder every minute.

'And I must admit,' I confessed, 'that I thought you might have had a hand in it.'

'Cross my heart and hope to die,' quoted Amy, making the appropriate gestures. 'Although, of course,' she added, looking rather pink, 'I may have mentioned your worries to James. Or, come to think of it, you often told us about them yourself when James was present.'

This was true enough. We awaited James's return with as much patience as we could muster, and prepared the tea tray ready for his arrival. The gingerbread had turned out satisfactorily dark and sticky.

James was his usual cheerful self, and greeted me affectionately. We were halfway through our tea when I broached the subject which meant so much to me and my school. James listened smiling, and then began to explain.

'First of all, I must make it plain that Amy knew nothing about it. I didn't tell her a thing, knowing she can't keep a secret for two minutes anyway.'

'Well!' gasped Amy outraged.

'But, *unknowingly*, she did set things in motion, because she told me about your two empty houses and how steeply they had dropped in price. Of course, my tough old business instincts were aroused, and I thought of the Trust.'

'But why at this precise time? Haven't you got other possible plans in this area?'

'Since Derek's death we've had a large amount left to the Hope Trust, as you know, and we wanted more premises in these parts. He was a great believer in the family idea, and the next big project is to found a whole village, rather like the Pestalozzi one in Sussex. But that's not going to be ready for many a year, and so we are carrying on with the policy we have already. We've found that a few children get settled very quickly in a community, and the local school can absorb them easily. That's why we keep the units to school ages approximately, some like the Fairacre one's from roughly five to eleven, then some from eleven to about sixteen, and of course there are a number of babies' homes. We learnt a lot from visiting well-established places like Barnardo's.'

'It's wonderful news for me,' I said. 'It makes the future really hopeful. When will they come?'

He laughed, and took a third piece of gingerbread. 'I can't see them sitting in your desks until next year at the earliest. We've got to interview the couples who will be in charge of each house. Luckily we've got a splendid list of applicants, but we take a lot of trouble in matching them to the neighbours as well as the children.'

It all sounded perfect, but I still had an uneasy twinge of guilt. 'James,' I said tentatively, 'you didn't do this for some quixotic reason, such as pleasing Amy and me?'

'You flatter yourself,' he said sturdily. 'I can assure you I started the negotiations for two reasons only. The first was to put into operation Derek's wishes. The second reason was that I could not resist a bargain, and we shall never see house property as cheap again. Satisfied?'

And with that I had to be content.

Just before they went, James said: 'I'm taking Amy away for a break. She's never really recovered from that bang on the head, and I didn't help by inflicting that little rat Brian on her. You can be sure *that* won't happen again!'

On Monday morning I broke the good news to Mrs Richards who was as thrilled as I was.

'So Fairacre School is safe?'

'It looks like it.'

'Isn't that marvellous?'

'Marvellous, indeed; and I'll let you choose this morning's hymn to celebrate it.'

She went to the piano stool and began to leaf through our shabby copy of *Hymns Ancient and Modern*.

'What about "Let all the world in every corner sing"?' she enquired, swivelling round.

'Perfect,' I said.

At that moment I noticed Joseph Coggs, framed in the doorway. He was looking hopeful.

'Yes, Joe,' I said. 'It's time for the school bell. You can ring out the glad tidings to everyone in Fairacre.'

ABOUT THE AUTHOR

Miss Read is actually Mrs. Dora Saint, whose novels draw on her own memories of living and teaching in a small English village. She first began writing after the Second World War, mainly light essays about school and country matters, for several journals. Her first book, *Village School,* was published in England by Michael Joseph and then in the United States by Houghton Mifflin Company in 1955. She has since delighted millions of readers with both the Fairacre series and her equally well loved series about the Cotswold village of Thrush Green. Miss Read and her husband, a retired schoolmaster, have one daughter and enjoy a quiet life near Newbury, Berkshire.

Books about the beloved village of Fairacre
AVAILABLE IN PAPERBACK

Village School "An affectionate, humorous, and gently charming chronicle."
— *New York Times*

The first novel in the Fairacre series, *Village School* introduces us to that cheerful schoolmistress Miss Read and her lovable group of children, who are just as likely to lose themselves as their mittens. ISBN-13: 978-0-618-12702-3 / ISBN-10: 0-618-12702-X

Village Centenary "Miss Read reminds us of what is really important." — *USA Today*

Village Centenary chronicles the year Miss Read's school celebrates its one hundredth anniversary with the help—and, in some cases, hindrance—of many of our favorite Fairacre friends. ISBN-13: 978-0-618-12703-0 / ISBN-10: 0-618-12703-8

Summer at Fairacre "A world of innocent integrity in almost perfect prose consisting of wit, humor, and wisdom in equal measure."
— *Cleveland Plain Dealer*

Summer at Fairacre charmingly recounts one hot—but very welcome—summer, when Miss Read tends to the problems and possibilities that unfold in the lives of her downland village friends against the background of Albertine roses, skylarks, and bees.
ISBN-13: 978-0-618-12704-7 / ISBN-10: 0-618-12704-6

Mrs. Pringle of Fairacre "Miss Read's novels are sheer delight." — *Chicago Tribune*

Through the eyes of Miss Read and other longtime Fairacre friends, we trace Mrs. Pringle's life from childhood through her stormy standing as the redoubtable (but beloved) cleaner of the Fairacre School. ISBN-13: 978-0-618-15588-0 / ISBN-10: 0-618-15588-0

Changes at Fairacre "Fairacre offers a restful change from the frenetic pace of the contemporary world." — *Publishers Weekly*

While Fairacre's new commuter lifestyle causes a sharp decline in enrollment at Miss Read's school, Miss Read focuses her attention on the ill health of her old friend Dolly Clare. ISBN-13: 978-0-618-15457-9 / ISBN-10: 0-618-15457-4

Farewell to Fairacre "Humor guides her pen but charity steadies it . . . Delightful."
— *Times Literary Supplement*

The beloved village schoolmistress, Miss Read, is suddenly taken ill and must consider leaving her longtime post at the school. But through the changing seasons in this gentle, humorous drama, the problems of Miss Read and her fellow residents of Fairacre are gradually resolved. ISBN-13: 978-0-618-15456-2 / ISBN-10: 0-618-15456-6

And look for more Fairacre titles coming soon in paperback from Houghton Mifflin:

Village Diary, Storm in the Village, Over the Gate, The Fairacre Festival, The Caxley Chronicles, Emily Davis, Tyler's Row, Farther Afield, A Peaceful Retirement, and *Christmas at Fairacre.*

Made in the USA
Middletown, DE
28 April 2018